The Freak Chronicles

The Freak
Chronicles

JENNIFER SPIEGEL

DZANC
BOOKS

DZANC BOOKS
1334 Woodbourne Street
Westland, MI 48186
www.dzancbooks.org

THE FREAK CHRONICLES

Thank you to the journals who originally published the following stories (some in slightly different versions):

"Advent," *The Seattle Review*; "The Freak Chronicles," *Fresh Boiled Peanuts*; "Free Dive," *Coe Review*; "Glasnost," *PANK* on-line; "Goodbye, Madagascar," *Frostproof Review*; "Killing Castro," *Camera Obscura;* "Lemon," *Switchback*; "The Mickey Rourke Saga," *As It Ought To Be* and *Nimrod*; "Missing Northern," *Waccamaw*; "Nipples Beads Mealie Pap," the winner of the Robert C. Martindale Educational Foundation Award for the Long Short Story in May 2001, originally appeared in excerpts on the Santa Fe Writers Project website; and "Zigzag Bridge," *New York Stories*.

Published 2012 by Dzanc Books
Book design by Steven Seighman

ISBN: 978-1-936873-70-8
First edition: June 2012

ART WORKS.
arts.gov

mc
aca
*michigan council for
arts and cultural affairs*

This project is supported in part by an award from
the National Endowment for the Arts and MCACA.

Printed in the United States of America

10 9 8 7 6 5 4 3 2 1

CONTENTS

Special Thanks to the Following Freaks and Non-Freaks:

Timothy Bell, my one and only. We're giving each other a run for the money.

Ron Carlson, who once drew a heart on my manuscript, wrote *Brontë* inside, and put a big X over it. I'm not sure what he meant, but it stuck with me nonetheless.

Kelly Fitzsimmons Burton, who—it's gotta be said—lives where the streets have no name. She's a true friend.

Steven Gillis and Dan Wickett of Dzanc Books. I like your books, I like your style. And, while we're talking about Dzanc, a huge thank you to Matt Bell, who skillfully edited this child of mine. In truth, I didn't expect our editorial exchange to be so emotionally intense. I'm grateful for his generosity and attentiveness.

Julie Hensley, a lovely person, a writer who inspires kindness and poetic prose, my first friend post-personal drama.

Robert Johnson, Jr., a cohort in writing and Gen X memories. He knows a good thing when he sees it.

Kyle Minor, who read something I wrote and remembered it, an inspiration and bastion of writerly know-how.

Penelope Krouse, my first reader, my first editor. She's got it down right, and I'm forever thankful.

Melissa Pritchard, graceful teacher. I still remember sitting on her couch while she held my writing in her hands and spoke seriously and lovingly.

Marilynn Spiegel, who doesn't need to talk about what it means to be a strong woman.

Alexandra Treat of Jonas and Treat Photography for her wonderful photo.

And, of course, ASU's Department of Creative Writing for invaluable lessons.

There are others who go unmentioned but not disregarded. I thank my friends (especially Anastasia Campos, Laura Cerny-Ciaccio, Jenny Keech, Sara Mahoney, Jolly New, and Meghan Pfister), my family (from Aunt Debbie to Joe), the literary journals who published these stories originally, Dzanc designer Steven Seighman, classmates in workshops, writers out there I really like who don't know I exist, and even Bono. Why not?

In memory of Harvey Spiegel

Given to laughing hysterically at old *Saturday Night Live* sketches, a lover of Twain and Salinger and spy thrillers I thumb my nose at, instructor in the ways of Battleship and hiking the Havasupai, Harvey once wrote on an empty vending machine the following important message: "Pretzel man, please add pretzels."

Desperate times call for desperate measures.

Goodbye, Madagascar

—For Timothy Bell

After preaching, Daniel gets frustrated.

Daniel, a zealous man, good with words, is asked to preach more and more. The pastor wouldn't be able to make it out of Durban this week. Sick child. Could Daniel do it?

It's Sunday morning in Port St. Johns, South Africa. Daniel and Isabel Harmond, missionaries, walk along the gravel road to a church in the township, looking about as missionary-like as they get. Which isn't very often. People expect collars up to necks, chaste hemlines, hairy legs regardless of gender, and hats or bonnets on heads. Daniel and Isabel often wear cut-offs. Today, Daniel wears pants and a button-down shirt while Isabel wears a sundress.

Entering the church, Daniel experiences a flush of disappointment. The church is filled with women and children. Men are rarely there. Daniel likes women—likes them a lot, in fact—but he finds the conspicuous absence of men disturbing.

Isabel sits in the first pew, looking like the dutiful wife.

Daniel stands in front of the Xhosa congregation. He rests his

3

hands on the scratched pulpit and, like a cliché, counts heads. He tries to breathe through slightly opened lips so as to avoid the stench of unwashed bodies. That he finds the smell disdainful shames him.

He opens his Bible. He has a powerful singsong Irish brogue, musical in contrast to African bird, Transkei song. People love listening to him just because he's Irish. He's married to an American, and that's a pity, but when he preaches, it's charming.

"Is God clearly revealed in the things created?" He looks around the church, trying to catch eyes.

The congregants look around, look at each other, wondering if this crazy Irishman wants them to speak.

Daniel applies pressure to his fingertip, touching a verse in Romans. He scans the Xhosa people. It's like hunger or a heart attack. He feels empty, pained. His skin is hot and he wants to shake someone violently. Maybe cut out his tongue to speak with his hands—remove the focus from his brogue. He looks at Isabel, his beautiful American wife. What can he do to distract people from paying so much attention to his Irish brogue and Isabel's long legs?

"Can *everyone* know God?" he asks.

The township church is rapt. He sees that his wife breathes through her mouth, too.

"Are *all* without excuse?"

The congregation listens to the hum of his voice, up and down, up and down. A lullaby.

"*How* is God clearly revealed?"

He stares at Isabel. He sees her there and his mind quickly moves over her terrain. This must be the way people experience God. He barely gazes upon a beautiful woman anymore. Every once in a while, he will. Maybe on a holiday or on his birthday. Most of the time, though, he just sees the woman to whom he's married. A good-looking woman, no doubt. That's God for the Xhosa people. Nice, when you notice.

"How do you know something is eternal?"

Eyes fall on him without understanding. A quietness fills the church.

Sympathy dissolves when he meets one blank face after another. "Isabel?"

She's startled. Her eyes lift to his. "Yes?"

"Is God clearly revealed?" Daniel knows he's subtly humiliating her. It's frustration: frustration from the immobility of people, the lack of evidence that the Gospel transforms the lives of individuals, the paralysis of minds, the fragmented church, the problematic church, his own small offerings, his wife's discontent. Despite the shame, Daniel persists. "Tell me, is God clearly revealed in the things created?"

Now alert, she sits with her back straight and her hands folded, feeling like Hester Prynne in *The Scarlet Letter*. The women and children look from Daniel to Isabel and from Isabel to Daniel with eyebrows high on foreheads, mouths open.

"Yes, God is clearly revealed in the things created," she whispers.

"And does that mean all are without excuse for not seeing?" Daniel leans forward over the pulpit.

"Yes, that's what it means."

Daniel wants, at that very moment, to race out of the church, to race away and find someone who will hold *him* together—because he has his hands full. He takes care of her. He takes care of the sick and the old and the poor and the black. He takes care of Port St. Johns. He wants someone to take care of *him*. And God, though God, doesn't always seem to be *enough*. That thought, again, sends the shame racing through his veins. *God is enough*, he says to himself, believing it, repenting, and finishing his sermon in a flurry of words.

"We'll pray on this." He doesn't have the energy to resolve any conundrums today. When he lifts his head from the closing prayer, his eyes go directly to Isabel's. She slowly stands, turns on her heels, and heads out the door. Down the township dirt road.

Daniel says his good-byes and races after Isabel.

Walking down the poorly paved road that leads to the Indian

Ocean, her dusty sandals flip-flop on the soles of her feet. Daniel
follows closely. They are aware that people are watching them, but
they don't care. They head towards the sea, towards the edge of
Africa. Daniel swiftly makes a grab for her elbow—reaching out his
arm, stretching out his fingertips. He just manages to graze her flesh.

"Don't fucking touch me," she snaps, jerking her arm close to
her body.

She quickens her pace and they continue down the road,
bypassing the run-down Hippo Café, missing the newly painted and
always empty Wild Coast Frozen Foods, ignoring onlookers. From
the side of the road, Mrs. Mvalo, big and black and garbed in bright
African colors, stops with her six grandchildren underfoot and looks
after them. She lets out a clicking sound in Xhosa. Simon, who
tells everyone he's related to Nelson Mandela, tips his hat in their
direction. Isabel ignores him. Daniel gives him an awkward salute.

These are the missionaries: Daniel and Isabel Harmond. They've
lived in Port St. Johns, the seaside town in the Transkei—a former
black homeland—in South Africa for two and a half years. Everyone
knows them and everyone knows their piety is different. No one
doubts their piety. They just know it's different.

Daniel gains ground on Isabel.

Reprobate, she thinks.

Just beyond the township that creeps up the coastline of Port St.
Johns, Daniel reaches Isabel and begins walking at her side.

"Why did you do that?" she asks.

"Frustration."

"That wasn't fair."

"You're right."

"It defeats your purpose."

"I'm sorry."

They walk in silence.

"You can be cruel, sometimes." She turns to look at him. "I'm a
lot of things, but I'm rarely cruel."

"I get tired. I get tired and you're the safest target."

"Well," Isabel begins, dragging her feet through the dirt, "don't count on that safety."

But he does, and she knows it.

Seven p.m. Daniel leaves the house, not telling Isabel where he's going. Isabel has been quiet all day. Daniel, frustrated. He walks to the mouth of the Umzimvubu River and pays a little boy two rand to take him across in a rowboat. River sharks swim in the river's mouth. He heads over to Chris and Georgina Vanderhoff's place, hoping for a cup of tea and some light conversation. He knocks on their door.

"Who's there?" It's Georgina's voice. Georgina's Afrikaner voice. *Pleasure*, she says on certain occasions.

"Daniel," he answers.

"Daniel," Georgina sighs. It sounds like she's standing on the other side with her forehead pressed against the wood. Her voice is sultry, oozing.

"Yeah, it's me." His hands are in his pockets as he waits in the dark.

Georgina slowly opens the door. Light escapes from inside and places Georgina in silhouette. "Chris isn't home—he went to Umtata."

Daniel takes a step backwards. "Oh."

"But you can come inside." She looks behind her into a big room.

Daniel passes in front of Georgina and into her home. Georgina pours brandy and he ponders alcohol. Beer with Isabel only. A bad rule for a lousy missionary. He takes the brandy.

Georgina looks at him. She thinks him lovely.

"Have another," she says, when Daniel finishes the first.

Her home is neither African nor European. Ndebele patterns meld with Guatemalan schemes. Daniel has seen it many times, but never under the influence.

He pores over Georgina's features much like he did earlier with the Xhosa women and children. Her skin is taut on the bones of her face. Her eyebrows are plucked to thin arches. She may have been beautiful when she was very young, but Georgina is no longer very young. Still, though, Daniel knows what's being offered. Georgina sits on the couch before him, one leg tucked under the other. She has thin legs like her eyebrows. She wears a long, paint-splattered shirt. Daniel remembers other women with paint-splattered shirts. He's sure that even Isabel has one. She never wears it, though. Georgina wears hers when she's alone. What does Isabel wear when she's alone? Georgina leans forward and Daniel sees straight down her paint-splattered shirt.

"Another drink?"

Isabel begins to worry around nine. Then it starts raining. She opens the door and tries to adjust to the darkness, see through the storm. She doesn't like it. She has no idea where he went, but she considers the possibilities. Neil's hostel. His hostel caters to the PC-hippie-love-tribal-tattoo-lit-crit-backpackers-of-middle-class-affluence—Generation X on the Green Hills of Africa. There's always a host of backpackers from Europe with all kinds of depraved tales to tell. They all congregate around the big wooden table in front of the fireplace and some play chess and some roll joints and all of them tell about the things they saw along the Garden Route or in Kruger or Zululand. They have stories about Mozambique and Kenya, about Vietnam and Laos. Daniel likes to listen and then tell his own tales.

Son of a bitch, she thinks.

He could be at Chris and Georgina's, discussing dialectics and antinomies, concepts that require the use of big words.

She's afraid, because she hates it when he's gone. It's pouring outside and already she has to think about stuffing towels under the doors to collect muddy rainwater. But she doesn't.

No, she doesn't.

Isabel slips on shoes and a rain jacket, heading out the door at a quarter till ten.

Daniel's no louse. He's just a drunk. He drinks the brandy and never says, *No thank you*. Georgina slithers over, unsure it's going to happen.

"Tell me about India. About Bangladesh," she coos.

At that moment, Daniel can't remember those places. The last place he remembers is Madagascar. "I only remember Madagascar."

"And what do you remember?"

"Leaving."

Georgina pours more brandy and moves closer. "Were you happy to go?"

"We were." He spins the brandy around in his glass. "But afterwards, we hated the leaving."

Georgina drinks deeply. "Never happy." She shakes her head, as if it's a pity.

"We try."

"Daniel."

Daniel thinks he may be blind in one eye. Some alcohol-induced confusion. He raises his hand to his right lid and prods it the way a child does after waking. He's sure he's blind. Georgina says his name.

"Georgina," he imitates her.

"Are you going to kiss me or what? I know one thing that'll make you happy."

Isabel arrives at Neil's hostel. She's drenched. She opens the door, doesn't step fully inside, and calls out, "Neil?" A bunch of backpackers look at her in wonder. Not shock. Nothing shocks these guys anymore. They think, *Hey, maybe she emerged from the sea. Maybe she's a mermaid. Maybe not.* They say, "Come inside. Do you want coffee?"

"No, thanks. Is Neil here?"

Neil comes from the kitchen. He's with David, the white witch doctor, and Simpiwe, his nine-year-old Xhosa assistant. They must be staying at the hostel for the night. Simpiwe runs up to Isabel and reaches for her hand, wanting to hold it.

"Is Daniel here?" she asks.

Isabel mesmerizes Neil in unparalleled ways. "No, he hasn't been here at all." Daniel likes to kid Isabel, whisper to her that Neil is in love with her. Neil is smitten, bewitched. Doesn't she see it?

"It's raining hard." She looks around timidly, touching her wet hair.

"Come inside till it stops."

"No, I can't. Really." She flutters about. She creates a puddle under her feet on his floor. "I'm making a mess for you, Neil. I'm sorry—"

"Don't worry." Neil approaches her. "Have coffee. Talk to the kids."

Isabel releases Simpiwe's hand, squeezes his arm, looks at Neil. "I have to go. If you see Daniel, tell him I'm looking for him. Tell him it's raining too hard for him to be out cavorting around. You'll tell him?"

"I will."

They look into each other's eyes. Neil reminds Isabel of a gentle old horse. One you feed carrots and celery to because you like him so much.

"I have to go." She leaves.

Daniel recovers a semblance of missionary-ness when Georgina suggests a kiss.

Daniel stares at the woman, stares at her lips. "Georgina …." Drunkenly. "I'm sorry." He struggles to stand. He's sure something's wrong with his right eye.

Georgina jumps to her feet. She doesn't want to be humiliated. She doesn't want him that much.

"I'll tell you what," he says. "I'm going to leave now and we're going to pretend these words weren't spoken." He heads to the door, walking with difficulty. "This way, we can live in the same town." He reaches the exit. "What do you say?"

He stumbles out into the Port St. Johns night.

Isabel stands in the rain on the bank of the Umzimvubu River. The boy who rows people over to the other side for two rand is no longer rowing. His rowboat, however, is tied to the dock.

Wondering if Daniel got stuck on the other side, she sees someone.

It's Daniel. Possibly drunk. She sees a man walk in the rain to the end of the bank and stand there, distraught. Then, the man plops down on the shore. He sits on the muddy ground with his knees bent and pointed in the air.

Isabel waves both arms over her head.

Nothing.

She does it again, her arms flailing in the dark and rain.

This time, a wave from the other side. Definitely Daniel. Definitely drunk.

She walks to the end of the shore where the rowboat is. Though she has never rowed a boat in her entire life, she unties it and moves it into the water. Dirty, shark-infested water splashes around her ankles, ruining her shoes. The rain beats down on the top of her head. *Unbelievable*, she says under her breath. She crawls into the skiff. It's more like she bodily throws herself in. She picks up the oars and, with great difficulty, rows. It turns one way, then the other. It goes nowhere, then it goes somewhere—slowly. Finally, after twenty minutes—the man still sitting on the ground with his knees to his chest on the other side—she gets the boat to move. Moving north, across the Umzimvubu River.

She rows and rows. The rain is relentless and she knows they're both going to be sick. It's a cold rain, but the good news is she can't see any river sharks.

After forty minutes—considerably longer than what it should take—Isabel Harmond makes it to the other side. She doesn't know, though, how to tie the boat to the dock, how to get to the man on the shore, what's next. For a moment, she pauses. She sees a drunken Daniel stand up.

She has no choice. Isabel jumps into the water and it swirls around her legs, thigh high. Despite her fear of river sharks, she begins to plod through water, pulling the rowboat behind her. It's ridiculous.

"Daniel Harmond!" she cries out.

Daniel begins to walk into the water. As he marches and Isabel tugs the rowboat, they are oblivious to the uniqueness of this moment. They are oblivious to Port St. Johns; to the Transkei; to the fact they are two missionaries born in different countries, living in South Africa in the post-apartheid era, when Nelson Mandela is president and where Xhosa, Zulu, Afrikaner and others are wrestling with politics, identity, and God. They are oblivious to the exquisite and extraordinary nature of their positions, standing in the Umzimvubu River in the rain.

Daniel, his ankles invisible, yells out, "Isabel!"

"Stop right there!" She points her finger at him, her legs made heavy by the whirlpools around them. "Stop right there, mister!" The word *mister* surprises her. "There's only so much I can do and I can't save you from drowning or from the damn sharks!" She's only a few feet away from him. "I'm coming there."

Daniel stops and watches her, dumbfounded. "Be careful, Isabel!"

"Yeah, *you* be careful." She reaches her husband then—rowboat in tow. "Get in the boat," she demands. "Hurry!"

Daniel collapses into the skiff, gangly and drunk. Isabel follows suit. They are a confusion of arms and legs. It takes forever to get them both sitting up straight, facing one another. They are breathless, wet, tired. Daniel reaches out to touch her. She begins to row, asking no questions.

Daniel makes efforts to secure the oars from her, but she doesn't let him. They struggle noisily, but Isabel, sober, is stronger. She holds onto them tightly and pushes him away. She doesn't meet his eyes as she thrusts the oars into the water. She works them vigorously, feeling like Sisyphus. *We better be going somewhere*, she thinks. Daniel twists his ankles around one of her legs. Their chests heave. He puts his hands on her knees.

"No one believes in God." He cries out emotionally through rain and alcohol. Isabel rows defiantly. "They don't believe." Daniel squeezes her knees. "Look what's around them, Isabel!" He releases her body and opens up his arms, as if to show her the river, the rain, the moon, the ocean, Africa. "They don't believe."

Forty minutes later, they crawl on shore. Isabel, demanding, militaristic, makes him stand on sand. She ties the boat to the dock and splashes noisily through the water. Still not saying a word, she heads home.

When they reach their driveway, she starts climbing. It's steep and rain-slick. Broken tree branches litter the land. At the top, she looks back to make sure he's behind her, and he is.

"Isabel!"

Though she hears him, she walks away. She moves towards the back of the house because that's the door that will have the least water under it.

"Isabel!" he cries again.

"What, Daniel?" Exasperated, exhausted, soaking wet, not knowing the story, not wanting to hear it.

Daniel reaches his wife. He falls to his knees and holds her around the waist. Isabel, with his weight against her, is forced to respond. At first her hands are in the air, floating above his head—not touching him. He holds her closely and she lowers her hands to his hair.

It's raining fiercely and the sky is black and the wind is blowing and they can hear rain hitting leaves, the branches swaying. They look like Ophelia in her death scene.

13

"Promise you'll never leave me. Promise."

"Daniel." She's fatigued.

"You have to promise me that."

She doesn't know where it comes from, if it's the drink or the sermon or whatever was on the river's other side. She puts both hands in his hair, holding his head to her body. She is crying now, unexpected tears—tears as fierce as the rain, tears indistinguishable from the downpour. She says something, a response to what's not even said. "But we're the missionaries. We're the missionaries."

Daniel holds her. While the rain hits their backs, their faces, their flesh in a torrential homeland storm, Daniel and Isabel are petrified, still.

"I'm not going to leave you," she says.

"Why a missionary?" Isabel asked. They were sitting in a booth at Freaky Fran's on Avenue A and St. Mark's Place, and Isabel and Daniel had known each other for three days. "Why not something else—like an organ donor or a Humane Society volunteer? I mean, it's so *drastic*." Isabel leaned against the wall and put her feet up on the booth.

Daniel wiped his mouth with a paper napkin, swallowed a bite of cheeseburger, and spoke with that startling Irish accent. "Once I decided to abandon *debauchery*"—the word fell from his lips with a certain relish—"to pick up the old cross, missionary work seemed like the most fitting thing." Daniel put his foot up on Isabel's side of the booth, making her feel trapped inside. She didn't care. "Look at me, Isabel. I'm not exactly well-suited for *Mr. Rogers' Neighborhood*." He opened up his arms, presenting himself to her. "And most of the churches I know are in that part of town."

Isabel *did* look. He was thirty and dark and attractive and he looked like he should be writing sonnets or wandering around used record stores or maybe buying heroin in Tompkins Square Park across the street. "I could never do it," she said. "I could never be a missionary."

"Sure you could."

"Do you miss the debauchery?" Isabel watched him carefully.

He wadded up his napkin and threw it on the table. He looked into her eyes. "I miss it all the time." He smiled. "But I don't miss the mornings *after*."

"I couldn't do it." She rubbed a fry in a spot of ketchup. "It isn't the debauchery I'd miss. It's the commitment I fear."

"It *is* a commitment. A kind of fidelity."

Four days after the storm and the earth is dry. For the first few days following the downpour, Isabel didn't want to hear how Daniel ended up sitting on the bank of the Umzimvubu River with brandy on his breath. It was like they were waiting for the dove to return with the olive branch after the water receded. The homeland storm is over.

"What did you do afterwards?" Isabel folds newly cleaned sheets.

"I left."

"Did you want to stay?"

Daniel runs his hand over his forearm. He's thinking. Isabel stops folding and watches. *He has to think!*

"I probably wanted to stay, Isabel." He walks up to her. "But it had absolutely nothing to do with *Georgina*."

She moves over to the window to stare at the sea.

He puts his hands on her shoulders. "There are other things I want, and I want them more than I could ever want that."

"I'm glad you told me." Isabel has the extraordinary ability to forgive. "Don't ever use the word *probably* again."

"Marry me." Daniel said it and meant it, even though he barely knew her.

"Marry you? I don't even know you, Daniel What-Was-Your-Last-Name?"

Daniel leaned over the railing and looked at the Brooklyn Bridge. She kissed the profile of his face. What the hell? Her life was in tremendous flux and, because of the impetuous nature of such periods, she'd marry him. She'd be a missionary, too. "Tell me where I have to go and what I have to do." She kissed him again. "I'll sign the dotted line."

On the front porch, Isabel places a bowl of peanuts on the wooden table with wobbly legs.

Paulina, a young Xhosa woman who works at the Coastal Needles Hotel, walks by with her baby tied to her back. From the road, she calls out, "Hello, Isabel!"

Isabel shouts a greeting, looking at the baby. In seven years of marriage, she's had three miscarriages. She turns from the woman on the road and disappears behind her screened door, thinking about Daniel's words last night: *We can adopt from the Transkei.* Isabel, staring at the ceiling, listening to the rain fall, thinking of bringing a Xhosa baby into her home, had said, *No, Daniel—we live here. It's too close. We can't adopt from here. Somewhere else. Madagascar, maybe. Anywhere but the Transkei.*

Their house consists of one large room, a small kitchen, a tiny bathroom, and a claustrophobic cubbyhole not big enough for a bed. Daniel's "study." When Isabel wants to work alone, she walks to the beach, over the rocks, to the sea. She looks at blue bottles and jellyfish washed up on the shore like luminescent shower caps. There, she contemplates paradise, Eden, the Infinite. Daniel, though, likes tight quarters to investigate grand designs. Their home is cozy; it's neither well-lit nor decorative. They like it.

"David called from Neil's. He wants to know if he can sleep on the floor."

"That's fine."

Daniel walks around the house, searching for a shirt. Chris and Georgina appear at the screen door. Isabel, generous with her forgiveness, walks over to open it. Transkei locals for the last decade, the rumor is that Georgina comes from money, which allows for lazy Transkei days. Chris writes and is occasionally published. Georgina paints and her studio is filled with beautiful, undiscovered, avant-garde Afrikaner art.

It's dusk and they drink beer. They can hear a rumble of voices rising from below—Africa with its catcalls, bird sounds, and clutter of rhythmic echoes.

"I could never leave." Chris is contemplative. "Not now, anyway. South Africa is too crazy. Where would we go?"

"It's pretty crazy here, Chris." Georgina raises her eyebrows. "Taxi wars, poverty, a whole mass of people who have no clue they're part of the so-called *New* South Africa."

"It takes a while for things to change." Daniel puts his arm around the back of Isabel's chair.

Neil Hammer of local hostel fame appears on the steps. Isabel stands. "I'll get you a drink, Neil." Entering the house, she calls back, "I thought David was coming with you. We swept the floor."

"He's talking to some backpackers."

Georgina shifts her body towards Neil, and speaks to him as if she were some kind of reporter, "So, Neil, tell us what you think about the Transkei's chances for stability now that it's no longer a puppet-state in the hands of a racist regime."

Neil moved to South Africa from New Zealand during the apartheid years and settled in Port St. Johns because it was Africa inside of a more or less Europeanized country. A supporter of the African National Congress, he has stories about the struggle, tales about being a white man in the Transkei. Now, with the democratic elections over, Neil knows about the Transkei's other struggles. The ones against poverty and crime. The backpackers come to stay in his earthy hostel, to smoke the homegrown pot, and to tell stories about their travels. "The Transkei will always be the Transkei—it'll always be the Wild Coast. It doesn't matter who's in Pretoria or Cape Town."

"That's why we're here." Chris turns to the Harmonds with a sardonic twinkle in his eye. "And that's why we need the missionaries. The natives are, after all, restless."

Daniel reaches for another beer and Isabel eyes him.

Neil crosses his legs. "Once upon a time, Port St. Johns was quite the white colonialist hot spot—it wasn't always just the dumping ground for hijacked cars and unemployed Africans."

"Yes, the Boers loved this place." Georgina absent-mindedly twists a thread on her skirt and pulls it. Only Georgina and Chris, two Afrikaners, can get away with the offhand use of *Boer*. The word reeks of nationalism, of an ugly history.

"Where's that David?" Chris turns to Neil. "I could use a little magic."

"We all could," Georgina adds.

David the Enigmatic.

"You know," begins Georgina, "a friend of mine called from Jo'burg and told me she read an article about a white witch doctor in the paper recently. It was all about how there's this white guy living among the Xhosa. But it had something else to say, too." She looks around conspiratorially. "He was apparently raving mad and on PCP and coke five years ago. They found him naked in Yeoville behind a garbage can."

Isabel dismisses Georgina's words with a wave of her hand. "Wrong guy, I bet."

"But, Isabel, how many white witch doctors do you think there are in South Africa?"

"I don't know. But they've got the wrong man."

David, the white twaza. A witch doctor-in-training. A creature of beauty. David Blare is thirty and he possesses a Michelangelo-sculpted form just like his namesake. He has unruly blond hair, and an unkempt beard and mustache with brightly colored strips of cloth and goat hair and beads weaved and braided throughout. He walks around Port St. Johns barefoot and practically naked—wearing just a sarong. His torso revealed, his stomach flat. He carries a walking stick and rubs it with grease to smooth it, the splinters disappearing. David Blare walks about, beautiful in shape, mostly naked, wild in appearance, and practicing magic. He's a witch doctor. A sangoma.

"He's a fucking lunatic," says Georgina.

"We like him." Isabel stares pointedly, bitterly, at her.

David sleeps on Isabel and Daniel's floor sometimes. Usually, he sleeps at Neil's, hanging out with backpackers. He lives in the village of Unxweme with a man he calls Dada in Dada's family kraal—rondavels, circular huts made of mud and dung. David lives as a Pondo (a subgroup of the Xhosa tribe), lives as a twaza, and dresses as one, too. He has ceased living like a white man altogether, forsaking its luxuries, dismissing its excesses.

"You know, he's marrying a Pondo woman in a few months." Georgina holds her hands out in front of her, checking her nails. "As soon as his training period is over." She snickers. "When he's a *real* witch doctor."

"He kills a goat and marries a Pondo," adds Chris.

"Fucking unbelievable," says Georgina.

"He's found his peace." Neil spends a lot of time with kids who seek peace.

"What do you think, missionaries?" Georgina turns to the Harmonds. "Has David, the white twaza, found peace?"

Daniel pauses and Isabel defers. "I don't doubt his sincerity," Daniel says. He uncrosses his legs. "I'm sure he's not trying to put anyone on with the magic or the trance-dancing or the healings. I'm sure he has good intentions."

"But?" Georgina leans forward, as if she were examining Daniel's face for darks and lights.

Carefully, Daniel tries to address the salvation found by a sangoma while maintaining his own Christian beliefs. "I don't think it's a satisfactory peace. I think it's temporal." Daniel speaks the way he has learned to—with quiet determination, non-offensively, unswervingly.

Isabel slaps a mosquito on her leg, killing it. "I respect his beliefs."

"How can you say that, Isabel?" Georgina is annoyed. "How can you say you respect his beliefs when you think you possess *Truth* and all other truths pale in comparison?"

"Stop being pejorative with the missionaries, Georgina." Chris gives his wife a sharp glare. "They're missionaries, for God's sake."

"Just tell me this," Georgina addresses her question to Isabel Harmond, not to the steadfast Daniel, Daniel with the answers delivered so quickly and calmly. "Can David heal the sick?"

Isabel, the one everyone wonders about—her faith dubious, her convictions untested—answers. "He may be able to heal the sick, but I *know* he can't raise the dead."

In the distance, David, herbalist and magic man, white and decidedly African, appears on the road. He walks towards the five people, the expatriates, the missionaries, the bohemians. The moon shines on his skin, blazes on his face. The people on the porch tilt their beers back, watching him approach.

This was how they met.

"Don't sit me next to that man," Isabel whispered to the hostess of a dinner party on the Upper West Side.

"Do you know him? Is he a jerk?"

"I don't know him." Isabel looked manic. Ever since she had decided to move back to California, she had sworn off meeting people. "I'm leaving in two weeks."

"You're insane. And he's off to Russia in five months. A missionary!" The hostess shook her head. A shame. A waste of good-looking man.

"I overheard him say that."

The woman touched Isabel's hand delicately.

Fate, karma, luck, predestination: they were seated together anyway. Over blackened salmon, Isabel leaned over. "What made you decide to become a missionary?"

Daniel, just out of seminary, tattooed and tainted, said, "It was either Christ or a gluttonous plunge into unadulterated sensuality— one of the two, I couldn't decide."

Isabel watched him speak, watched his body slip into her space. Daniel, looking piercingly into her eyes, had a voice weighty with secrets. "I decided."

"I'm supposed to leave New York in two weeks," she said.

"That's nice. Why didn't you want to sit next to me?"

Three days later, Daniel (electric and kind) pushed Isabel (fragile and passionate) back against a graffiti-covered wall in the Bowery and kissed her.

He was perfect for her. Excessive. Stringent.

She was doomed.

They saw each other daily. She postponed the move. He proposed. They agreed to go to Russia together.

She hadn't wanted to sit next to him because she had heard him talking about uncharted promised lands and the vows he meant to keep.

They married in a time of flux. Flux isn't a part of Isabel and Daniel's daily routine anymore because every day in this part of Africa is a beautiful day, and every day in this part of Africa demands the same things of you the previous day demanded.

"What kind of calling?" Daniel is under the covers in his bed, next to Isabel. David the Sangoma is sprawled out on their floor. He has only a blanket, refuses anything else.

"It was Dada." David has a thick Zimbabwean accent. During the late eighties, when Neil was giving up his yuppie existence in New Zealand, when Chris was writing postmodern poetry, when Georgina was painting the most chic Afrikaans art to date, when Daniel and Isabel were strangers, David Blare was living it up in Johannesburg. He had it all: he was young, sexy, jet-set, and a drug addict. "I decided to get out of Jo'burg. But that wasn't the calling. I felt pulled towards the Transkei. I dumped my earthly possessions and went cold turkey on the drugs."

"Then the calling? Then Dada?" Daniel is flat on his back, a hand tucked under his head. The calling. He's really interested in the calling.

"I met Dada through other people—through other white men who lived in the Transkei. They told me I had to talk to this guy. He was a healer, a magic man, from the Pondo people, gifted in prophesy."

"A sangoma?" Daniel tries to picture the meeting between the gaunt white man and the black Transkei witch doctor.

"He told me all my secrets." Growing up in the former Rhodesia, now Zimbabwe, no father. His less-than-magical encounter with a girl. The loud and unmemorable music in the background as they approximated lovemaking, bottles rolling around their feet in the back of a truck. The child David doesn't know, has never seen, a rumor, a picture once sent. That was what Dada talked about.

"Spiritual authority does tend to belong to the bearer of one's secrets." Daniel's voice lowers in nocturnal cadence. "And then?"

"He said I had healing powers and I was called to be a twaza." David Blare, former playboy: *Turn Back, O Man.*

Isabel, awake too, whispers to Daniel, "Who has your secrets?"

Daniel whispers back, "Only you and God, Isabel."

Isabel—not in the privacy of her own home—reaches over and touches his stomach. "I have no secrets," she whispers.

"What?" David asks.

She raises her voice. "I said, 'You need healing leaflets.'"

"Sounds entrepreneurial," David responds.

Daniel thinks about the magic man. He faces Isabel in the dark, runs his hand over her neck, across her breasts, down the length of her body. "Only I know the truth about you," he whispers in her ear.

"Mostly, I tended bar in London hotspots," Daniel explained his pre-missionary life to the woman he was marrying as they packed up her New York apartment.

"And now you're an evangelist." Isabel reached for packing tape. "We'll have a stormy relationship, Daniel Harmond. We'll cash in on a mutual proclivity for excess and stringency."

Daniel was pleased with her response. "Promise?"

"I do." She tore off some tape with her teeth. "What did you do before you tended bar?"

"I emerged from the University of Dublin with a degree in history and a supreme case of wanderlust," he said, "that had less to do with geography and more to do with philosophy and women."

He did acid with a girl named Patty for nearly a year and a half, their psychedelic sexual intimacy so staggering they'd lain for days on a mattress in Patty's London flat, weary and spent. Patty professed her undying love for Daniel, but for him it was already over the moment the curtains fluttering in the breeze stopped resembling multidimensional passages leading to six or seven spiritual truths.

There was Sasha, a beautiful backpacker he met in India on holiday. That was when he got his first tattoo. They practiced Buddhism for the summer; then the weather turned and Daniel had to admit to the ever-meditating Sasha that it never really made sense to him. Daniel dipped into Hinduism (Lindsay), Gnosticism (Kristina), Mysticism (Barb), and Nihilism ( ).

He covered Isabel's hand with his. "I went from one relationship to another. I read Confucius, Camus, and Kierkegaard. I became a vegan, a pacifist, and a drunk." They sat on Isabel's floor with boxes surrounding them. "Having traveled the world and the gamut of great religions, I returned on a cold winter day to Dublin—empty and bruised—and took up my old Catholic albatross." He held her hand tightly. "Convinced that only a Creator with a Son made sense, I went to confession." He was there confessing to a random liaison with an earthy but fine-boned Finnish relativist. "During confession, I thought I heard a hint—a subtle note—of licentious greed in the priest's voice. *Tell me more.*" With fingers woven between Isabel's, he lifted his other hand to her chin. "And that was it."

Her eyes met his. "What was it?"

Daniel, possessing three tattoos (each illustrating a major theistic religion), feeling sober, had jumped to his feet, nearly hitting his head in the confessional, and had sprinted out of the Catholic Church and into the streets of Dublin, his own beloved city. "I must have looked like a madman, Isabel. I literally ran out in the streets renouncing salvation by works and the priest's intercessory role."

Isabel stared at him. "A conversion experience?"

He held her hand. "Yes."

Isabel froze. "And?"

"My wanderlust ceased. I got an AIDS test, stopped sleeping around, read the Bible in a month, went to seminary, and made plans to become a missionary." He dropped to the floor beside the boxes.

Isabel didn't know what to say.

Isabel and David the Sangoma walk towards the center of Port St. Johns on a bright early morning. Port St. Johns has a rich history and a ragtag African countenance. Once a busy port, once a mining town, and once even a hotbed for illegal ANC military training, now Port St. Johns is impoverished and crime-ridden. The marble mines dried up long ago and the Afrikaners left in droves the moment the Transkei was declared a black homeland during the apartheid years. Now, it has a township with hills and hills of Xhosa villages surrounding it. The so-called Trendsetter Supermarket has a certain selection of fine foods. Dairy products are questionable. Tab and Coke are available. There's a post office that's notoriously unreliable. The bank always has lines in it. If you want dinner at the Hippo Café, you should not expect a choice between mutton and beef and chicken, though they're all on the grease-spotted menu. Whatever is served, it'll come with rice or samp, a porridge-like substance. One can stay at the Coastal Needles Hotel, occupied almost exclusively by blacks, which is unusual in South Africa, despite the fact they are the majority. Great for darts, great for singing. There are a few stores, a bunch of fruit stalls, a hostel. That's about it. Everyone is fully-clothed. Only a few carry tribal weapons. Xhosa is the dominant language. This is a seaside Transkei town, a little remote, a little primitive, a little unruly, and in possession of a couple of unusual missionaries.

"Why did you two leave Madagascar?" David strolls in his bare feet.

"Orders from above." Isabel shields her eyes from the sun, recalling how the assignment came one hot African day when they were in Madagascar. "Daniel was sitting at his desk, studying Ecclesiastes, feeling like a great theologian in our tropical outpost, when—quite suddenly—the fax began to receive."

"God sends faxes?" David winks.

"Pittsburgh does." She wipes her forehead. Her fair skin and red cheeks have given way to a brown, sweaty glow. Isabel still wears her American tennis shoes and her American clothes. *White woman*, says her apparel. *From America*, it explains. "We would get very excited about faxes."

As they walk, Xhosa men and women wave to them. It's as if the representatives of two camps are walking together—an herbalist who argues his magic is not contradictory to Christianity, and a Christian who argues it is. In Western eyes, one looks like a savage. In African eyes, the other looks like a billboard advertisement for toothpaste.

25

"It was from Pennsylvania," she says.

"They sent you here? The Transkei?"

"Well, the other couple was expecting a baby and they wanted out of Port St. Johns." Isabel waves to someone. "Maybe the carjacking and dagga scared them."

Isabel thinks of Madagascar. She always misses what she has left. *It isn't so bad,* the fax had said. Both of them would teach Sunday school and lead Bible studies. Isabel would teach history at the primary school and Daniel would provide counseling services to adults. They already had a pastor, but he was rarely around. His sermons were decent, but he only came to town on Sundays. He really lived in Durban. Hence, they moved to the continent. Good-bye, Madagascar.

"Have you met those guys?" David points to two white boys headed towards them. "Michael and Sam?"

"Who are they?"

"Brits backpacking from South Africa to Kenya. Nice kids."

They look about twenty. One looks like a skinny-ass English kid, crew cut, goatee, has the tattoo thing going. Ruddy. A pierced body part. Isabel doesn't even know what this body part is called—the part just below the lip, but not yet the chin. The inflection of skin in between. A silver stud. The other one looks like a real boy, long bangs; he probably doesn't shave yet.

"How do you know them?" Isabel watches the boys approaching.

"They're staying at Neil's place."

"We'd love to go on that hike with you to your village. How do you say it?" says the one with bangs when they reach the two.

"Unxweme." David's Xhosa is perfect.

"Yes, Unxweme." Sam, the boy, makes a valiant effort at correct pronunciation. "Michael and I would like to go."

"Good." David nods his head and turns to Isabel. "Would you like to join us on an overnight hike to Unxweme? Trance-dancing is possible."

Isabel is taken aback. She has lived in the Transkei for years and she has been to villages that can be reached by car, but she has yet to sleep in a mud and dung rondavel and she has yet to abandon the dirt roads for the hills. "Well, you're very kind to extend the invitation, David—"

"You can't refuse." He jams his walking stick into the ground. "John the Baptist didn't exactly live it up when he was preparing the way, did he?"

Damn these white Africans with their warped Christian backgrounds, she thinks. Isabel is embarrassed by the familiarity of their communication in front of Michael and Sam. They don't know what it's like to be a missionary in Port St. Johns. They don't know that certain rules don't apply, certain stereotypes give way. "Yes, but his head ended up on a platter."

"Yours won't. Bring Daniel." He brushes matted hair out of his face. "I'm sure that wiry Irish man can protect you from what lurks in the heart of darkness."

Michael and Sam look on, curiously.

When they first arrived, Daniel made Isabel walk by herself through the township overlooking the sea. He made her walk alone through the black and impoverished shantytown. "You have to get used to it. This is where we live."

It's a township situated directly on the mountainside, amidst beautiful dark green vegetation and purple and orange wildflowers, directly between the town of Port St. Johns and Second Beach (First Beach having been washed away years ago). The Wild Coast, the Shipwreck Coast, the Transkei—virgin sand and rocky cliffs overlooking the bluest of oceans. On this lush coast, which touches the Indian Ocean with its craggy fingertips, a mud and stone and tin and rock house/shelter/shack community lies like bruises on unblemished skin. Dirt roads weave through the township and fires burn in yards. Children in torn pants and T-shirts with holes in them and American sports teams splashed across stained surfaces stomp their feet in the dust. Children with chocolate skin and black woolly hair and graceful little limbs race around, pounding the ground with the flats of their feet, kicking their heels up and running in circles, making noises, street sounds, song. Dirty children, lithe and beautiful—their eyes alive and on fire—with dancing going on in their minds. They race ahead of each other and then back again, the other way. Hills climbed without strain, homes slept in without disgust. Dirty children who have never been fully immersed in hot, soapy water and who live in a virtual paradise. *My God,* Isabel and Daniel had thought.

Isabel, new to South Africa, wondered if the inhabitants considered the Transkei beautiful. Could it be so to them?

On that first time Daniel forced her to walk through the township alone, Isabel chose her gait carefully. She assumed confidence, comfort, nonchalance. She stepped forward as if she knew where she was going.

The children approached. They flocked around her like a swarm of bees. She took a step and the swarm moved with her, expanding in front, trailing after. Their hands were all over her— all over her body, in her pockets, on her rings, reaching for her sunglasses, for charms on necklaces, for earrings in ears. "Give me your money!" they demanded. "Treat!" they begged. *Give us something, white woman.*

Isabel thought, *I can't do this. I'm not made for this.*

"I don't have any money." She opened up her hands, flipped over her wrists, lay bare her palms. Nothing.

Madagascar, she wished.

She pushed through the swarm of children with their flashing eyes. She pushed through them and only one little boy persisted in the onslaught. Smiling, mischievous, already hating her for the ring on her finger, the earrings in her ears, the tennis shoes and blue jeans and clean white T-shirt on her veggie-burger-sparkling-water body. "Give me money," he said.

"I don't have any," she answered.

He was five or six. He danced circles around her, jumped out in front of her. He reached up and tried to get the sunglasses off the top of her head, his arms thrashing by her face, his hands reaching high.

"Candy," he said.

"Nothing." She showed him she was empty-handed.

This child, his child-face animated in secret mischief, balled up his tiny black fists into tight little orbs. He took those fists and he came at her—he came at Isabel Harmond, and those fists went into her groin. He hit her hard and Isabel, alarmed and feigning control, knew this little boy could sense her fear. She reached down, grabbed his hands, took them in her own, looked him in the eye, and said—softly, deliberately—"I don't have any money." Then, she released his fists.

The child gave her another punch in the groin, just for the hell of it. Then, like a torpedo, he spun around and ran away.

I'm not cut out for this, Isabel thought.

It's two and a half years later.

Port St. Johns is home.

Isabel walks along the dirt road that cuts through the township on her way to Second Beach, where she meets a group of women twice a week to discuss nutrition. Many of the people know her and call out as she walks by. "Isabel Harmond! How do you do?"

The township kids, seeing her stroll, seeing her with her bag of books and a pear, run to her. They are filthy and their clothes are stained and ripped. They smell like urine, like dirt. Little boys with ripped pants run by. Girls in old party dresses skip over. Boys, touching their penises, reach with those same hands to hold hers as she walks through their shantytown. She sees their hands go from their genitals towards her white fingers, her thin wrists, her delicate hands. Isabel Harmond, not made for this, takes their hands in hers and walks through the township.

This is her life. She seems made for it.

It's raining again, a storm from the sea, and water is seeping through the bottom of the front door, the back door, the windows, too. Eleven-thirty at night and thunder roars and Isabel's feet slap against old wooden floors as she pushes grimy towels in cracks. Isabel wipes hair out of her eyes with her forearm. Her hands are dirty from muddy rainwater.

Daniel watches from his place in bed and then gets up. He walks over to Isabel and begins wringing towels in buckets and shoving them underneath all openings. Thunder booms in Port St. Johns and it seems to start from somewhere far away and approach like a mad dog, hind legs meeting front legs in fury. Daniel and Isabel pause in their wringing of towels for its dramatic show to finish and they smile at each other.

"Are you tired of being a missionary, Isabel?" His voice and the question surprise her.

On hands and knees, she looks up at him. "Why?"

Daniel sits on the floor in front of his wife and Isabel cringes when his boxers touch wood. She points to the place where bottom and plank meet, distracted from the topic of conversation. "Now you have to change your boxers before getting back into bed—"

"Are you feeling restless?" he asks.

Isabel pushes towels under the door like she's kneading bread. "It's late and there's water all over the floor, Missionary Man."

They're silent for a while. The rain hits their roof in a steady tap-tap-tap-tap. Isabel squeezes out rags. Daniel does the same.

After Daniel and Isabel had been married for several years, after they had spent many broken wood beam, moonlit, tall reed, ocean-breeze evenings in the company of multi-hued folk from villages and towns and islands—after the lazy comfort of these things—he would point out to the people with whom they shared their stories on shores and porches and around splintery wooden tables that Isabel is indulgent and constrained. She is like a creature at the bottom of the ocean. So still, so suspended by the density of its surroundings—moving gently in the sea's embrace—until the touch, the sensation, the flush of danger that sends still creatures under rocks, up walls, towards surfaces, anywhere other than where they had rested in pristine tranquility. Isabel is like that, like a creature at the bottom of the sea, given to flashes of terror. Daniel would joke about her tendencies for compulsive behavior with the indigenous population and expat community, saying, "It makes her a brilliant lover, but a lousy recreational drug user." This would make them stop and think. Now, Daniel looks at her, wondering if she'll flee, indulging terror.

She makes circles on the floor with her cloth, not looking at her husband. "Don't worry, Daniel."

Daniel swooshes towels around.

"David invited us to go on an overnight hike to Unxweme." Isabel empties the bucket. "With two British boys."

Daniel doesn't say anything for a moment. Then: "How about if you go alone?" Other husbands suggest an evening class, a membership at a gym, lunch with friends, a *We'll get a babysitter* night. Daniel suggests an overnight hike with a witch doctor.

"Why alone?" Isabel looks up.

"You can get away from me."

"I don't want to get away from you."

"Come on, Isabel." He crawls over to her. "A trial separation. A little trance-dancing." He nudges her ribs, grins. "David, half-naked. The next best thing to Chippendales."

"How will you get along without me? Who would stir your instant coffee or make sure you got a peanut butter sandwich for dinner?"

Daniel thinks. "There's always mutton, mutton, or mutton at the Hippo Café."

The rain pours on Port St. Johns. Daniel and Isabel stuff towels, listening, listening, listening.

Isabel Harmond stays up late and hand-washes bras in the sink. She takes a long, hot shower while it rains and she thinks about belief in God. She wonders if her credibility as a missionary rests on the fact that she sleeps with Daniel and wears his ring around her finger.

Eventually, you do it alone.

Twenty-eight, Daniel waiting for her in London with marrying words. Isabel rushed home to California with all her worldly possessions. Her family looked at her, thought the usual. Isabel, home for three weeks, with belongings and explanations. Her dubious faith, they whispered. Isabel not-yet Harmond drifted ghost-like among family members and old acquaintances. *I am going*, she said.

In her childhood room, she packed away old possessions that took years to collect, to pay for, to have. And then, thinking of Daniel and the life that awaited her where possessions meant nothing, she remembered that when you didn't own anything, you really didn't miss having something, either. Isabel, driving in the car, during those three weeks when her faith was counted as dubious and her wanderings rootless, knew she didn't need possessions. She packed them away. Compact discs for parents.

Isabel, aloof. Friends invited her to dinner. She was already living out of a backpack. Twenty-eight, they'd whisper. You're twenty-eight and you live out of a backpack. *What kind of man is this?* Isabel, not the kind of woman to bring flowers or wine or candies along with self to dinner parties, handed over a string of beads from Côte D'Ivoire—grabbed from the basket at the side of Daniel's already-sold couch. *I brought these for you*, she said.

Isabel, sitting in living rooms with matching furniture, paid for by two incomes. Sitting down at tables with cloth napkins and placemats. Isabel, feeling single despite being betrothed. Remembering Daniel—whom she barely knew but would certainly marry—and the way he didn't promise her a home or a garden or health insurance, good schools, or a grocery store nearby. Isabel watched as dessert was served, scrutinizing the form and content of the dish: an ice-cream casserole—*a casserole of ice cream*—with a Ritz cracker crust and crushed Whoppers on top.

A conspiracy between Ritz and Whoppers.

Isabel, wondering why she wasn't the kind of woman who knew how to make casseroles.

Isabel, calling Daniel, in London, the man with whom she would spend the rest of her life, letting him know the secrets of her discontent and taking on his history of stained sheets, his future of washing feet. Telling him about the ice-cream casserole.

You are more of a couscous kind of a girl, anyway, he said.

Isabel, during those three weeks at home, running on a treadmill, thinking of the things she will miss. *I will miss American movies and sun-dried tomatoes. I will miss college friends and* The New York Times. *I will miss my parents and a few TV shows. I will miss big bookstores and cups of coffee to go and songs about the end of love. There is nothing else I will miss.*

Isabel's stormy relationship with God. This positioning of her decisions as apart from God, apart from the monolithic church. Daniel's convictions, Daniel's motives—were they not enough to absorb hers?

Isabel believed, in her heart of hearts, this God would take whatever motives were hers and turn them, twist them, conform them, break them, make them His own. Isabel believed, in her heart of hearts, that whatever she was about to undertake was what she was meant to undertake.

Eventually, you do it alone.

David brings the Xhosa boy on the overnight hike. From what Isabel gathers, Simpiwe has the option of being a twaza himself when he becomes an adult. Now, at nine, he's an assistant. Wherever David goes, he goes. He's part of the sangoma package. A walking stick, a goat skin, and a boy. Because David is a white man who likes to come down from the hills and hang out with the Port St. Johns whitey crowd, Simpiwe has this unusual English education. He likes Coca-Cola, chocolate, and Europeans who sit around. He's a sweet little boy and beautiful, really. When the group gathers, it's Michael and Sam, Isabel, Simpiwe, and David. Georgina Vanderhoff is a surprise addition.

On an autumn day in early May, David (half-naked) and Simpiwe (Chicago Bulls garb) show up to collect Isabel (shorts and tee) at her house. Michael and Sam are already in tow. Georgina will meet them on the side of the road. Putting her backpack on and tying her hair up, Isabel says good-bye to Daniel.

He helps her with her pack. "You've got your cell phone, right? Your beeper?" Daniel jokes.

"Yep." They kiss and she whispers, "If it rains, leave the towels on the floor. If David gets naked, you're just going to have to believe me."

When the group begins their trek, Daniel yells, "Make her sweat!"

David is the Pied Piper. Always barefoot, he walks quickly, ahead of everyone with Simpiwe close by. They speak in Xhosa, while the American woman and the British boys follow jabbering in English.

This odd group stops at the Trendsetter Supermarket and the Xhosa people stare at them as they huddle. Isabel no longer stares back, used to the bundles on top of heads, babies tied to backs. The three whiteys—David now Xhosa—go inside the store, where Isabel usually shops. All three buy sticky, sugarcoated peanut brittle candy bars, which they argue are the trail mix equivalent in the Transkei.

Outside the Trendsetter, David and Simpiwe sit on the ground, eating take-away food. It's meat and rice in a Styrofoam container. The whiteys stand around (not sitting) with their arms dangling at their sides while David and Simpiwe eat. It's a dynamic process, involving finger-licking. Though she pretends not to look, Isabel watches them eat. David and Simpiwe use their hands, scooping food up with finger and thumb to spoon it into their mouths. Food on David's beard. Grease on their fingers. Bones are thrown in the road and Isabel flinches. It's the act of discarding garbage. It's the act of David discarding garbage. *Why*, Isabel thinks, *is this part of the authentic lifestyle he embraces?* Isabel watches him contemplate the grease on his fingers. He takes his walking stick and rubs the grease into the stick, smoothing the wood, conditioning it, massaging it with the oil.

Then they continue walking.

Georgina waits at the edge of the road with Chris. "I've brought my sketch pad." She wears a turban, reminding Isabel of *I Dream of Jeannie.*

They leave Port St. Johns, departing from the road and heading into mountains.

Once inside the hills, it's another world. In villages buried within the Transkei, there are people who have never been to a town the size of Port St. Johns. Umtata, only an hour or so away by car, is unimaginable for most. Jo'burg, another planet. This part of the Transkei is the developing world inside the already-developed. They walk through a wet rainforest, with a creek of fresh water rumbling from an unknown source. They hike hills covered in a tall, pastel green grass. Cows with red, shiny coats graze, their flanks warmed by the sun. The deeper they hike, the more Xhosa kraals they see. Groups of rondavels spot the land. The Xhosa beckon David over— here, they do not know Isabel. He kneels before them, removing seeds, herbs, plants from the pouch at his waist. Then he spreads them on the ground, moves his hands in dance-like gestures, and returns to the foreigners.

The hills are progressively larger; people stare longer.

"Isabel." Michael jumps around when he speaks. Isabel can't help but stare at his piercing. He makes her think of New York, of late nights and Washington Square—her body wrapped in cellophane dresses, head hurting, everything in her dying for a good conversation. "Have you smoked pot in the Transkei?"

"I haven't."

"That's why people come here, you know."

"Not me."

"So, you're a missionary?"

Isabel watches him speak, watches him move. He looks like Daniel-Gone-Wrong, like *Trainspotting* means something different to him than it does her. "Yeah, I'm a missionary."

Michael smiles. "We should smoke together, don't you think?" He watches Isabel. "I'd love to get stoned with a missionary."

"Sure," she says, sarcastically. "Before you and Sam take off, come to dinner one night. We'll eat something Western and smoke a little pot."

"If we weren't leaving afterwards, I'd take you up on that."

Later, they pull out peanut brittle and eat it, sticky and sweet. They run their fingers in the current to clean them, splashing their faces, dousing their hair. The afternoon sun lowers, softening the light on the green hills, the red cows, the pastel rondavels.

Michael is wide-eyed, fascinated by Isabel. "You don't mind if I ask you questions about the whole missionary thing, do you? We don't get to talk to very many."

"It's fine." She tries to be careful in the way she steps in mud. "You aren't writing a book, are you?"

Michael laughs. "No, but Sam keeps a journal." Sam turns red. "And he studies theology," Michael adds.

"I've taken a few theology classes."

After another hour, they sit. David is strange to them. He tells them about life among the Xhosa. "My existence prior to this means nothing." He leans back, his hands spanning over rock. "Everything turned out to be meaningless." It's a language with which Isabel is familiar: the language of spiritual transformation. She listens, watches him, watches the others absorb his words. David lights a joint, smokes it. This isn't doing drugs; it's organic living. It's more vegetarianism than addiction. Simpiwe runs around, skipping stones along the stream. Isabel thinks about sincerity and insincerity.

Family, friends—they think her faith dubious.

No one doubts David's sincerity.

Is there a qualitative difference, she wonders, *between her dubious faith and his honest sincerity? Does it matter which system is more closely aligned with truth? Or does it all hinge on the strength of the believer's convictions?*

"David." She stares at him.

David, looking at Isabel as if she were most definitely a Western invention, some condemnation in his eyes because she is both Christian and soft-skinned, both narrow-minded and glamorous. He pulls guavas from his bag, bites into one to check for worms, and hands it to the missionary. "Hmm?"

She takes the worm-free guava from his hands, the same hands that rubbed the stick with grease and went from meat and rice to mouth and beard, and she holds the fruit in her palm. He has bitten it in half. Isabel takes a bite.

"What accounts for your calling to be an igguira?" Isabel uses the Xhosa word for witch doctor.

Like the others in town, David has seen this woman being chased down the dirt road, chased to the sea by her husband. He has slept on her floor and heard the sound of her breathing in the night. She is one of the few white women in town. She is something to watch, something compelling—the way one finds a marionette, a firefly, or a hummingbird compelling. She is disturbing and suspicious in her whiteness, her femininity, and especially her Christianity.

David wants to be a Pondo ixhwele, an herbalist, a sangoma, not a white man. He doesn't want to find her compelling.

"It's pre-ordained." He plays with a leaf in his hands. "Usually, the calling manifests itself in a supernatural way and the one called has suffered tremendously."

"Can you do magic?" Michael asks.

"I have the ability to sense others' angst or ailments." David looks broodingly towards Simpiwe. "It's a penance. It's a penance to feel someone else's sufferings."

Isabel twists a twig in her fingers. "There are certain commonalties among religions—the connection between suffering and enlightenment, the idea of knowledge being a penance."

"I'd have to argue with you, Isabel." David drops the leaf.

"No commonalties?" She raises her eyebrows.

"No religion—this isn't a religion. It's compatible with religion. The trances, the herbs, the magic—it's a way of life. It can go hand-in-hand with your Christianity."

"So what do you believe? What goes on in your head when you're trance-dancing?"

He hesitates. "It's like you're absorbing all this energy, this unbelievable amount of energy, and just when you think you might explode, you give it up and let go."

"David, you'll have to pardon me for saying this ...." She speaks cautiously. "But I don't understand that. I don't get what you mean when you say you're *absorbing* all this energy."

Michael laughs, "You're obviously doing the wrong drugs."

"You know my own religiosity has very little to do with any supernatural sensation," she says. "There was never a blinding light, a tingly sensation, or an overwhelming calm." She pauses. "Just a conviction of truth."

"I've heard others of your kind say they've at least gotten a tingly sensation," Michael tells her.

"So do you believe in God?" she asks David.

David simply says, "God is everywhere and everything."

"Hmm." They're quiet. They stare into each other's eyes. "What are the purposes of the trances?" She twists sticks in her hands.

He strokes his beard. "We're communicating with ancestors. It's like prayer."

Isabel squints. "Christianity draws a distinction between God and the earth. God is infinite; the earth is finite."

"You don't know the earth very well."

"Why do you say that? Because I don't think it's divine?" Her eyes lock with the twaza's. "I still believe the earth was made by a divine source. I know the earth for that."

"It's a living thing." David puts his hands flat on the ground, like he's feeling for a heartbeat.

"You've got to smoke it to know it," Michael says.

Georgina abruptly turns to David. "It's like you're Christ and this is Galilee and we're hearing the Sermon on the Mount, except you're a sangoma and this is the Transkei and Isabel keeps interrupting."

They get to their feet to continue. "We want to get there before dark," says David.

David tells them about the Xhosa. How they exist on subsistence farming, how the only cash crop they have is marijuana. He tells them about boys getting circumcised at puberty, about marriages being arranged but informally based on affection, about the combination of Western medicine and herbalist endeavors. He speaks of the importance of ancestors, the practice of polygamy, the existence of a hierarchy in society, and the general lack of interest in politics.

They eat guavas. They stop on the side of the trail, their shoes covered in a thick wet slosh of mud and dung, and Simpiwe climbs a tree and throws down ten guavas. They check for worms by biting into them, spitting out seeds. Their hands are dirty with mud and guava juice and they wait until they reach a stream to rinse them.

The sun gives way to the moon, casting a gold and lavender tint on the land. They've been hiking for six hours. Isabel falls behind. She hesitates to watch the sunset and the pale blue and soft pink kraals bathed in light.

A boy joins her. He's wearing a suit—a boy's suit—old and tattered. The hand-me-downs of another boy, now a man.

"Hellooo." He walks next to her and smiles broadly, staring into her face. He stares at her backpack, too.

"Molo."

"Unjane?"

"Ndiphilile, enkosi," Isabel answers. *I am well, thank you.*

"Is that your backpack?" he asks in English.

Isabel remembers the fear two years ago when the child in the township punched her in the groin. "Yes."

"Oookay," he answers. "Where are you from?"

"America," she says. "The United States," she adds.

"Oookay." He smiles broadly.

Isabel is struck by the differences between these remote villages and the Port St. Johns townships, which are apartheid-constructions— geographically-confined, labor reserves for whites, holding grounds for the poor. In contrast, these villages, though poor, are not necessarily built on hatred, though they may be maintained by it. The hills, the rondavels, the livestock, the farms are not the product of oppression, but of underdevelopment. The sight of this child immediately creates trepidation within her, fear of fists to groin. But he has no intention of doing anything of the sort. Isabel can see that now, with his "hellooo" and his "oookay."

The boy suddenly veers off from the sunlit mud path and heads into the tall grass, walking towards a pastel rondavel. "Good-bye!"

It grows darker. Simpiwe comes back, taking her hand to guide her. Finally, they stop at the kraal of the witch doctor and his family. This is where David lives. They are in the village of Unxweme.

There are three rondavels. The center one, the makosini or sacred hut, is used for trance-dancing and ceremonies. Another, a communal hut, is used for cooking and sleeping. A third is used when the weather is bad or when David brings people home from Port St. Johns. The kraal is built on a bog. Soft mud is everywhere. A giant pig wanders around, along with a chicken and her chicks.

Isabel, Michael, Sam, and Georgina are ushered into the third rondavel and David leaves them alone. Later, they will eat dinner and see trance-dancing. It's a nightly undertaking, part of the training process for the sangoma. Left alone, the four of them sit on blankets spread across the dung floor. There is no electricity, no running water, no plumbing, no furniture, no decorations. It's a Xhosa rondavel, circular, barren, made of dung and mud.

"I'd choose Isabel's puritanical impulses over the pigs and bogs," says Georgina after ten minutes. "I suppose this kind of deprivation must serve some purpose, right, Isabel?"

"I don't feel deprived, Georgina."

"You don't feel deprived?" Michael leans towards her.

"By my beliefs?" she asks.

"Look at you and that husband of yours." Georgina's comment is tart and sudden. Everyone turns to Georgina and waits for Isabel's reaction. "You live in Port St. Johns. Your friends are this provisional crowd of backpackers, hippies, and anarchists. And when you become close to them, they leave you because they're really on their way to Durban or Pretoria. I mean, Isabel, you read the Bible. You teach black children things they'll never have any use for. We know you're unhappy." She puts her chin in the air. "We've seen you running towards the water like you might drown yourself just for the drama of it."

"Georgina." Isabel pauses. "I only run because I know Daniel is following." The British boys are quiet.

"Molo?" David peeks his head into the rondavel. "Would you like to eat?"

The moon is high in the sky and a thousand stars light up the firmament.

Before they gather in the communal hut, Isabel stands outside and watches Umfazi make the mealie over an open fire. Umfazi is twenty-years-old and delicate-boned, thin-limbed, with perfect black skin. Her face is serene; her cheekbones are high. Already, she has given birth to two children. Dada, her husband, is Isabel's age.

Isabel watches the stoking of the orange fire with corncobs, the thickening of the corn in the black pot. She watches the woman stir the mealie, build the flames, chop the wood. Isabel thinks of deprivation and what it is that makes her morose. Not deprivation. She is not deprived. Her cup is full. She lacks nothing. Isabel watches the young woman work, noting her expertise; she thinks of ice-cream casserole dishes with Ritz cracker crusts and Whoppers crushed on top. In America, it's a cracker-box dessert served with *Good Housekeeping* ingenuity. In Africa, it's mealie served by willowy child-brides.

They sit in the makosini with the African magic men. In the center of the rondavel, a fire burns. The men inhale herbs. Drums are beaten steadily, rhythmically—in frantic, sexual pulses. The foreigners watch. The men fall into trances. They rise above the flames and begin to dance. Chicken necks are stuck to the inside of walls in gory testament to magic practiced. Small animals hang from ceilings. The fire burns and the drums beat; the witch doctors stomp their feet on the ground and then lift them, kicking them high and hitting the surface in hard thuds. The rhythm is intrusive, overpowering. Bodies are everywhere, black and shiny. They are convulsing, stomachs becoming hollowed pits as muscles strain and bellies jut forward again. Legs meet heads. Eyes disappear, rolling into skulls. The witch doctors inhale weed. The whites of their eyes show, their bodies are vessels for something outside of themselves, the dances are uncontrollable. Michael watches, his jaw slackening. Sam stares, enraptured; the whites of his own eyes revealed. Georgina is watchful, but not put-off. Isabel is transfixed. The drums beat into the night, fire lighting wet flesh, pounding, pounding, pounding.

Three in the morning and Isabel tries to sleep on a grass mat on the dung floor in a dusty blanket.

A pig snorts outside. She turns to the left and looks at the child, sleeping soundly. "Isabel, are you awake?" Georgina talks over the bodies of the British boys.

"Yeah."

"May I ask you a personal question?"

The women don't look at one another. "Okay."

"Do you love Daniel?"

Isabel feels the weight of the question, the longing in the asking. "Yes, I love him."

"Why?"

"I love him—," she begins. She thinks, drawing on memory, on things he holds onto, things he leaves behind. "I love him for his *changeability*. I love him for—," she pauses. And then she settles on it. "Daniel is dedicated to his epiphanies."

Georgina sighs. Two hours later, Isabel sits up and looks at the sky through the open door. She hears roosters crowing. A myriad of stars are still visible. It's more magical to her than any trance. The sun begins to rise. She hears people waking. Coughs that strongly suggest the onslaught of tuberculosis are rampant. Georgina is a cat waking, yawning instead of meowing. Michael and Sam stretch their arms and say good morning to Isabel Harmond, still a missionary.

They drink tea, sweetened with sugar and made spicy with chili powder. "I'd like to show you the cornfields," David says.

They take the three-kilometer walk to where maize is harvested. Kraals adorn small plots of land, occupied by lazy animals or measly crops.

Dada, Umfazi, and others are spaced out along a ravine. They comb the sides of the chasm, picking corn off stalks and peeling away each ear from its leaves. Through thorns and insects, they stretch to reach precarious shoots, bending them towards their bodies, pulling the corn off in a loud *crunch* as it disconnects. Then they throw the corn into piles on the hills. They pull oxen up the hills and gather piles as they go. Their clothes are covered in burrs and their hands are scratched. The corn kernels are yellow and white with an occasional purple one, shaped like little pearls. Mama laughs at Isabel when she sees her standing with hands at her side staring at the Xhosa like an exhibit.

Returning, David and Isabel walk ahead.

"You gave up everything to live as an ixhwele," Isabel says.

"You did the same. You, too, are a healer."

"I do it because I believe."

David exhales deeply. "I do it because it seems to be the purest form of living."

Michael calls out from a few yards behind them. "Hey, Isabel?"

"What?" she yells.

"Do you and your husband only do it in the missionary position?" Hysteria rushes up to meet the twaza and the Christian.

"Only since we became missionaries," she yells back. To David, she says, "We're missionaries, but I don't know if we're spreading the

Word or looking for it." Then, deciding, she says, "We're looking, but we know it's there."

When they return to the kraal, they find the children gnawing on sugarcane. They chomp on the stalk, suck its sweetness through their teeth, and spit it out when the sugar is pulled from the roots. Georgina pulls out her sketch pad. Isabel sits down and opens a blank journal. Udad'obawo, who stays home to watch the children while the family harvests corn, breaks off a piece of her sugarcane and hands it to Isabel, staring at her. Suddenly, she says something in Xhosa.

"What did she say?" Isabel asks.

"She wants to know what you're writing." David easily moves between Xhosa and English.

"What did you tell her?"

"I told her you're writing down everything you see."

Isabel turns to the old black woman, thin and wrinkled. The old woman kneels before Isabel with sugarcane in her hands and her skirt touching the earth. She doesn't smile at Isabel, she just looks into her eyes.

Udad'obawo speaks again.

David translates. "She wants you to remember the name of the village. She wants you to write it down correctly. Unxweme."

Isabel carefully writes.

The old woman speaks again.

"She says," begins David, "this is the clan of Iyeza in Unxweme."

"The clan of Iyeza in Unxweme," Isabel repeats.

Isabel writes down the old woman's name. She writes Udad'obawo. *Great Mother.*

The old woman stares at Isabel from her position on the ground. Then, while Isabel stares back at the old woman, Udad'obawo begins to pick burrs from the fields off Isabel's clothing. She pulls thorns off, one by one. Her hands dance over Isabel's socks, removing thorns with nimble fingers. She does it gently, with care. Isabel, moved, doesn't know how to respond. This gesture is too large. She joins the old woman. Their hands work together—old, black, withered; and young, white, soft. As the last burr is pulled from Isabel, she looks into the eyes of the old woman and stares deeply into the woman's face. She wants this countenance to be etched into her mind. She is humbled, overcome by the hands of Udad'obawo.

"You should be heading back," David announces.

Georgina says she'll stay an extra night to sketch, if David doesn't mind. David's friend, a young Pondo, will drive the other three to Umtata, which is about an hour and a half from Port St. Johns. In Umtata, the British boys will take off for Durban. Isabel will catch a minivan taxi to Port St. Johns.

Isabel sits in the back of a truck with the British boys. Michael looks at the clouds, smoking a cigarette. He's distant now, already headed somewhere else. Sam opens his notebook and reads the things he's written. The young Pondo drives the yellow pickup to Umtata, where he works in a vegetable stall. Umtata is the largest city in the Transkei, a black city with almost no whites there. Everyone has warned Isabel against taking taxis from Umtata alone and she didn't tell Daniel about this last leg of the trip. It's out-of-the-way and not particularly wise.

She looks at Sam.

"I don't believe in God, you know," he says.

Isabel smiles at the confession. "But you study theology?"

"Just because it's interesting. Do you believe humans have the capacity to commit themselves?"

Isabel feels like touching his forehead. "I think humans will forever try. We *want* to commit."

"Do you?"

Looking around her, she says, "I do."

They get closer to Umtata. Michael looks at Isabel. "I wouldn't go out there if I were you."

The number of cars on the highway has increased.

"Come with us." Sam speaks enthusiastically. "We're catching the Baz Bus." The Baz Bus, the backpacker mode of transportation in South Africa, travels from Cape Town to Johannesburg and back again, dropping off kids as it goes. "You can get off at Durban and then figure it out. Call your husband or that Neil guy."

Isabel turns quickly to the right and left. The streets are bustling in third-world frenzy—an open bazaar, a flurry of color and filth and ratty clothes and inefficiency. Behind them, an armored vehicle follows. There are people everywhere.

Shit, she thinks. This isn't for her. She can't do this.

She finds herself asking the British boys for advice. "What would you do?"

"Do what you want," says Michael. *What happened to his missionary obsession?*

"Come with us," says Sam.

"I don't have a Baz Bus ticket."

"We'll argue." Sam looks around. "They aren't going to leave you here."

Isabel's mind races. She can just go, call Daniel from Durban, apologize, ask him to pick her up, offer to trade eccentric sexual favors or fresh meat, a steak, whatever he wants.

"Don't do it." Sam catches her eye. "It isn't worth it."

Isabel is frightened because she's in the streets of Umtata and she feels so white and the fact that she's afraid of color distinctions horrifies her. She jerks around, straining to see the city. She's been to Umtata before, but never alone.

The truck pulls up to the taxi stop. Isabel is beside herself. There are masses of people. The British boys freeze.

The young Pondo man jumps out of the cab. "I'm going to find you a taxi headed for Port St. Johns." He's just exhausted his English.

Isabel climbs out of the truck and begins searching her pack, searching for the Greyhound schedule she knows she has somewhere. Durban, she can get to Durban. She'll call Daniel from there. She rustles through her belongings. She can't find it. She finds it. She's missed it. She looks around maniacally. The boys are watching her. They look at her as if she were a scary movie.

"What's your surname?" Sam says.

"Harmond. Yours?"

"Paskins."

The Pondo man comes back. "I've found one."

"May I check it out?" she says.

He doesn't understand her.

"I'll go with you." Michael hops out of the vehicle.

They walk over together, Isabel Harmond, the missionary, and Michael, surname unknown. They arrive at a minivan jam-packed with at least fifteen people.

Michael says a few words in Xhosa to the African driver.

"What did you say?" Isabel turns to Michael in the noisy taxi-stop. People call out foreign words while vehicles backfire, tires spin on dirt, and vans accelerate away. Isabel and Michael shout. They watch each other's lips. People push them to get by.

"He's to take care of you." Michael faces Isabel.

"What do you think?" Isabel asks.

"I think it's okay."

Isabel doesn't move. There's no time to decide. There are taxi wars and drive-by shootings. There are perils to being white in the Transkei. There are dangers in being a missionary in Africa, of choosing your fears, of choosing the things to which you will be loyal, of defining what it is that matters to you. She looks at the driver. She can see neither good nor bad in his face. He's just a man.

Eventually, you do it alone.

"Okay," she says. "I'm going."

Michael and Isabel rush back to the truck and it seems very apocalyptic. She grabs her backpack, throws it over her shoulders, and looks at the British boys.

"I'll remember you, Sam Paskins." She follows Michael.

It's all very *Casablanca*. Michael races her to the minivan, races her away from Sam and the Pondo man and into the taxi. "Goodbye!" they shout to each other.

She sits in the back, breathless. She's the only white woman, the only white person. One man is packing a gun. Realizing she hasn't eaten all day, she bites off a piece of leftover peanut brittle from her bag and eats it slowly. Everyone takes his or her turn shifting around to check Isabel out.

She leans back and thinks about the British boys and their perpetual journey; the way Michael looked off into the horizon, having already moved on, saying, *Do what you want*; Sam's relegation of her to nostalgia, the missionary he met in the Transkei. She's their memory, a note in a travel journal. An adventure had. She eats her candy. It's sweet and she's thirsty. She thinks of sacraments. She thinks of Daniel, who loves her now and later. She thinks of God who doesn't abandon her. She thinks of dilapidated townships. This is her life. She seems made for it.

Isabel Harmond arrives completely unscathed in Port St. Johns in a dirty minivan with numerous black people. What one fears in South Africa and what one should fear in South Africa are two different things.

Isabel thanks the driver and begins to walk down Main Street, parallel to the Umzimvubu River, towards the Indian Ocean. It's dark outside. She can hear shouts from the Coastal Needles Hotel—boisterous cries and song. She passes the Trendsetter, almost shuffling her feet. She walks to the fourth street, stepping over rocks, trying to avoid catching herself on hanging branches. She heads up the sixth driveway.

At the top, she twists the front doorknob. It's locked. She has keys, but they're buried deep in the pack, so she circles around the house towards the backdoor. She notices the light on in Daniel's nook. Nearing the window, she drops her pack to the ground and approaches it.

Peeking inside, she sees him. He sits at his improvised desk of broken wood working by candlelight. He's bent over open books, Bibles and concordances, commentaries and tomes on sanctification, eschatology, and the sovereignty of God. He has one hand on the back of his neck, which he rubs inattentively. He stares down, his gaze fixed and intense. He doesn't notice the woman outside his window.

Isabel stands to the side and watches Daniel. He reads, writes notes, flips pages. Isabel stops and feels her heart beat in warm rhythms. She is unable to move. She stands still and watches his hands, watches how he twists the pencil in his fingers, rubs out words and rewrites phrases. Isabel watches his eyes, how intent they are on paper, on candlewick and flame. He closes them and opens them slowly. The lines around his mouth tremble in hopeful deliberation. It's Daniel and his aspect thrills her.

Isabel believes in the capacity for human commitment. It has nothing to do with geography, with borders and demarcations, with spatial relationships. Absent of color like the center of the candle flame on Daniel's wood beam desk, it is white light in darkness, sanguinity in the midst of discontent, faith in the midst of faithlessness.

Advent

On our way there, we saw the whores. They wandered the streets, hovered under roofs of buildings engraved with dates like 1923 and even earlier. All along Main Street, skinny girls in miniskirts with dark bare legs strutted lazily with kick-like steps—high-heeled feet jerking forward following after bony knees. While their legs jutted ahead, they clung with folded arms and concealed hands to their own rib cages garbed in mismatched sweaters. As people drove by, the girls met eyes with the spectators.

"The whores are all colored," Miles commented.

"They must be cold," I responded. It was April and winter had arrived early in the Western Cape. I resented it because I hadn't brought the right clothes.

We fucked all Easter weekend. I didn't pray once. Fucked through Good Friday. Missed the church Easter egg hunt. Would have fucked through Advent, if Advent had been in April. On Easter Sunday night, we had dinner at a Portuguese restaurant. There was nothing Portuguese about it.

The restaurant was dark. I was drunk. Miles had his hand on my thigh and I covered his hand with mine. I pressed firmly. Pictured his skin turning white with the pressure. Wished he wouldn't go away. Wished he'd stay. Miles.

"I don't like Americans." Kobus was speaking. He sat across from me. He was Afrikaans and Miles had known him since the time they were working together in London. "Find them insincere."

I spun the wine around in my glass with limp wrists and false laughter. I barely knew him. Met him one other time before. At a party. He had pointed out I was the only American in the room. I had said, *Goody for me,* and then I had raised my glass and said, *God Save the Queen.* None of it had made any sense, but Kobus had laughed and Miles had raised his eyebrows in pleasure. *See what a clever girl I have.* Everyone had toasted the Queen.

Now Kobus was with an English woman named Billy. He looked over our heads and deep into the restaurant and said to no one in particular, "Get the child."

Miles put his mouth against my ear. He whispered, "Kobus was a drug lord for nine months in London." His lips hummed against my ear. "I don't know who the hell Billy is."

"You're lying to me," I laughed, eyeing Kobus, who scanned the restaurant. I ran my hand up the inside of Miles's leg.

"He went everywhere with a chauffeur and two bodyguards."

I pictured Kobus in London with an entourage. In my head, he was wearing a black jacket with large lapels. Maybe sunglasses, too. I laughed aloud.

Kobus had his finger pointed in the air and his chin lifted high, trying to get the attention of this elusive boy. Miles moved his legs together and trapped my hand inside. Billy was digging through her purse.

A child approached the table. He had olive-colored skin and white blonde hair. Thin, delicate limbs. I stared. Couldn't help it. His white-blond hair was almost in curls around his head. Like a Greek sculpture. I whispered to Miles, "He looks like a little boy from Ancient Greece. Like he ran in the first Olympics with fig leaves around his head in a wreath. A little god. He should be in marble."

"Don't stare."

"He's beautiful."

"We need more ice in the ice bucket." Kobus tilted the bucket so the child could see it was empty. "Would you bring us another?" Kobus was elegant and affected. London did it to him. Certainly not Bloubergstrand, where he grew up eating boerewors and smoking dope. "And another bottle of this wine."

The child picked up the empty bottle and hurried away.

Miles moved his legs apart, releasing my hand. "This place makes me want to swoon," I whispered. I fell into him, into his body—a body that was mine, then not mine. Tonight, mine.

"You *are* swooning." Miles winked. "It's the wine."

"It's the child."

"It's the wine."

"Am I drunk?"

"You are."

The child returned with the ice bucket and the new bottle of wine. "Thank you." Kobus took the bottle from the boy's hands.

"He's Lolita," I said to Miles. I watched the boy maneuver around the table. Billy whispered in his ear and he nodded his head in understanding. I stopped staring and looked at Kobus. "Kobus, what do you do now in Cape Town?"

"Flying tours over Namibia."

"Who goes?" I pictured the red sand dunes, the desert, vast and empty. Miles lit my cigarette.

"Germans, Dutch, Americans."

"What do they pay?"

"Between seven and ten thousand rand."

"That's a killing."

"For them, as well."

The boy checked our ashtrays, our water glasses, the candles. He gave Billy some matches. My eyes followed him as he worked.

Miles dipped his hand into the ice bucket and let it sit there until it must have been painful. He moved his icy fingers over the back of my neck and I recoiled, rolled my neck, moved it like a swan.

I reached for his hand, dried his fingers on a cloth napkin, and turned it over in my palm. "You're wearing a thumb ring." I looked into his eyes. It was silly—but naughty, naive. Miles smiled. I looked down again. He watched me scrutinize his hand, twisting the thumb ring around his finger and contemplating the etchings in silver.

"It's Israeli," he said.

"It's sexy."

"Mmm." His eyes were half-closed and a smile crept over his lips.

"Your Israeli thumb ring," I repeated. Miles draped his arm around my shoulders, pulled me towards him. "I'd like to suck it right off." Kobus was staring at us, but I knew he couldn't hear what we were saying.

"So you've been a drug lord," I said to him, so he could. Miles slapped my thigh under the table.

Billy didn't even blink. "Let's order." She peered over the edge of her menu. She was tall and thin and I was certain Kobus didn't love her because he never looked at her like he did. "We can have ribs," she said. "Or we can have prawns. Or we can have ribs *and* prawns. What do you want?"

"You want ribs or prawns or ribs *and* prawns?" Miles asked.

I knew that Miles didn't love me either.

I drank more wine. I leaned against Miles.

"I want them both." I clapped my hands together, like a happy girl. Kobus lifted his finger in the air. The child rushed over.

"I find him devastating." I grabbed Miles's leg and squeezed it tightly.

"What are you two whispering about?" Billy asked when the boy left.

"The child." I reached for my water glass.

"He's lovely, isn't he?" Kobus poured more wine and didn't look up when he spoke.

"Yes." I tried to read his face to see if Kobus knew how lovely the boy really was.

"Sarah, how long are you in Cape Town?" Billy pushed a lemon rind through the neck of a bottle of cider. Then she sucked her index finger.

"Until June." I felt Miles lifting the hair off the back of my neck, his fingers tripping softly over my flesh.

The food arrived. Plates of ribs and prawns and chips. Obscene amounts. Little finger dishes of chili sauce. Something oily that glistened in the candlelight. Everyone reached his or her hands over each other and dipped ribs into sauce bowls. A chaotic feast. My vision was blurred, my head fuzzy. I could see Miles ripping the meat off the bones with his teeth. There was Billy, pinkies in the air, biting the prawns with shells still intact, tails discarded afterward. Directly in front of me, I saw Kobus eating a rib and eyeing me, knowing I was drunk. Miles whispered over to me, "Where are you sleeping tonight?" All over the restaurant, posters with the words *I am Portugal* on them.

I had a rib in my hands. "I *really* have the urge to suck that thumb ring right off your finger."

"Too bad I'm not wearing it on my—"

"Shhh."

"Do you want to disappear in the alley for a minute or two?"

"You're being lewd."

"You like it."

"Are we still in Portugal?"

"We were never *in* Portugal."

"Do you think that Kobus ever had anyone killed?"

"I doubt it." Miles put down a meatless bone.

"Ask him." I elbowed his side.

"Eat your ribs and then let's go in the back. It'll only take a minute."

"Don't be lousy, Miles. I demand more."

We threw the bones onto little plates in the center of the table. They stacked up. A pile of bones in the middle of the table. The child hovered like a little bird. He took away the plates of bones.

"Are the Portuguese Catholics?" I asked the entire table.

Kobus nodded.

"This child should be in bed. It's Easter, for God's sake." I reached across the table for a clean napkin. "A big Catholic holiday. Resurrection. The Second Coming right there. What's the deal?"

"Maybe he gets Christmas off." Kobus slid the napkins towards me. "Here comes the band again." They were a cover band. They played popular songs that everyone knew. "Sympathy For the Devil," "Stairway to Heaven," "Knock Knock Knockin' On Heaven's Door." We loved it. Miles and I got up and danced. But it wasn't really dancing. I moved my hips into his and wrapped my arms around his neck. He winked at me when we sat down and I thought to myself that he uses that wink as a remedy for everything. I smiled when he did it, but I wished he had said something instead. Something *nice*.

Billy was smoking one cigarette after another. Kobus was thinking of more reasons to summon the boy. Miles had his fingers in the ice bucket. I pressed my palm into Miles's leg and moved up towards his groin. Kobus said, "Whenever I fly Americans to Namibia, they always compare the landscape to the States—nothing can be just as it is."

"Are you trying to say something about Americans?" I asked with simulated languor.

"Not really."

"I want to *fuck* an American," Miles whispered. I had known Miles for one year. We had met at a hotel in Johannesburg where he was doing business and I was spending a small inheritance from a dead relative.

"You fucked an American all weekend."

The band started the second set. Kobus had one arm around Billy and the other tapped in time with the music. Miles kissed my jawbone and told me where he wanted to touch me. In the year that I had known him, he had never told me he loved me. It didn't matter. I sipped my wine and listened to the band. Slipped my hand under Miles's leg.

We sat there and listened. We sat there until the plates had been cleared and the wine had been replaced with Irish coffees, thick with cream. Our bodies were turned in our chairs towards the cover band, fingers drumming the table in steady beat.

The child was done with us.

In the corner, by our table, he dragged a barstool over to the wall. He stepped on the first rung. He turned around and sat down. His legs dangled off the stool. His shoulders were hunched and his hands were folded in his lap. He listened to the band play and his mouth dropped open a little.

Kobus twisted his neck around when he saw me staring at the boy. "Did you want something, Sarah?"

I had one hand under Miles's leg and the other wrapped around the stem of a wine glass. "Why?" I didn't know what Kobus thought I could want.

"I see you staring at the boy. Did you want more wine? An ashtray?" He stopped and smiled coyly. "A wet towel to wipe your dainty fingers?"

"No." I paused. "Thanks."

Kobus eyed the boy. The child's little shoulders were hunched, his legs swung haplessly, his mouth open unselfconsciously.

"He looks so innocent," I said.

Kobus lifted his finger in the air and spoke aggressively. "Hey, you—"

"No, don't, Kobus—" I reached my arm out to grab his wrist across the table.

The boy turned around, as if wakened from a dream. Slowly, his mouth closed and his shoulders lifted, and he was like a nursery rhyme to me, more suited for haystacks and plum pies than bars at midnight with bones and wine.

"This lady would like something," Kobus said, nodding his head in my direction.

The child didn't say anything. He looked at me, shyly.

"Tell him what you want." Kobus looked at me and opened his eyes widely.

Miles straightened his body and then wrapped an arm around my shoulder, smiling suspiciously. "What *do* you want, Sarah?" He moved his hand from my shoulder to my breast and I pushed him off me, embarrassed.

The child waited for me to speak.

"I don't want anything," I said to the boy, smiling. There was an awkward pause. "You don't have to get us anything."

Kobus stared at me from across the table. "No more wine, Sarah?" The boy still stood by the table.

"No." And then to the boy, I mouthed, "Thank you."

Kobus gave the child an empty coffee cup. "You can go now."

The child took the cup and walked away. I lowered my eyes. I folded my arms across my chest. Miles pounded the flat of his hand in time with the music. I looked up. Billy smoked and Kobus stared past us into the crowd. We sat there a long time, drinking.

"Excuse me for a moment." I stood.

"Where are you going?" Miles asked.

"To the restroom. I'll be back in a second." I touched his cheek and walked towards the back of the restaurant. My balance was off. I held onto furniture as I made my way. Touched a wall, touched the back of a chair, held onto a table, tried to look elegant. My eyes fell on one *I am Portugal* poster and then another. *What makes one Portugal?* I thought. *Am I Portugal?* I found the bathroom and entered it. I leaned heavily against the sink. Looked at myself in the mirror with my heavy eyelids and wild hair, my demure days over with whiskey and soda, Irish coffees and red meat right off the bone. Black lashes licking my lids, leaving makeup dust to be rubbed away in absent-minded ecstasy later that night with Miles's gasps and groans which sounded more to me like *A one, and a two, and a three.*

I pushed off the sink like I was pushing off the side of a pool, felt myself glide backwards in space—drunken space, where movement is soft. The good side of being drunk. I headed towards the door and opened it. Cold air and cover songs. "Strawberry Fields Forever." I balanced against walls and stopped.

I could see them at the table. Miles, a hollow body. Kobus, a quick sardonic wit. Billy, a neglected and forgotten soul. *Oh, I am being dramatic tonight,* I thought. *Where is my little* Death In Venice? I looked around. Where was he?

From across the restaurant, I saw him. He sat on a stool in the corner. His small mouth dropped open like children who are asleep. His shoulders hunched again, his eyes fixed, absorbed in songs long sung. *He is a little boy*, I thought. *Only a little boy.*

From across the room, a shout. "Sarah!" Kobus was waving from the table. "We're over here." He enunciated each word with exaggerated clarity. "You are not lost."

I smiled. Walked over in my soft, inebriated space. I sat down. I said to Miles, "We should leave."

Miles looked surprised.

"I want to leave now."

"Why?"

"What more is there?"

"Sarah, you're drunk."

"I've had my fill."

"I'll take you home."

"Yes, that's where I want to go."

Miles smiled and stood up.

On our way home, the moon hung in the sky. The sun would rise in a few hours. I looked for the colored whores, imagining they would still be there, still hovering under roofs of ancient buildings, still gaudy in the shadows of crumbling eaves with ornate detail.

"We should stay up and watch the sun rise." My eyes locked with a lone whore's, the only one left. I thought of the possibility of a red horizon, dawn—something epic and biblical. "What do they call the day after Easter Sunday? Do they call it something special in South Africa?" What happened to the rest of the streetwalkers? Did they turn in for the night, finding someone who spoke kind words and left their bodies whole? Did they gather on the beach, sitting in a circle, maybe holding hands, waiting for the sun to lift slowly and dramatically across the sky in the colors of a burn or a deep bruise? Where did they go when it got so cold?

We quickly passed the solitary whore, but her face continued to glow in my mind, reflecting off the window. Her cheeks were a little shiny now, her forehead slightly glossy. Just as it was with the old buildings, delicate lines fractured the smooth make-up surface of her skin. A long night: a long night on a holiday weekend.

I thought about the child, no doubt asleep, tucked in, breathing loudly through his mouth.

Miles leaned over the steering wheel to look at the stars. "Easter Monday." He turned back to me. "That's what we call it. Just Easter Monday."

Zigzag
Bridge

—For Robin Bernard

How to run a nonprofit: First, pick a geographical hotspot where the food is good. Second, make sure the Executive Director is rich. Third, get a moody sidekick who enjoys foreign taxis and using hotel soap. Fourth, consult fundraising types. (Otherwise, the rich Executive Director is in trouble.) Fifth, find a TV station willing to throw a dinner party.

"The shuttle's coming," says an Asian woman.

"So is the messiah," the American guy responds. "Ten more minutes, and we take a cab."

We're waiting for the hotel shuttle at eleven at night in the Shanghai airport. I (moody sidekick) roll my eyes and whisper to Beth (rich Executive Director), "Get a load of *this* guy."

The shuttle arrives five minutes later.

Beth and I sit behind the man and his wife, whore, or girlfriend. We'd normally never make such assumptions, but it's late. We're tired.

The guy looks like Spalding Gray, whom I find mildly attractive After five airports and three countries, I don't find him attractive at all.

Spalding and the woman cuddle, so she's probably a whore.

From airport to hotel, it's twenty minutes. I stare at the couple; I stare at Shanghai, a city bathed in a purple electric glow that throws lines over our legs in crisscross, waffle-like patterns.

We sit in contemptuous quietude. There's something lurid about Gray, who also resembles James Carville and a white Spike Lee. He most likely has an Asian woman fetish, which my Korean friend says is gross and demeaning to all women everywhere. And, there's an age difference. The relationship will never last. She's too pretty; he's too old. Beth and I raise our eyebrows at each other as the Asian chick leans into his middle-aged arms.

Outside, Shanghai. While light dissects Spalding and his lover, it illuminates the city beyond. Unnatural and lavender, it floods buildings, alleys, and matchbox apartments. Billboard advertisements like movie projections shower identical living rooms, kitchens, and bedrooms. I see Chinese people within, stiff-legged and moving in slow motion, cast in plum. Volkswagen and tennis shoe ads beam across indistinguishable floor plans. These are vertical human ant colonies, futuristic like Orwell or Huxley novels.

"Scary." I turn to Beth.

"Eh." She shrugs. Beth's been to China three times. She and her husband have adopted three little girls over the past five years. Then she started this nonprofit last spring, Girls in School, Inc. We're here on business: we'll interview rural schoolgirls, take their pictures, write down their stories, make fundraising pamphlets, and come back next year with money.

This time around, Beth's putting down the cold, hard cash.

The streets are alive. Shanghai is like back home, like Manhattan, oblivious to hour, sleep, celestial body. The stars are invisible anyway. Just bicycles, old people, Communist people, countless people. People upon people upon people. They squat in semi-circles, talking. They sit on chairs, on stoops, smoking, thinking, planning. They ride their bicycles too close to cars, proving some people still have blind faith.

Beth clutches the laptop to her body. "We're here." A luxury hotel looms to our right. "We'll change money and shower."

We're like refugees running across a border, a blanket over our bodies, spotlights racing overhead. We grab our bags and head to the safety of check-in, breathing in little of the Shanghai night air, watching Spalding throw his weight around.

In our room, Beth towel-dries her hair. I count my money on the bed, worrying about the Pepsi I recklessly spent money on at the Tokyo airport.

"Tomorrow, we have an afternoon flight to Nanning. I've got Valium." Beth studies her toiletries. "Should I call Mark?" Her husband.

Beth is forty and a real New Yorker in an uptown way. She's enviably thin with long, almost black, hair. Usually, I'm a measly copyeditor for a nonprofit magazine on nuclear waste. Beth hired me to accompany her to China to write her interviews for Girls in School.

Not a very catchy name. Too safe, too conservative. Beth, who exists on the philanthropic scale somewhere below Bob Geldof and Mother Theresa, is a little on the safe side.

Girls in School raises money to send female children to school in countries where there's rampant gender discrimination. She doesn't want to step on anyone's toes, however. We're in China because girls are really screwed here, but Beth would qualify this: "China is one place—certainly not the *worst*, certainly not the *only* one—where girls lack opportunity."

Uptown, all the way.

China screws girls, I'd say.

She abandoned a lucrative career as a web page designer to start Girls in School.

I'm not a great writer, but Beth likes me. I remind her of when she was thirty. We share philanthropic instincts, though they differ. She's heart; I'm head. Whereas she *feels* like something should be done, I *know* we gotta do it.

Sitting on the edge of the bed and combing wet hair, she says. "We'll go to Old Town tomorrow before our flight."

Then, we're gonna do what's right.

Introduction to China. We find the Bund, Zhongshau Road, which runs along the Huangpa River. People and businesses are everywhere. I've never seen so many people.

"Let's wander around and take pictures of beautiful women," Beth says, a true feminist.

We scope out beautiful women. Like Spalding, we've got a fetish.

In Old Town, a maze of narrow alleys and ancient architecture, our faces are politely placid. There are unearthed and teeming vestiages of dull gold and staid red wood, feng shui courtyards, pagodas, temples, a gong. We see old men playing mah-jongg on crates beneath goblins carved in stone walls, beneath paper windows. Under the swoop of the eaves, vegetables still attached to dirty roots, live chickens, and noisy ducks are stacked. The people are swarming. They stare at us; we stare at them.

"Did you see the flies on that meat?" I snap a picture of laundry that looks terribly exotic.

"Liz, look at something else. Don't take a picture of that."

"I'm not photographing the meat," I protest. "I'm photographing the laundry."

The chickens cluck; the ducks quack. Bicycle bells ring; motorbike horns honk. Chinese words rush past us—a harsh language, dissonant to the ear. My senses are bombarded.

Beth and I spend a lot of time watching things. In the Guangzhou airport where we have to catch a connecting flight, we sit for three hours barely speaking.

"Babies don't wear diapers here." She disrupts my private travel reflections, lifting her chin towards a mother bouncing a toddler on her lap. "They have little slits in their clothing, and the mothers just *know*."

"Wow." I'm impressed.

This is the extent of our conversation.

Across the way, a white guy—he could be anything, German, Australian, Swede—hunts through his backpack. That backpack is more desirable to me than Beth's flat stomach. I want to hit the road, bum through Asia, stop off in India. Because we're both Anglo, the guy and I stare at each other. He makes me nostalgic for *Lonely Planet* travel guides, co-ed youth hostels, and those fake-deep conversations with strangers you have before kissing them—I mean, *really* kissing them. "Beth," I begin, "don't you miss traveling?"

Beth and her husband traveled a lot before they had kids.

"What do you mean? I travel. We're in China, for God's sake."

"Remember the backpacker thing? What it was like going town to town on no money?" I wink. "Oh, yeah—you always *had* money. But don't you miss it?"

"Liz." Beth looks motherly. "You romanticize it. I loved it. I really did. But you know what I remember most?"

"What?" I tilt my head.

"The people who do it—who pick up and leave with nothing but a backpack—those people." Beth crosses her legs. "They desperately want to be *inclusive*, to feel like they're a part of the world, to align themselves with the impoverished and the peasantry and the village folk." She pauses. "Soon enough, those same kids realize they're just passing through. Despite going native, they've got round-trip tickets." She hugs the laptop to her torso. "For them, it's a hiatus from their civilized existences. They have the luxury of eating bugs and sleeping in mud, but they're totally vaccinated."

Poverty porn, I've heard it called.

"What are we doing then?" I ask.

"What do you mean?"

"Doesn't our work just reaffirm the idea that we're rich Americans here to save the day because the poor Chinese don't even diaper their babies? Aren't we trying to be inclusive, but ultimately waving our flag around? We're totally vaccinated," I throw my hands into the air. "I'm on malaria pills."

Beth uncrosses and crosses her legs, shifting the laptop around. "What else can we do?"

Five boys in army green uniforms with splashes of cherry red on their sleeves enter the cockpit, displaying stern and soldierly faces. The plane has yet to leave the ground.

"What's going on?" I peek over seat tops.

"No clue." Beth squirms.

The police boys walk down the aisle. They stop four rows in front of us, speaking to a male passenger in the middle seat.

"What are they doing?" I stop dipping into the bag of dried peas with the wasabi zing, the honey-roasted peanuts' equivalent on Southern China Airlines.

"I can't see." Beth leans back, still harnessed into her seat belt.

The passengers are jumpy. Everyone tries to look respectable, helpful. The guy shows the police boys his airline ticket.

Suddenly, he rises, grabs his carry-on, and leaves with the police boys.

He's escorted right off the plane.

"My God." I eat a wasabi pea.

The plane still doesn't take off. Flight attendants search the empty seat and overhead compartment. Nearby passengers feel around the bottoms of their chairs. A captain-like man comes over to take a look.

It's pantomime for Beth and me. We have to guess what's happening.

"Bomb scare?" I raise my eyebrows.

"I'm asking." Beth unbuckles her belt and stands; she's in charge.

This is my favorite way to live: I like the pretense of independence, but the reality of having others in control. It only works if I trust people. I trust Beth.

She returns.

"What did they say?" I watch her buckle her belt.

"The attendant barely spoke English. He kept saying, 'This plane and the passengers are safe.' He just kept repeating that. 'This plane and the passengers are safe.'"

I lean back, closing my eyes. "So maybe we'll die."

"I'm taking drugs." She pops the top of her Valium bottle.

My eyes are still closed. "I wonder if he's a political prisoner and they're taking him away to torture him till he dies. What d'you think?"

The plane begins to move. Beth holds my wrist. "Prepare to meet your Maker."

Over the loudspeaker, a voice says something in Chinese. Then, there's an English follow-up: "We are sorry for the delay due to special condition."

"Ahh, Valium," Beth croons.

I open my eyes after a couple minutes. "We're alive?"

"Yes." She pauses. "And there are still girls in China who need to go to school."

I pull out *Crime and Punishment*.

"Liz?" Beth whispers in my ear, sounding like thunder at a picnic.

"Hmmm?" I put down Dostoyevsky.

"Why do you support Girls in School?"

We get to do this, Beth and I. Since we have no one to talk to besides each other, we have the privilege of asking one another personal questions.

"It's education-oriented and it appeals to over half the world's population." I'm not much of a feminist and this drives Beth crazy. I look to see how she's taking it. "You?"

"Rage." Again, the motherly concern. "I'm obsessed. The population is fifty-one percent female. Does world leadership reflect this? No. Women change their names when they marry. My mother won't see a female doctor."

Neither will my mother, but I'd probably hyphenate my name. "Gender discrimination is just an ugly part of human nature," I say.

"You think it's innate? Men and women are more than just biologically different?"

I look out the window. "Yep."

"Nature versus nurture." She shakes her head. "We can't do anything if it's nature."

"I don't think nature is unchangeable. It's not *futile*, Beth." I stick my bookmark in Dostoyevsky. "I used to think the differences between men and women were strictly biological, but after a couple bad relationships, I realized men are just *different*." Disgust washes over Beth's feminist face. "Girls in School is compelling because over half the world's population—regardless of race, religion, sexual orientation, economic level, political affiliation, philosophical inclination, or belief in a soul—is female. You either are a woman, or you know one. You either are a mother, or you have one." I elbow her in the side. "Use *that* for your T-shirts."

Too snotty for philanthropy.

Peter, our Chinese translator, picks us up at the Nanning airport. As we toddle off the plane, Beth whispers, "He's very religious. Don't say *fuck*."

In the car, she explains, "Peter works at an orphanage. He's moonlighting. His real name is tough to pronounce."

Trees line the streets of Nanning. Bulbs like Christmas lights are threaded throughout green leaves. Like Shanghai, the avenues explode with cars, bicycles, and motorbikes; hordes of people race everywhere.

"Welcome to the Majestic." Peter opens the taxi door at our latest luxury hotel. I wonder what he thinks of us for staying here. The hotel is huge, blocky, Stalinesque. "You're tired?"

"A little." Beth nods.

Peter takes us to our opulent room. When I travel, I'm used to sleeping in sheets sewn up like potato sacks.

He wears a big cross of jade around his neck. "I'll pick you up tomorrow morning." He places Beth's suitcase on a chair. "We have school visits in the Na Ma district."

When he leaves, Beth wanders around, peering behind heavy curtains, picking up room service placards. "I have to eat something or I'm gonna die."

"It's ten-thirty." I point to the alarm clock between our beds.

"Let's go to the restaurant."

We trudge towards the elevator. The hotel seems empty.

Beth points to her menu when the waitress approaches. "We'd like two orders of toast."

The waitress leaves.

After a minute, she returns. "We only have one toast. Would you like French bread?"

"That would be fine." Beth grins at her, and she walks away.

At ten-fifty, we drink delicious glasses of mango juice, one order of toast, and one order of French bread.

"This is damn good mango juice." I lick my lips.

Beth pushes her empty glass away from her plate. "I forgot. We shouldn't have had it."

"Why?"

"They use human shit for fertilizer."

"Where'd you hear that?" I squint.

"I read it." Beth wipes her mouth with a Majestic napkin. "We also have to be careful with meat." She flinches when I pull out my camera. "Stick to bread."

The Na Ma district looks like Cambodia or Vietnam does in my head. Brilliant wet-green rice paddies and pineapple plants spread over gentle emerald hills. Farmers in straw hats work the paddies, sometimes only the tops of their heads visible against verdant, sumptuous countryside.

We arrive at a school far away from urban clout. A million degrees Fahrenheit with out-of-control humidity, we step outside the car, sweating. Beth told me to wear a schlocky outfit. She would, too, she said. Hers is from Banana Republic. Mine is from the floor of my closet.

The school is an old building with peeling white paint and red Chinese letters scrawled on the walls. I assume it says something about coming all ye faithful. In a shaded area, ten little girls sit lined up in ten little chairs. To their right, a Greek chorus of mothers hovers.

Peter directs us to the chairs for big people. "I've arranged for girls and their mothers to be here." It's July and school's out, but Peter managed to spread the word: Americans in town! One has money! The other takes notes! Show up! Say something memorable!

The girls have serious faces and sad eyes. They wear dirty pants, ripped shirts. They're pretty children, obscenely quiet. Beth looks upon them with kind eyes.

"Shall we start?" Peter rubs his hands together. The girls don't look at me. They're so small—their feet don't even touch ground. The mothers smile, broken and missing teeth showing from behind cracked lips. "We'll go around so that everyone gets to answer each question." Peter waits for me to do something smart and international.

I look at the somber children. "What do you want to be when you grow up?"

Peter translates.

It hits me the way Gray did: its outrageousness, its *garishness*. My questions are meaningless, American. American children want to be doctors, lawyers, even the President of the United States. In the Na Ma district, there's little room for *want* or *desire*.

Occasionally, a little girl breaks the silence and tells us in hushed Chinese, "I want to contribute to the good of the country," or "I want to contribute to the four modernizations."

One little girl says something unorthodox. "I want to be a writer."

Oh. My. God. Beth and I are delighted. We beam; glow; pull out cameras, pens. We want *that* little girl's name.

The mothers freak. So this is what the chorus is for. They shout sharp orders like unruly football fans. Beth and I look at Peter helplessly.

He translates. "They're telling her she wants to be a worker."

"Worker! Worker!" the mothers yell.

The little girl bows her head, examining the hands in her lap. "Worker," she says.

I open the window in the back seat as we drive to the next school. The emerald rice paddies blur like French Impressionism. Beth, in sunglasses, looks like Jackie O on a yacht.

"What are the four modernizations?" I ask Peter.

"Holdovers from Mao's Cultural Revolution," he answers.

Beth nudges me in the ribs.

"I thought the Revolution was over," I say. Evidently, word is still spreading in rural areas that the revolution failed.

Peter doesn't respond.

"What are the modernizations?" I ask.

Beth elbows me again.

"Industry, agriculture, science and technology, and the military," Peter says.

"Sounds fun." I try to picture China during the Cultural Revolution. I see Mao posters, a few clippings from recent Chinese films, some hoes. I don't have much to go on.

Beth sits quietly beside me. Both of us are dehydrated because we don't drink all day in order to avoid bathrooms in the boonies.

"The girls have no language in which to say, 'I hate math'—they can only express themselves in platitudes," I say. "They can't *really* care about the four modernizations."

"They're afraid of repercussions," Peter responds.

"Repercussions!" I lean forward. "They're children!"

"Their words could haunt them, Liz." He turns his head to look at me.

"What do you think they'd say if they could say anything?" I ask.

"I don't know." Peter, too, must wonder if Big Brother is watching. "But it would be different."

Beth whispers, "They'd probably say *fuck math*."

More little girls in the afternoon. The teachers bring watermelon slices, but we refuse in case the fertilizer is made of human shit.

We're somewhere remote, hidden in the Na Ma countryside. In the distance, farmers pull water buffalo through rice paddies. The village is brick and medieval. There are no drawbridges, moats, or royal seals—just a lake, a cesspool, really. Swans float on its dirty surface. Children run around muddy banks, the soles of their feet caked in boggy brown paste. A brick wall surrounds a hole in the ground, the toilet. Flies buzz.

And yet it's also oddly beautiful, with ancient brick castles against plush green and an overcast sky.

In school, girls assemble before us—withdrawn, grave, economical in gesture, avoiding eye contact.

There's a megaphone for announcements so the children are informed that Mao is dead and the rebellion crushed. The classroom is bare, but the ceiling is bordered in pictures of communist heroes. Instead of the alphabet, Mao and Lenin. One wall is covered with a world map, China at its center.

The girls look like they're in trouble or ashamed.

I stand next to an official. "Have any other Americans visited?"

"No foreigners since the Japanese invaded."

Together, we laugh. He puts his cigarette out on the classroom floor.

When we begin, it's the same.

"What's your favorite class?"

Who the hell knows? We have no preferences. We're just like everyone else. There is *nothing* that distinguishes us from any other child here. We're the same—working for the good of the country.

"If you could have three wishes, what would they be?"

Are you crazy?

"Do you think you'll go to college?"

Surely, you're fucked in the head.

"What do you do after school?"

Feed the pigs, fetch the water, sweep the floor.

"I think we're done."

Peter, in Chinese: "They're done. Thanks."

The girls stay in the room while we talk to their parents. They all have siblings despite the one-child policy. Rural folk seem to keep trying for boys. Girls? Big disappointments. Often they're abandoned, or made to work so the boys can go to school. This is why Beth adopted girls.

No one's giving boys away.

"I can't afford to send all my children to school," a man with his fly down explains through Peter. "Of course you send the boy."

"Why not the girl?" I bite my pen.

"If you send a girl, it only benefits the family she marries into."

Crossing his skinny legs, another father leans forward and motions his cigarette towards his three present daughters. "Their mother drowned herself out of shame. She produced only girls." The children look down. Their legs dangle off miniature chairs. In silence, they listen to this revelation about their tiny selves.

I'm no Jackie O in my dusty sandals and sweaty paisley-print dress; I'm more like a water buffalo cooling itself in mud. Heading back to Nanning, I look in my notebook and sweep hair away from my face. Mostly, I've written down names. Intermittently, there'll be some comment: *feeds chickens, likes all school subjects.* "I can't believe the parents speak like that in front of their children."

"It's nothing." Peter shifts in the front seat. "Greater humiliations are suffered. Children write articles about their parents. School rankings are posted for everyone to see. This is nothing."

In the afternoon, Beth and I walk through Nanning's Renmin Park to White Dragon Lake.

"There's the zigzag bridge," Beth points. "We'll cross it."

The bridge is wooden and angled in sharp zigzags like a lightning bolt. Children and parents hang over railings, feeding giant orange goldfish that slap their bodies against the water—jumping up eagerly for mysterious food people toss in.

"You know the pictures you see on TV of African babies with bloated stomachs?" I lean over the rail, mesmerized by orange fish.

"Yeah?" Beth stares at her gold watch reflected on the water.

"Do you think we're doing anything different with these girls? Are we exploiting them?"

She turns to look at me. "Liz. I have to do *something.*"

The goldfish are a little grotesque in their flip-flop dance. It's gotta hurt. "You think there's an afterlife, Beth?"

"Here we go." Beth turns and props her back against the railing. "I lean in the no-afterlife direction." She points a finger at me. "If you do this to get into heaven, I'll kill you."

"I don't. I *hate* that. But I do this because I think there's a God— not because it's my ticket to heaven."

"What?"

"If I believed there wasn't a God, I wouldn't do a damn thing. If I believed there were nothing but African babies with bloated stomachs and Chinese girls who are their mothers' shame and self-indulgent American capitalists, you know what I'd do?"

Beth lifts her sunglasses off the bridge of her nose. Very Jackie. "What?"

"I'd have a lot of sex, eat only chocolate, and spend all my time in the Jacuzzi." A boy throws food away from the spinning vortex of clamoring goldfish. The little brutes swim like freaks towards the food. "I guess I think justice and goodness eventually win." My vision blurs in goldfish chaos. "So I don't only eat chocolate or spend all my time in a Jacuzzi. Let's not talk about sex."

"Helping others doesn't necessarily have to do with any belief in God. For me, it's a compulsion. I had a lousy childhood—I don't want for it to be that way for others." The sun begins to set over White Dragon Lake. "Just like there's no Santa Claus or the Tooth Fairy, there's no triumph of good over evil. We just do what we can."

"Mere Band-Aids? Sticking our fingers in holes before dams burst? I'd rather have sex and eat chocolate."

Beth bends over to look between the wooden planks of the bridge floor. "People like us—we have no choice. This is what we do." She stands upright. "You know why these bridges are built in zigzags?"

"No."

"The Chinese believe evil spirits can only cross bridges in straight lines."

"Trying to foil evil spirits, hey?" I eye the horizon, a soft mesh of yellows and pinks.

"A little evil spirit trivia."

We leave Renmin Park. The pace of the Nanning streets is hectic like a Brooklyn street corner. Storefronts, dentist's offices, and beauty shops open onto road. A sweet, bready, nauseating smell permeates the air. Red bean buns. Roasted meat hangs in windows. Batteries are sold in bulk next to cameras and formal gowns.

"I think we should rename our community outreach program," Beth says.

"To what?" I ask.

"Schmoozing for Girls?"

"The Schmooze Project?" I suggest.

"Project Yenta?" She furrows her brows.

"Project Vagina?"

"Let's stick with 'Focus on the Community.'" She points at a window. "Feel like a little chicken foot?"

The girls are always the same. The only difference is that we stop asking about their three wishes.

Peter takes us to dinner; Beth pays. We go to a happening restaurant in the heart of Nanning. Peter orders quail, snake, pigs' feet, intestines, guts, spring rolls, stomach, sweet potato leaves, snails, and fried banana.

Beth, looking deeply disturbed, says, "Pass the fried banana."

I swallow sweet potato leaf. "So, Peter…" Beth tenses up. "What was the Cultural Revolution like?"

Peter speaks quietly. "Bodies filled rivers. People turned each other in."

I picture bodies rising in White Dragon Lake, orange fish slapping around, clothes on corpses puffed up with air bubbles in the medieval Na Ma village cesspool—their backs to the sun.

Beth kicks me hard under the table. I eat stomach in silence.

Walking back to our hotel, I tap Peter on the shoulder. "What are *your* three wishes?"

He laughs heartily, this round Chinese man in American clothes with a jade cross dangling from his neck. "I'm Chinese!" he protests. "I don't have to tell!"

In the Nanning airport, we see a woman hack up a wad of phlegm and spit it on the bathroom floor.

This powerful image stays with us for a long time.

We board a plane for Guangzhou. As I buckle up, Beth whispers, "Is it me, or have you noticed there's a lot of sneezing and coughing going on?" Two seconds later, she whispers, "Do you smell fried fish?"

A goofy toddler bounces on chubby legs in her mother's lap.

Beth must miss her own Chinese babies, because she's staring and making silly faces at the kid.

"Cute, huh?" I put Dostoyevsky down.

"Her personality will be squashed by the age of four," Beth says. "By then, her only goal will be to contribute to the good of her country."

Beth has a meeting with someone at the U.S. consulate office in Guangzhou. We stay at the White Swan Hotel, which is crawling with Americans adopting Chinese girls because they're required to stop at this consulate office prior to leaving the country. Apparently, every American adopting a baby is loaded—I've never stayed in such a nice hotel before. A waterfall and gilded cage with blue, yellow, and green parakeets adorn the lobby. Parakeets chirp their little parakeet heads off.

Americans walk around grinning and clinging to their kids. The babies are totally confused. Sometimes, they'll reach out to a random Chinese person passing by. It's hell to be a newly adopted and cognizant Chinese baby with American parents.

Beth's meeting gets cancelled, so Guangzhou is vacation. We wander through alleys and opium pipe markets, picking up Mao's *Little Red Book*. We see fish in buckets, dried bats and lizards and seahorses wrapped around sticks like gothic popsicles. Old crooked men carry golden birdcages containing blue finches. At the end of a maze of pickled snakes, little boys urinating in street gutters, and signs promoting the one-child policy (all picturing girls), we find a jade market.

"Look!" Beth points ahead. The Golden Arches. "McDonald's!"

We order Big Macs. "Careful with the lettuce," she says.

We eat every last bite, including the lettuce.

Back in Shanghai, we visit an orphanage. In the cab, I put my hand on Beth's arm. "Don't worry—the publicity interviews will be beautiful."

"We'll lie. We'll make up a little girl named *Li Li*."

"Li Li Flower Drop Soup. Or Li Li White Dragon."

"I like it. We'll say, 'Li Li's dream is to own her own panda farm. Girls in School is making this possible.'"

I clap my hands because I can see it, and it's lovely.

At the orphanage, which resembles a stark dormitory or prison featured in a *60 Minutes* episode on institutional abuse, we see only one room. The "special needs" quarter is skipped, and we're escorted straight to "healthy babies." Walking between cribs, I'm horrified; it's like going to the zoo. Infants and toddlers—all girls—lie on their backs, usually lethargic or asleep. They wear plastic bags for diapers (here, they get diapers), while grim nurses pace and watch us closely.

"Can I pick up a baby?" Beth stands by the cribs; the babies are like a litter of kittens.

This is when I get sick. I don't know if I can do this, if I can muster up the will to foil evil spirits. We don't do enough. This isn't enough. It's all or nothing. Either we save the world or forget it.

What if I just forget it?

Beth picks up a child. "They have rashes on the creases of their necks," she says.

I wait for a nurse to blow a whistle, saying, "Okay, time's up! Put the babies down!"

When we walk out, I say, "They can't keep their heads up."

Beth stands frozen in the orphanage courtyard. "You have to be quiet, Liz. Every time we show hostility, they clamp down on American adoptions. Then what happens? Is that what you want?"

How to run a nonprofit: First, pick a geographical hotspot where the toilets are clean. Second, make sure the Executive Director is rich and willing to spend her own money. Third, get a moody sidekick who romanticizes travel inconveniences. Fourth, don't count on donations. Fifth, get media support.

A TV station throws us a dinner party.

Beth is presented with an award for good works. And there's a catered bash, filmed for late-night viewing in Shanghai.

A feast: duck, turtle soup, deep-fried crabs, jumbo shrimp with black eyeballs intact, a fish from the Yangtze River, broccoli and scallops, sweet corn and crab soup (dessert!), a wiggly pink slab of meat, chicken with thick skin, someone's kidneys.

Out of the corner of my eye, I watch Beth. She's having a tough time. This is harder for rich broads than poor ones. She looks like she may vomit. She murmurs, "I'm trying to stick to the fried batter around the crab shells."

This is how the officials say, "Thank you."

On the final day, we walk around Shanghai. It's so hot we fear death. "Why aren't you wearing shorts?" I have my hands on my hips before Beth.

"I *hate* shorts. No one in New York wears shorts."

I think about this. Her friends *summer* in Martha's Vineyard. "*Everyone* I know in New York wears shorts."

Nanjing Road, the Shanghai Museum, the Bund, and then straight to the Hard Rock Cafe for burgers.

I drink a chocolate malt. I'm twenty pounds overweight in a starving world. I'm middle class, I'm white, I'm educated, and I've been to the top of the Eiffel Tower. I drink my malt with relish. It feels the same way it does to bury *Crime and Punishment* in my suitcase. Must I be reminded of sin and guilt?

Beth orders her burger rare, worries about its pinkness, and eats the whole damn thing.

Americans! What are you gonna do with them?

We sip hot coffee in the Tokyo airport.

"You have a great husband, beautiful kids, meaningful work. You've been all over the world. What's the deal?" I wind my watch.

"I'm nuts, I know. My husband says I should just give up searching for meaning."

"I bet you couldn't," I say.

"Well, you know what Judaism says about it."

"What?"

"I forgot," she smiles forlornly.

"Beth?" I study her face. "Do you really believe you can make a difference?"

"I told you. I don't believe there's *world* peace or *world* justice."

I breathe deeply. "I don't know why you bother, then."

"Leave me alone, Liz. I want to send them to the grave smarter, okay?"

I drain the remains of my coffee. "It's not enough for me—this doesn't cut it." I can't be a mere voyeur, a peddler of poverty porn. "I don't want to simply make provisional plans to foil evil spirits."

"We can't obliterate evil spirits."

I rise. "You've got a good heart, Beth."

"But?"

Here I am, thirty, well-meaning, under-employed, jaded by mediocrity and standard heartbreak, slightly uncouth. Full to the rim with things. "It isn't enough. We send five girls to school and there are five thousand others who stay home. I need to believe in world peace and justice, the triumph of good over evil."

Beth pulls me down, not saying anything at first. Her lips twitch. She turns to me. "What will you say in the interviews?"

"I'll say we're throwing curve balls at demons. I'll say this isn't a losing battle. I'll say Li Li dreams of owning her own panda farm—a beautiful, *possible*, panda farm with a grove on it where the mangos are edible."

"You'll lie?"

"No. I'll tell the truth." I stand again. "I'm getting more coffee. You want some?" How to run a nonprofit. "I'm right about this, Beth. I'm right."

The Freak
Chronicles

Freak (\frēk\)

1 a: a sudden and odd or seemingly pointless idea or turn of the mind
b: a seemingly capricious action or event
2 *archaic*: a whimsical quality or disposition
3: one that is markedly unusual or abnormal: as a: a person or animal
with a physical oddity who appears in a circus sideshow b *slang* (1): a
sexual deviate (2): a person who uses an illicit drug c: HIPPIE d: an
atypical postage stamp usually caused by a unique defect in paper (as
a crease) or a unique event in the manufacturing process (as a speck of
dirt on the plate) that does not produce a constant or systematic effect
4: a: an ardent enthusiast <film *freaks*> b: a person who is obsessed
with something <a control freak>

—Merriam-Webster Dictionary

Jennifer majoring in biology, age 19

We sit outside Patty Wagon, messy charbroiled burgers on whole-wheat buns and pickle spears before us like food sacrificed to idols. It's right across from the university, so there's this constant flow of students and weirdos who thrive on sexual longing and artistic freedom. Everyone eats burgers and discusses Hegel, Freud, *The Grapes of Wrath*, *Sir Gawain and the Green Knight*. There are no vegetarians on the premises.

Tammy orders her jack cheeseburger medium rare: "A little bloody," she says. I balk, but she pays me no attention.

This cat, tiger-striped and dusty, slithers over to our table and rubs against our collegiate legs.

"A stray," I declare, without originality. "On this busy street." I look at the poor thing. "I hate that."

Tammy bends down to touch it. She makes a loop with the thumb and index finger of her left hand, ringing it around the cat's tail and pulling it along its length. "Hey, kitty, kitty," she says. Tammy always touches animals, especially cats.

The cat jerks, turns, hisses.

"What's going on?" I ask, surprised.

The cat, though, is already back at our legs, a buzzy purr in her throat—happy again.

Tammy, examining the feline for obvious marks of the beast, says, "Oh, look, Jennifer. Her tail is kinked." Sure enough, the tip of its tail is misshapen, the fur gone, the flesh tweaked—like a sausage squeezed in the middle. "Someone must have slammed her tail in a door." Tammy touches the cat's back and it porpoises up, trying to shimmy under her palm.

I turn away, looking at the cars zooming by. "You know," I say, "I can't even look." It makes me too sad to know cats with kinked tails are wandering the streets.

My parents had a cat they kept outside for twelve years. Her name was Henrietta, but originally she was called Henry. Henrietta just showed up one day, starved. My parents were the kind of people to keep animals inside. Dogs slept on couches atop their own Ziggy blankets. Cats ate on counters, licked cream sauces off silver spoons near stovetops, and waited patiently for someone to turn the faucet on for a drip of water to fall into their mouths. Henrietta, though, endured lightning, thunder, and rain by crouching in the purple bougainvillea by the front door, uninterested in living room foyers or even the garage.

In twelve years, I touched her maybe six times. It was easier that way.

Tammy reaches across the Patty Wagon table with her free hand. She rests her fingers on my arm. "Jennifer." Her voice is quiet, comforting, forceful. "It probably only hurts when you touch it."

I stare at the headlights of the cars, my burger getting cold. The cloudless sky is darkening, a thick gray; this college town seems ominous for strays.

Jennifer during med school, age 24

I leave the hospital, still in my white coat, not quite smelling of flesh but rather like bleach. The smell of the sterile and the dead. I picture bodies in fetal positions with eyes closed and the drone of machines in steady terror. Nightmarish dioramas, abnormal hallucinations. This time it was a hit-and-run, the body mangled, the heart failed.

I enter the diner and sit in the back, hovering over my cup of tea. The tea clears nostrils, opens pores. I drink and watch.

I am a voyeur.

Hair on the floor in the corner by a booth. Maybe someone pulled a year's worth of hair from a brush and, then, a diner employee, a haggard waitress, an oily chef, someone from the Bronx, pushed it into the corner with a dry mop.

This place reeks of things left behind, neglected.

At the hospital, people wonder what we do with the possessions of the dead. Not everything is claimed.

Do we sterilize trinkets?

Burn datebooks?

Divide cashmere and velvet?

Is it like casting lots for Christ's clothes?

I stare at the memorials surrounding me. Sticky counters, chipped coffee cups. A pale shade of lipstick pressed onto the rim of a cloudy glass.

Whose lips were wedded to that cup?

Will I meet her in ER?

In detox?

In rehab?

Or, in the morgue? In body bags?

I smell negligence. I smell grease. It isn't even the new grease of French fries and onion rings. It's the old grease of spatulas scraping off fried egg, the grease that makes laminated menus glisten, slippery to the touch.

Obscenely extensive laminated menus. One can get sirloin, prime rib, butterfly shrimp. Who orders those things from a place like this?

What can such a person possibly be thinking?

What goes through his or her mind?

Is it an act of hope?

Is this what they mean by taking a leap of faith?

Look at her, winding her way through countertops and moldy cakes. Like she's been here forever. Like time has no meaning for her. She's Alice or Vera or Flo, but Alice doesn't live here anymore.

You poor-ripped-nylons thing in sensible flat shoes, readied for your nonsensical life. Serving these ignorant working stiffs the worst best meal of their lives.

In my hospital, the one in which I follow around old men in long, white coats, they give you a choice. Every morning, if you're one of the sick or dying, you fill out a piece of paper. Grilled Chicken Breast with

Asparagus Tips or Veal Parmesan, various cuts, assorted sautés. You'd think you were in the south of France or the north of Italy.

I eat cod. I remove skin. I cut off parts that look like fish. I remove bones. Every dissection an injury, an operation, an incision, and I lose my loathing for grease and hairballs and the remains of a kiss on a cloudy glass. I am consumed by the slicing of fish and the transformation it makes from thing living to thing dead.

I eat it like a sacrament.

When I'm done, I pay the bill and leave. Today, I saw the dead, but I smell very clean.

Jennifer thinking about her past, age 28

People judge me, I can tell.

It was the middle of the night, just after my residency.

Two a.m., for God's sake! It's never anything good at two in the morning. I'm a doctor; this is something I know.

He called, like he always did, sounding sleepy, maybe drunk, probably clinically depressed but rather articulate. He liked to catch me in that semi-conscious stage because, he said, I was such a good listener when my eyes were closed and the covers were pulled up over the phone, over my head.

We went back, back to the Patty Wagon Days of Collegiate Lust. There, in campus hideaways and earthy bars, we spouted Byron, Shelley—our cheeks flushed, our skin moist, the smell of the dead not yet present on my skin, trapped under my nails.

Yes, we went back. We dated then; we split up then; we dated again; we split up again; we dated other people; we split up with other people; we talked about dating again. He lived in San Francisco, and I lived in Tempe, Manhattan, Denver, Anaheim.

When I thought about him, which wasn't all the time, I remembered one late night in the desert when we went swimming while it stormed, sitting in a Jacuzzi at some random apartment complex at which neither of us lived. It was black outside, the pool was smooth except for the crystal pinpricks of rain water, the sky thundered, and we were eighteen and beautiful. We were! I was afraid we'd be struck by lightning, but it didn't happen. I wore his shorts and my T-shirt because I didn't have my swimsuit when we set out to rent a movie. My shorts hung low on my hips, heavy with water. The wet T-shirt clung to my skin like I was a porn star. We were running barefoot through wet grass to the pool. We were running down a grassy knoll with rain clouds above, and there were frogs in the grass.

You'd think the frogs would have grossed me out, but for some reason I loved this image, this picture: the wet grass, the rainy night, the pool, the frogs, the two of us running, me in his big shorts, the drenched T-shirt. It seemed like a music video; we were seraphs, winged, able to fly.

When he called at two a.m., post-residency, that image not present in my head, he said, "I just wanted to tell you. I took a razor and I cut my chest. I'm bleeding."

That definitely woke me up. "Badly? You're bleeding badly?"

"Yeah."

"You're gonna die!" I pulled my legs out from under the sheets, lifting myself into a sitting position.

"I'm done. I'm saying good-bye."

The *melodrama*!

My feet were on the floor now. "You can't do that. You can't just *say good-bye.*" I took a deep breath. "Are you home alone?" I asked.

"No. Jason is asleep in the next room." Jason was his roommate. He played drinking games and volleyball. We liked each other nominally. He looked slightly retarded to me. Once, when leaving the apartment, he patted me on the top of the head, not as if we were playing Duck-Duck-Goose but as if I were the family pet. I had a hard time forgetting that.

"Go get him," I said. "I need to talk to him."

"I did love you, you know." He hung up.

I called him back. The phone rang two times before he picked up. "It's me," I said.

"What are you doing?" He was annoyed. He would die annoyed with me.

"Get me Jason," I shouted.

"Goodbye, Jennifer." And the receiver clicked.

This time he picked up after one ring. "I'm going to keep calling. I'm going to wake Jason if you don't get him for me now."

He sighed heavily, and I pictured him in his bed on his back, looking sort of like Saint Sebastian, bloody, the sheets white. His eyes were blue. He'd be staring up at the heavens: it would be a moving scene—his image, forever lovely in my head. "Jennifer, don't. Okay? Please don't."

"I have to," I answered. "Don't you see that? I can't *not* call back—"

"Yes. You can. Stop. We'll see what happens."

I sat there in my cold room, my feet still touching the floor. I hesitated. "If that's what you want."

"That's what I want."

We'd see what happened.

I didn't call back.

Frankly, he'd been a lot of trouble.

Frankly, the existential angst routine, coupled with the dead poets and political alienation, had left me not only philosophically bankrupt but also an articulate Commie. Hadn't we outgrown this?

Frankly, there wasn't much left to say.

The state of semi-consciousness had left us dumb. He could've unplugged the phone. I could've called for help.

Neither of us did a thing.

He lived. We spoke the next day.

Eventually, we tried to lose touch.

Finally, it worked.

Now, I live, knowing I would've let him die, Hippocratic Oath aside.

Jennifer on potlucks, age 30

There's a four-to-seven-day-long potluck following a death. Someone dies. Your mom or uncle or distant cousin tells you to bring a bundt cake quick or bake a dozen cornbread muffins stuffed with real pieces of corn. A dozen, at least.

When my father dies, the people come. They arrive by dusk, simply saying, "I'm sorry." I don't want them to say anything else.

They bring food. Bagels and cream cheese with chives. Those sesame sticks you always want but never buy. Brie, brownies, buckets of Kentucky Fried Chicken. Greek olives, stuffed ravioli.

I open the fridge and see it there, the big stainless steel pot of chili my father had made before a drunk driver sideswiped him. I see the chili, and remember that my dad was meticulous about culinary endeavors. He claimed to have a secret ingredient. The secret ingredient is locked inside a body we will donate to science.

I heat it up. I let it simmer. I bring out shredded cheddar. We have a lot of cheese; people bring cheese.

And then I put it on the table.

A deliberately busy table: a loud cacophony of falsely cheery voices, the juggling of plastic kitchenware and casseroles. The chili pot has its day. Meaty bowls of thick chili make their way around the perpetual potluck; all survivors dig in. Those not eating sing hymns. Someone announces there is no more salsa.

It's Aunt Tru who says it: "Oh, this chili is delicious! Who made this unbelievable chili?" Her eyes are wide, her dress old-fashioned. At that moment, she looks like a Walton.

I look around, look at my still-young mother, a widow in her fifties. I look at Aunt Tru and Aunt Sarah and the friends I went to college with and the people I've seen once or twice in the neighborhood, people who trim trees and walk dogs. I look into their eyes; these are nice people who brought us food.

"My dad made it," I blurt out. "He made a big pot on Saturday so it would last all week."

Silence. No one knows what to say. No one knows how to react. I turn to my mother. She stares at me—her remaining family—and she smiles. Then she laughs. She laughs and laughs. And then the family and the college friends and the neighbors finish every last bite of the dead man's chili.

Jennifer trying to figure out what to do with her life, age 31

Say you're a doctor and you find out you only have six months to live. Do you stop trying to heal?

Do you stop dieting? Do you stop praying? Do you stop vacuuming?

I mean, what do you do when you realize you're gonna die? Really, what do you do?

Jennifer on identity, age 32

Rules for freaks:

1. If you're single and over thirty, never get gray hair or a fat ass. Blond is for teenagers and celebrities; red is fine till forty; black is witchy; go with brunette. Do whatever you have to in order to avoid the fat ass. Exercise, if you must.

2. If you get visibly excited over Richard Scarry books or TV miniseries from the eighties, avoid instances when they're brought up in conversation.

3. Don't watch *The Graduate* with others, because you know you lose it when they go to that bar and the topless dancer dances behind

the girl, the tassels on breasts spinning overhead. Your weeping may disturb people.

4. If a man says to you, "You look like a woman who's used to getting her way," don't be coy and say, "Looks can be deceiving." Don't show him any scars or war wounds. Just throw your head back, but only slightly, and laugh, but only a little.

5. If a man says to you, "You're the most beautiful one," he's lying. You may want to ask him, "The most beautiful what?" You may want to help him out, fill in the blanks: "The most beautiful woman strung out on student loans and NutraSweet? The most beautiful NPR listener? The most beautiful person who's ever seen David Copperfield and Barry Manilow perform on consecutive nights? The most beautiful what? What? *What?*"

6. If a man says to you, "Single women over thirty are jaded," tell him to fuck off.

7. Admit to yourself that you like "Kiss" by Prince. Admit to yourself that you believed Elvis was alive for a couple of months after seeing a special on Oprah. Admit to yourself that Anastasia's fate fascinates you, as does JFK's death and the ill-fated marriage of Tom Cruise and Nicole Kidman. Admit to yourself that you have a massive collection of scratch-and-sniff stickers, and you're still upset that your parents never bought you an Atari.

8. Jennifer, don't cry for the dead. What can be done for the dead?

Jennifer on life after potluck, age 33

Now I read the obits. I look for people who die young. And it gives me some sad, secret, *perverse* pleasure to count them up, to know that many, many people have died, as they say, "before their time." *Whose time are we talking about?*

Jennifer on disappointment, age 34

I wish my name were *Jada* or *Charlotte* or, if I were a boy, *Sponge Bob Square Pants,* because it's fun to say. I wish I made nerve endings detonate like citrus slices pulling apart perfectly. I wish I smelled like orange blossoms in the spring. I wish I tasted like coffee houses and cheesecake. I wish I sounded like Bono in the eighties, like Billie Holiday drunk, like an English person saying anything—even if it were only directions to the loo or a recipe for soda bread. I wish I looked like a sand dune rolling smoothly towards a baroque sunset. Wishful thinking. What are you going to do?

Jennifer on faith, age 35

I'm a believer in disaster,
a convert to catastrophe.
When I see cars on fire,
I know they're gonna explode—
Wildfires?
They'll spread.
My plane will crash,
terrorists will use nukes,
my house will get robbed,
my computer will crash,
that dark mass in the water is a shark,
that cloud of brown in the sky is toxic.
You shouldn't lick envelopes,
caffeine causes cancer

(which I'll get—
if not now, then later),
rock concerts will leave me deaf,
I'll total a car,
spill the red wine,
get VD.
I don't own a gun
because I'd accidentally shoot myself—
in the head.
I don't live in California
because I'd usher in
the Big One.
I don't fall in love
because I know about hearts,
and how they break.

Jennifer on gravestone possibilities, age 36

Here lies freak?
Freak Within: Get Over It?
Beloved Freak?
I have to confess, when people say to me, "You're a freak," I think
of it as a good thing.

Jennifer on being a freak, age 38

If I fall in love, what becomes of me? What part of me do I lose? The
best part? The special part? The *freak* part?
We meet in Portland at a medical convention.
The first thing I notice are the scars on his wrists, the ribbons of
buckled tissue—vertical, the way they're supposed to be when you're

cutting to die. We have this in common: incision, flesh dramas—medical and otherwise. I notice this, and his slight resemblance to a young James Woods in *The Way We Were*.

"I don't believe in chemistry," I tell him over a Mongolian grill. His scallops and chicken and peapods have turned an identical shade of mushroom brown. Entropy: all things lead to sameness.

"Didn't you major in it?" he says.

"Biology." I wind a spiraled noodle around my fork and look him over. Michael, an oncologist from Boston. "You went to school in Massachusetts?"

"Undergrad, yeah. I went to Vanderbilt in Tennessee for med school—a boy from the northeast."

"I don't know the South," I confess. "It's all mint juleps, Appalachia, and Georgia peaches to me. What was your first impression?"

He thinks a moment. "First, I was surprised to find that there really *are* people named Bubba." We laugh, and I'm not sure we're supposed to. Our inappropriate laughter rolls over us, an explosion marking the quietude of the Mongolian Grill. He continues, "Then, an administrator's wife at some campus fund-raiser—all dressed up—stopped me when I was talking about surgery and chemo, and she said, 'Young man, look at me when you speak to me.'" Michael pauses, a little dramatically. "Scared the hell out of me." He looks me in the eye, like the administrator's wife must have done. "Kinda direct."

I reach out then, probably surprising him, definitely surprising myself. I trace the textured river running down his wrist and stop like I'm taking his pulse. "Where did you go to undergrad?" I ask. I am searching for the things I like.

"Hampshire. The architect who designed the dorms also designed insane asylums."

I go over my mental checklist: Sense of the Absurd. *Check.*

He continues, "But we also divested from South Africa during the apartheid years before anyone else did. And there's the *Scooby*

101

connection. Velma went to Smith, Daphne went to Mount Holyoke, Fred to Amherst, Shaggy to Hampshire, and Scooby, UMass Amherst."

Global Morality, Pop Culture Finesse. *Check, check.* "You don't look like a Shaggy-kind-of-guy." *Check.*

"Vanderbilt fit better, despite the foreign surroundings."

A Sense of Otherness. *Check.*

"Are you taking my pulse?" He looks at my fingertips on his vein.

"In a way."

We go to Powell's that night. I buy Mary Shelley's *Frankenstein.* He buys *The Maze of Ingenuity: Ideas and Idealism in the Development of Technology* by Arnold Pacey. We drink coffee and he asks, "Are you being yourself?"

Myself? Am I showing you the *real me*? I didn't tell you I think the book you bought looks boring, did I? I didn't tell you I'd like to lick up one of those scallops right off your plate, did I? I didn't tell you I'm measuring you, keeping a list, tracking your freakiness. Did I? "Not completely. Are you?"

"Not wholly," he admits, nodding his head slightly and smiling.

"What would make us be ourselves?"

"Touching a lot."

Check.

Putting lids on our coffees, I say, "When did you try to kill yourself?"

Michael leans into me. "A very long time ago."

On downtown streets, he puts his hand on the small of my back. It's the first time we've touched. "I'm a believer in recovery, a convert to contrition," he says.

I pull my sweater around me. He takes my hand in his.

Three days later, we say good-bye at airport security. I have a big red mark on my upper lip, broken skin—my flesh so unused to being touched. "Once," he told me, "I tasted blood."

And here we are, at the end of a weekend I hadn't anticipated: "Okay, then," I say. As if I'm blasé. As if I'm not reeling. As if I'm not stunned by possibilities.

"We can speak tonight." He taps his watch. "I'll call you."

"What does this mean?" I ask. "I have things to do, personal time I need to spend alone." Surely, the things that make me *me* are threatened. "What am I without my spiritual lows, my black humor, my appreciation of darkness?"

"Well, you *will* be different—I'm not going to lie." He kisses me gently, lips touching bruised flesh.

On the plane, I run my tongue over the red mark, trying to taste the wound.

I taste it. A small part of me is lost.

But, despite its absence, I still feel like me.

Glasnost

—For Penelope Krouse

I t's late-night in Leningrad, the strange gray haziness of the White Nights enveloping a city already muted—made dull gray by passing centuries and utopian decay despite its one-time garish color—and she is going home from the wild Soviet circus, having said good-bye to the seven other summer language students at the metro station, the five Americans and the two Danish girls.

Elizabeth is a girl abroad. She is pretty but unmemorable. At seventeen, she has never been away from Orange County, California, without her parents. By the end of the year, Soviet Communism will fall, and Elizabeth will leave for college, never to return to her parents' world again except for short-lived visits that will leave her inexplicably gloomy and noisily independent, examining things like student loan payment plans and doing things like crying aloud during blockbuster movies that aren't particularly sad. But, for now, Elizabeth and the Soviet Union lack sovereignty. Soon, Boris Yeltsin will replace Mikhail Gorbachev in high drama; Russia will be re-born, resurging in fine Russian-novel fashion; and Elizabeth will move to Irvine, California, less gloriously but very well-organized. Perestroika and glasnost: restructuring and openness, indeed.

Her home is somewhere in the projects—she couldn't tell you where, as she only travels underground, possessing no visual of the city's layout—in a hotel called the Chaika, which she thinks means "The Seagull." Wherever the Chaika is, the projects seem endless, monolithic, and hopeless. Soviet apartment buildings, ashy in color, patches of weeds, shards of glass, garbage bins tipped—none of the hidden grandeur of the inner city's baroque past, its high-society-dinner-party days. But Leningrad was obviously, ostentatiously, once beautiful, and its beauty haunts *everything*.

Elizabeth rides the metro, staring at Russian people who ride trains at night. She doesn't hide her overt interest in their business. While the trapeze and the tamed tigers and flashy sequins leave a powdery filmic dust in her mind and a hum in her ears, she is quickly mired in her immediate surroundings. She looks from face to face, contemplates the clothes of Russians, the eyes of women and men. The train empties gradually.

Elizabeth scrutinizes people, a habit she has only just begun but one that will persist until her death some sixty years later in New Haven, Connecticut. On the one hand, Elizabeth will be called *perceptive*, which she'll quickly learn isn't the same as being called *intelligent*. On the other hand, Elizabeth will be called *presumptuous* and *arrogant*. Gift or vice, Elizabeth Crowe spends a lot of time trying to read the nuances of faces, the subtleties of gesture, the punctuation of silence, the layers of unspoken and spoken word, and the terrain of vocal pitch.

The questions are these: *Who can read the face? And how open is it to being read?*

And here it is, so clearly seen in the hazy gray of the White Nights in Leningrad, on the cusp of democratic revolution: Elizabeth's analogous Achilles' tendon, her weakness in the midst of strength, her hair like Samson waiting to be cut by the likes of a Delilah. While she believes it wrong to judge the hearts of others, to second-guess motives and intentions, she is also aware of the aesthetic beauty and alarming majesty of noticing what is beneath the surface of things.

Elizabeth Crowe will become a successful playwright because of this possibly reckless observation skill—her plays will be profound and funny, smart and popular. Some critics will rave; others will call her unabashedly vain.

The train stops, the doors open, and two middle-aged men with bulbous features and soft bodies stumble in, falling together on a seat already occupied by a youngish woman in a drab dress, once pink. The bodies in her drab-dress lap startle her. Hadn't they seen that someone was sitting in this spot? The movements stand out starkly in the overcast bleakness, like the minimalist tableau of an episode of *The Honeymooners* on black-and-white TV. The men pay no attention to her presence and she pushes away as if assaulted or maybe goosed, jumping to her feet in surprise. The woman is up and gone, banished to another corner of the train, and Elizabeth is wide-eyed and stunned. Elizabeth quickly forgets the woman. She watches the two men.

Who are drunk. They huddle together and one of them is crying. Their attention is so fixed, so privatized, that anyone can safely stare at them and they don't notice, which is good for voyeurs like Elizabeth. Over and over again, one of them says in Russian, "Son of a bitch, son of a bitch." He is weeping and the other man has his arm around him. They notice nothing. The one holds the other. The world around them is not present while one consoles and the other weeps. The intimacy between them is staggering, and Elizabeth finds herself holding her breath.

"Son of a bitch, son of a bitch." A whisper throughout the train.

She is transfixed. Elizabeth is mesmerized by the solitude they have forged out in a metro on a hazy gray night. Their huddling over one another's bodies, wrapping themselves around the thing that makes the one cry. The act of comforting. The fierceness with which the one without tears attacks the angst of the one crying.

The brakes squeal and Elizabeth has to transfer to another train. She doesn't want to, but it's late and she's alone. She stands, walks through the doors, and watches the train take off with the two men in each other's arms. They are gone.

Elizabeth will marry an intellectual, a thinker. He will teach mathematics, understand thermodynamics, be a better cook than she ever will be. Unlike her future husband, she is an average student and a weak debater. She measures emotion. He will be able to determine trends in human history, analyze philosophical arguments, and pull apart faulty assumptions. She will decipher hidden agendas, predict human responses, and choose friends wisely. Her husband will find this to be her single-most attractive feature, because finally here is a woman who understands a man. But, for now, she is mere voyeur.

So Elizabeth stands, waiting for a train in the underground station, her mind working quickly in habitual perception, passing over holes in nylons and wrinkles around eyes. She waits on the platform only for a few seconds. When the door to her train opens, she steps in and sits across from a couple in their late thirties. The three of them are the only ones in the car. The couple doesn't even glance at Elizabeth, who can pass through crowds without anyone noticing her at all. Maybe another virtue; maybe a vice. People often don't remember meeting her. When she walks into department stores, she has to search for help.

The couple is quiet. They sit next to each other, their bodies pressed together in serene silence. A pastoral painting. The woman has her eyes closed and she leans her head back against the window. Her face is peaceful, a hint of a smile across her thin lips. The man looks at his callused hands in his lap, turning them over quietly. They look the way Russians look when they dress up and have no money. The flowered dress and the brown overcoat, paupers, Russian Pygmalions, high cheekbones and clear complexions, his sharp jaw and her colorless hair—passive and wounded beauty. Elizabeth wonders if they are lovers, determines they are.

The train stops, the doors open, a pause, the doors close, the train rolls forward. The rhythmic movement disrupted by the jarring screeches of brakes, of gears, of doors. The woman keeps her eyes shut, maybe counting stops in her head. The man continues looking at his man-hands. At maybe the seventh or eighth stop, the man quickly rises to his feet, dashes out the door, turns around suddenly, and stands there on the platform looking at the woman, who finally opens her eyes. She stares at her lover—her face in suspended animation, a figure in intaglio print. The doors are about to close; everyone knows it. The woman lifts her eyebrows, her face serene even in surprise.

Elizabeth again holds her breath. The doors begin to close, the woman's lips part as if she'll speak. The doors slowly glide together, and then just before they shut completely, the man steps back onto the train. Behind him, the doors close triumphantly. He smiles. He doesn't take his eyes off the woman. He moves to a corner, leans against the wall, and stares at her serene face.

Elizabeth burns red. She is embarrassed by her presence; she trembles because it's so romantic, so noir.

The woman covers her mouth with her hands, reminding Elizabeth of a child—and she begins to giggle. Then the woman removes her hands from her face and throws her head back against the glass and laughs aloud. A laughter that transforms her, abandoning the innocence of the concealed mouth, embracing vivaciousness and sexuality, too. She suddenly stands and walks over to the man in the corner and Elizabeth tries not to look.

But she can't help it.

The couple embraces. They kiss. And Elizabeth just watches, pretending not to see.

The train stops and the man releases the woman. His hands trail after him, towards her body, as he exits. A touch of Degas. This time, the doors come together and he's gone. The woman takes her seat again, closes her eyes, and smiles.

Elizabeth *flushes*.

A night at the circus.

———

Having just graduated from high school, Elizabeth speaks conversational Russian. This gets her pretty far in her travels, but mostly she is still voyeur rather than eavesdropper. It's fine, because she's still more interested in what isn't said as opposed to what is.

When couples ride escalators in Russia, they face each other. The man will step on first, the woman will follow, and then the man will turn around. The escalators go down, and the couple is immobilized—locked in their own moment. Children, too. A child will often sit on his mother's lap stone-faced in some public place and then, without any warning, he'll reach for his mother's face and hold her cheeks in his hands with a crushing and unanticipated tenderness. There is, at times, this virtual explosion of intimacy—intimacy between lovers, intimacy between parent and child.

Elizabeth, just a girl, will eventually have one child of her own. Also a girl. One thing that will strike her, *slay* her, actually, is that when her little girl is three, she will want Elizabeth to rehearse aloud the details of her infancy. Her daughter will say, "When I was a baby, did I cry for my mommy? When I was a baby, did I wear pajamas with feet? When I was a baby, did I want to sleep in bed with mommy and daddy?" Elizabeth will answer each question till, at last, her daughter will move into her arms to be held like the baby she still will be.

Elizabeth has been in the Soviet Union for almost a month and she's about to leave. Her perceptions have not yet run dry, but one needs something by which to interpret them. So at the end of her trip, she wears shorts—which are taboo. She feels like asserting her independence of taboos. She's only seventeen.

Elizabeth walks along Nevsky Prospect. She heads over to Pushkin Theater, passing old men who fought in World War Two and still wear rusty old medals pinned onto jacket lapels. She pushes through widows, soft bodies like *babushka* clichés. The streets swell with impassive soldiers and young women with bad hair-dye jobs and crazy-colored stockings with seams down the back of legs, sexy and sad at the same time. Leningrad is a tangle of tram wires overhead, elaborate architecture blanketed in brown haze, and people who look exhausted. Orange, blue, and yellow buildings crumble, hinting at the past splendor. It's a world of longing.

People stare at Elizabeth. It's the shorts, her shaved legs.

Elizabeth walks past the icon merchants, T-shirt sellers, and trinket peddlers. She doesn't really want to buy anything, but she asks how much things are anyway.

A kid approaches her. When he sees her pick up an icon, a wooden Mary, he steps in front of her. In English, he asks, "Do you like it?" His eyes sparkle, despite his grimy countenance.

"Da," she answers. She puts it down and moves onto something else.

"You are American?" The kid wears brown pants, a striped shirt. He's thirteen or fourteen.

"Da." She is American, and she *feels* American. Though nondescript, plain even, she's a billboard here, all legs and white teeth. Elizabeth is, however temporarly, a romantic figure.

He steps in front of her, and then he walks backwards facing her. "Why are you in Leningrad?" He gives up on English and speaks in Russian.

"I'm studying at the University. I'm leaving soon." She enjoys the attention, despite the annoying way he jumps around in front of her, getting in her way.

He holds a finger in the air, indicating she should wait for him for a second. He runs off. Gone. She looks around, confused. Then, in a flash, he returns with the icon she had been looking at.

"A present for you," he says, opening up his hand as if he held a precious jewel.

"No," she protests. "I can't take this." He pushes it towards her and she resists but it becomes very silly, so she takes it. They walk together and she refuses to stop and examine anything, afraid he'll give it to her. He watches her carefully, calling out to old Russian men as they go,

"She's my American girlfriend." He turns to her, "I want to get you something else."

"Nyet," she says. "I don't want anything." She shakes her head, her hair whipping around her shoulders seductively and luxuriantly; she is suddenly rendered beautiful by the host of Russian male eyes.

Twice, he disappears. He brings her a T-shirt, a Pepsi. She begs him not to buy her anything. Old men laugh as the kid dances before the American girl with shaved legs.

"How old are you?" Elizabeth drinks the Pepsi.

"Sixteen." Not possible.

"What do you study in school?"

"Business."

"Where did you get the money to buy me such nice things?"

"Business." The boy winks at her. Then he says something with such rapidity that Elizabeth can't catch it. It's either licentious or criminal. He snickers, and Elizabeth snaps his picture.

They approach the area where the portrait artists congregate. All at once, there's a crowd of men surrounding Elizabeth and the boy; the artists are eager to paint her portrait. She has hard currency and denim shorts.

"She's my American girlfriend," says the boy, possessively.

"I want to draw you," one artist pleads.

"No, I'll draw better," says another, holding her hand.

"I'll draw you and you don't have to pay." This one looks straight into Elizabeth's eyes. He's ruddy. She *notices*. He's wearing a T-shirt with indecipherable English words written on it and dirty blue jeans. He has sandy blond hair and a few lines on his face. A big smile. "Please," he says, softly. He opens his palm to her, as if helping her out of a carriage, as if she is Cinderella.

It's a strange moment, unaccompanied by any of the wry cynicism Elizabeth will eventually have. Instead, she is charmed by his *please*, seduced by the lines on his face. And he's an artist!

Elizabeth knows she'll have to pay. The boy stands protectively at her side. The artist and the woman stare into each other's eyes, examining each other's faces. The boy is like a puppy at their heels.

While they are like a couple on an escalator.

"Please," the man repeats.

Please.

So Elizabeth—flattered, really—sits down on a chair and the man sits on a stool before his easel and begins to sketch. She is a woman who can easily slip in and out of crowds, self-conscious under his eyes. He smiles a lot. He stares at her face—reading her, interpreting her, figuring her out.

The questions are these: *Who can read the face? And how open is it to being read?*

Elizabeth's own future profession still obscure, she finds herself doing the same thing to him that he's doing to her—reading, interpreting, figuring things out. There is no paintbrush or palette in her hand, no pen or paper. She is mere voyeur, mired in romanticism.

The boy stands behind the artist and gives her a thumbs-up when she looks at him. The artist finishes, and Elizabeth is abruptly faced with his version. It doesn't look a thing like her. There is no resemblance whatsoever. She gives him a five-dollar bill anyway. He says, "I'm Roman."

"I'm Elizabeth." They shake hands, and he holds onto hers. "Come back in an hour and I'll take you for dinner."

Elizabeth smiles. She hesitates.

Roman smiles at her and again says, "Please."

Elizabeth wonders what it would be like. "Okay," she says. "In an hour."

"In an hour," he repeats.

Elizabeth turns to leave. The boy runs after her. "I'll buy you ice cream," he says.

"Okay." She smiles down at him, amused.

As they eat ice cream in a dirty ice-cream parlor, an old man walks by and points his cane at her legs and delivers an angry speech. The boy shoos him away.

"What did the man say?" Elizabeth asks, ignoring the cat that runs past with a rat in its mouth.

"Nothing," says the boy, shaking his head. *Nitchivo.*

"Tell me." She squints at him.

"No," he says, shaking his head some more. "He didn't say anything."

It occurs to her that the old man called her a whore.

She eats her Soviet ice-cream cone. A vanilla ice cream with a chocolate exterior and, on top, a little yellow flower that tastes of sweet cream. Then, with the boy at her side, she goes to meet Roman, the street artist, who says, "I want to stop by my apartment." He packs up his stuff.

Elizabeth, Roman, and the boy hop in a cab together. "Can't you ask him to leave?" Roman whispers to Elizabeth, as they squeeze into the back seat of the Soviet taxi.

"I've tried to get rid of him," she lies, speaking softly. "But he won't go." And, turning to the boy, while Roman talks to the driver, she whispers, "Don't go."

In the cab, the artist and the boy speak rapidly to each other in Russian. It sounds like arguing. Roman doesn't look at the boy; rather, he stares out the window.

To Elizabeth, he says, "You're very pretty."

"Thank you." She is a picture of demure naïveté, even as her mind spins.

They arrive at his apartment and Roman turns to the boy. "You wait here."

They climb a narrow staircase in a decrepit building, somewhere. She doesn't know where. On the second floor, Roman inserts his key and Elizabeth enters the apartment. She's uncomfortable, but she does it anyway. She'll force it, try it. Others do it, do *this*.

There's an old woman in the kitchen. She looks at Elizabeth the same way the old man at the ice-cream parlor did.

"I rent a room from her," Roman says.

She thinks I'm a whore, Elizabeth thinks.

She follows him, and he locks the door behind them.

Paintings and sketches cover the walls and Elizabeth pores over them. He tells her he's twenty-four, and he studied art at the University and he's going to Florence, where he has friends. Elizabeth looks at his room in the old lady's house. She looks at the drawings on the walls and the unmade bed with its linens strewn across the mattress. He points to his sketches and her eyes linger on them and she looks back to the room. *It's Raskalnikov's room*, she thinks. The woman is probably a pawnbroker.

"They're very good," she says, referring to the sketches, but they aren't. They don't really interest her. She doesn't even wish they did. Now, she knows: *I can't do it*, she thinks. She has to get out of here. Romanticism run wild, perceptions just impressions, meanings made clear: *I can't do this.*

She walks to the window. The boy is waiting for them across the street, looking up at the window with unwavering patience.

"The boy is waiting for us downstairs," she says with little inflection in her voice.

"You don't want to talk to kids like him," he says, with surprise vehemence. "He's no good. You can't trust him. I know kids like him." He mutters something else and Elizabeth catches the word *thief.*

"But he's waiting for us," as if that's all that matters.

"We can tell him to leave."

"We can do that," she says, saying words and not meaning them. Elizabeth's eyes shift around the room. She's uneasy. That old woman in the kitchen. That locked door. She can't make love with a struggling artist. She just can't do it.

"We'll tell him to leave—" Roman heads towards the door. He's going to unlock it.

"Okay." She obediently follows him, no longer scrutinizing her surroundings. She is bent on escape.

They gallop down the stairs. Wild horses. They exit the decrepit building and cross the street to the boy who keeps his eyes fixed on the second-floor window, even as they approach him. The man and the boy exchange harsh words. The man wants the kid to leave. The tension between them escalates.

"I have to go—" Elizabeth interrupts.

The man and the boy stop. They turn to Elizabeth. They stare at her.

"There's something I've forgotten to do—" she says, looking confused. "I just remembered—" She steps back. "I'm sorry. *I have to go.*"

Then she's heading towards the metro. Any metro will do. She knows what's beneath the ground, even if she's not sure from up above, from this perspective. Roman and the boy follow. All three of them move quickly, pushing through soldiers and widows.

"We'll walk you to the metro," says Roman. "Let me give you my phone number." The boy at their heels. "I can show you beautiful parts of Leningrad. You won't be sorry."

"I'll take you all the way to your metro station—" says the boy.

"I'll pay for a taxi—" says Roman. "I can meet you somewhere tomorrow."

"No. It's all right." Elizabeth, moving down the street. Roman, buying cherries from a vendor. Elizabeth, refusing them. The man and the boy, sharing the cherries.

All three head into the metro station. They head down the escalator. Roman gets on the step below hers and turns to face her. The boy is next to them.

Elizabeth stands face to face with this man. His rugged face and his dirty blond hair. He smiles broadly. In her arms, she holds a T-shirt, an icon, a portrait, and some cherries. Their faces are so close. Are they reading each other?

They ride as far as her station. With her gifts cradled to her chest, she steps off the metro and turns to the artist and the boy. They stand before her, waiting for the doors to close. Their eyes are bright and expectant. Elizabeth, possessing an unmemorable presence, says to the two of them, quickly, "Good-bye."

What Elizabeth doesn't know: She doesn't know why the two men on the metro that circus night were so drunk, what drove them to drunken myopia. In truth, the one had turned to the other after his child, his only child, had died of influenza. She doesn't know who the lovers on the train were, or what would become of them. In truth, their relationship was illicit, though they eventually married. They would, however, each have additional affairs—cheating on one another, as they had once done to previous spouses. She doesn't know why an artist named Roman would want to paint the likes of her, a seventeen-year-old girl given to gaping. In truth, he wanted to paint Elizabeth because he thought her exceptionally beautiful. He eventually did move to Florence to paint, but his art really wasn't very good.

She doesn't know, additionally, that she too will be regarded as an artist, at once called *perceptive* and *presumptuous*, forever begging questions. Who can read the face? And how open is it to being read?

Lemon

Tess paid two black boys with Wimpy's chips to watch the company van in the Cape Town airport parking lot. On that first balmy sub-Saharan night in 1998, she looked exactly like Margot remembered her from their years together at Northwestern—same long hair, same long legs—but with amazing bronze skin. "Guess which car is mine," Tess said. She worked for a health care nonprofit that did a lot of grassroots work in the townships. Her boss was an ex-Catholic priest from a groovy part of England.

Two kids ate fries by a combi with a bumper sticker on it that said, "Condoman says, *Use Condoms!*"

"Um, *that* one?" Margot said, pointing to the van.

This would be Margot's first memory of South Africa: children guarding a combi, fried potatoes for currency, "chips" instead of "fries," Tess with a tan.

Dear Ben,
    I'm somewhere over the Atlantic; I'll be in Miami by dawn, Vancouver by dusk.

Ben, this is for you. I tread lightly over the details. I do so for you, you burly Afrikaner ex. We ended badly; we ended well. I tread delicately, desiring no vengeance, harboring no hatred. Ben, old friend, I never gave you anything except that carved wooden chess-set I bought for your birthday on Greenmarket Square at St. George's, the same place I bought that cheap beaded necklace I wore every day for a year and Zulu Fire Sauce for my dad. You didn't even like it—you didn't even like the chess-set; you only wanted to return to the humdrum, you-win comforts of your beloved backgammon. No, I never gave you anything.

Both of us were aware of clashing sensibilities, aware we never felt strongly enough about one another to overcome contradictory convictions, aware that—when it came down to it—we were better patriots than lovers. Even then, both "patriot" and "lover" struck strange chords in my internal organs. The former suggested a sentiment I scorn; the latter, an arrangement I despise.

Inevitably, we would leave each other.

Just the same, this is for you.

Things happened quickly. Margot was not exactly a backpacker, nor was she a squatter—though she traveled with a backpack and without money. On the cusp of turning thirty, she came to South Africa to live, for a while at least. She liked when people called her an expatriate, but *she* wouldn't call herself that. It sounded pretentious, though conjuring up images of Hemingway pouring back red wine from wineskins was perfectly desirable.

After about two months, she moved out of Tess's Camps Bay bungalow and into a small home in Rondebosch with her new Afrikaner boyfriend, Ben. Tess, doing her own expat divinations, pushed her out the door with a quiet warning. "Even though no one truly knows the real you in this country, there's only so much escaping you can do." With that, Tess turned Margot over to Margot's new flame.

Margot had been dismissive of the counsel, waving her hand and snapping her tongue against the roof of her mouth. Later, when Tess's role in Margot's life had diminished considerably, she'd remember her college friend's words. She'd regard them as among the most memorable she had heard.

Ben was, he said, "A New South African." In other words, knowing that apartheid had to go, he touted democracy.

Like most whites, however, he had a maid. So, really, Margot had a maid, too.

Once, she lost an earring, a little dangly thing with a blue gem hanging by a silver wire. Ben, wearing a bikini swimsuit, entered the living room from the backyard. "I can't find one of my earrings—did you happen to see it?" she said to him.

Ben, still dripping from the pool, took on this stern, composed, bulldog look. "Let's go into the bedroom."

"I'm sure I just misplaced it—it's probably in my purse." Margot trailed after him. "For God's sake, put some clothes on."

Ben led the way down the hall. Passing the kitchen, he said to the maid, "Patience, follow us." A half-naked Afrikaner, a Canadian woman, and a young Xhosa woman in an apron paraded down the hall in single-file. Many maids had named like Patience, Justice, Joy.

Margot knew next to nothing about Patience. She didn't know if Patience was married, if she had children, what she did on weekends. Patience was a black woman, maybe around Margot's age, rather pretty. They moved by one another like apparitions. Margot lifted her legs if she sat on the couch when Patience vacuumed. In the kitchen, if Patience chopped while Margot sliced, Margot thought about talking to the maid. Then, figuring herself white, and thinking that Patience might view her disruptive attempts at discourse as feeble, false, and impossible—Margot stopped. She said nothing. Margot sliced while Patience chopped.

Ben walked directly to Margot's jewelry box on the dresser. "It was here last?" He fingered pearls, some trinkets.

"Yeah. I can't find it," Margot answered. Ben stood before the two women. He was the opposite of Margot's usual romantic fare. No lanky body, no wire-rimmed glasses, no boyish charm, no political agendas. Ben was solid, cocky, tough, and he seemed like he'd be good at keeping one warm around a campfire. He could definitely build the fire himself. Where Margot was from, the boys had *heard* one could start a fire by rubbing two sticks together, but, thankfully, everyone had a lighter.

Patience, wiping her hands on her apron (she wore a uniform straight out of American sit-com TV in the fifties), had to know what was coming next. Suddenly, Margot did, too.

Ben turned to her. "Patience, have you seen Margot's earring?"

Margot was paralyzed.

Patience didn't seem to notice Ben's bikini. The two women weren't even looking at the same man.

"Miss Margot lost her earring?" She always called Margot *Miss*. "When?"

"I wore it yesterday." Margot couldn't meet her eyes.

Patience did what she had to. This tall, graceful Xhosa woman sunk to her knees, wearing her pink dress and white apron, and she ran her hands over the carpet. "This it?" She held up Margot's earring.

"Yes." Margot reached for it. For a second, the two women's hands touched.

"Thanks, Patience." Ben smiled, his hands on his hips.

Patience left, no doubt relieved she could still feed the babies, the husband, maybe an ailing mother.

Ben walked over to the bed and sat down. He pointed his finger at the doorway out of which Patience had just walked. "*That girl doesn't steal.*"

"You didn't have to do that," Margot said in a loud whisper.

"Do what?"

"Accuse her of stealing."

"I didn't."

Margot fiddled with hairbrushes, combs. "You did. And now you're making it sound like it's a lesson for me." Margot looked into the mirror over the dresser; she looked at herself. *"That girl doesn't steal."* She caught his eye. "Do you even care about Patience?"

Ben looked straight at her. "Of course I do. You don't occupy the same space as someone without caring." Walking to the door, he asked, "Do you not care?"

For the life of me, I can't remember Patience ever using the bathroom.

I suppose she must have. I mean, she had to.

Ben, where did the black woman go to the bathroom? Was she allowed to use our bathroom?

In the spring, Margot went on a jaunt alone, a safari-and-camping-spree à la organized tour involving binoculars, big animals, and campsite showers. Though she had a job as an administrative assistant, she still took off at a moment's notice. Her responsibilities abroad, she knew, were minimal. If she needed a little time off, she'd take it.

On the trip, she met an English guy who told her African travel tales which he wove together like *One Thousand and One Nights,* with magical Xhosa equivalents to Aladdin, Sinbad, and Ali Baba.

"You should go to Coffee Bay in the Transkei," he said. He was refreshingly first world with his buzz cut and penchant for granola, raves, and alternative rock. "It's gorgeous: rolling green hills, black people, red sunsets, the ocean." He wanted to kiss her, Margot could tell, but she felt committed, even if mildly, to another. There were subtle things that made her less backpacker, more transplant: she *did* hold down a job, she *did* have a monogamous relationship, she *did* live in a house. This English storyteller was looking for backpacker experiences, romance on the road. Margot considered, but found herself more interested in Coffee Bay.

Coffee Bay was a seaside Transkei town along the Wild Coast in the Eastern Cape Province, largely populated by members of the Xhosa tribe. Legend had it that a shipwreck littered the beach with coffee beans; hence, the name. It was probably as true as *One Thousand and One Nights*, but the image of white sands bejeweled with coffee beans filled Margot with inexplicable longing.

"It sounds like real Africa," she said. They were sitting together on a tour bus driving through Swaziland. His eyes were wet and dewy.

"It is," he said.

"Thanks for telling me."

When Margot got home, she announced to Ben she was going to the Transkei next month. "Alone. I'll hitchhike, take the bus, whatever."

"You don't want to do that," he said. "It's not safe."

"What do you mean?" Perhaps this was the *real* Africa: arguing with a white man about the rest of the continent.

"Carjackings, murder. White people only go there for one thing."

"What would that be?" She squinted at him.

"The pot. Best in the world."

"It's supposed to be beautiful."

"It's not safe for a white woman, Margot." He put his hands on her cheeks, pulled her over, and kissed her on the lips.

"I'd like to see real Africa."

Ben, do you remember when I first arrived? How we met at cafés downtown and I asked you one question after another?

I'd ask you anything. Who are the women you've loved? What do you think about Mandela? Are you going to leave the country? Where will you go? Who do you love, Ben? Have they loved you? What can you tell me, Ben? Tell me about love.

It amused you—I amused you. Our relationship was built on the enchantment of difference. We had no commonalities, none at all. My wide-eyed, no-holds-barred questioning charmed you; I was enthralled by your blunt answers. Never before had I encountered a man so willing to answer my silly questions, so willing to entertain my absurdities and eccentricities.

We sat next to each other at cafés, both of us very serious. I asked, "Do you take advantage of the fact that Dutch, Danish, British, and American girls are coming to your country in droves now that apartheid is kaput?"

"Only four times," you replied, seriously.

This amused me. You amused me, Ben.

Once upon a time, South Africa had designated "homelands," pockets of land reserved for blacks. One needed a visa to get by border control. Homelands were third world sites within an industrialized second world country. Often, black men would go into the cities for jobs, leaving behind wives and children for months and months—maybe years, lifetimes. Back home, in rural wastelands, families would founder under the weight of extreme poverty.

But despite its want, the Transkei, one such place, was supremely beautiful with endless lime-green hills and a blue sky ripe with billowy white clouds. Kraals, pastel-colored circular huts , spotted the ground. When the sun set, the world was golden, like an African Van Gogh. Before Nelson Mandela became a Johannesburg African National Congress outlaw, before he became a political prisoner on Robben Island for twenty-six years, before he won the Nobel Peace Prize, and before he became the first democratically-elected president of post-apartheid South Africa, he was a child in the Transkei. Also called the Wild Coast and the Shipwreck Coast, the Indian Ocean flanked the geography and sharks lurked in dark waters. The terrain was feral, lovely, simultaneously blessed and cursed.

Margot went to Coffee Bay because she liked its name.

Getting off the Baz Bus, the backpacker mode of transportation that journeyed between Cape Town and Johannesburg, she was surprised. Most people didn't bother moving from their seats when the bus stopped. Right in the middle of a country of wineries and resorts, a shocking African world spread out under an endless sky. Everyone was black. Their faces were painted with clay to stave off sunrays. Women washed clothes on the roadside. Some sold pineapples. Many carried huge bundles on their heads. Cows and sheep, bone-thin, wandered aimlessly. Burned-out, rusted, and wrecked cars had been dumped everywhere, maybe casualties of carjacking.

This was the Transkei; she was used to croissant sandwiches at Café Bardelli in Cape Town served by women about to launch modeling careers.

"The manager of Coffee Bay's youth hostel will meet us here," said the driver, also not moving from his seat.

"Here?" Margot asked. "On the highway?" She twisted around, looking out the windows.

"Yeah."

Margot took a deep breath, preparing to exit the bus and look around. Another woman, Central European, would be getting off to go to Port St. Johns a bit farther north. She hesitantly joined Margot in checking out the surroundings. Together, they stepped onto the edge of the highway.

Xhosa children and an old woman immediately approached the two women, asking for money. They didn't understand the language, but a rampant clicking of tongues escaped Xhosa lips: the sound of bottle tops popping off. A click, click, *ng, nd.* The old woman's face was painted white. Hands stretched out to the white women like they had something to offer. A click, click, *nt, ny.*

Margot looked at the Central European woman. There was panic in the woman's eyes. "Is this what you expected?" Margot asked.

"No." The woman smiled weakly but bravely, too.

People had warned Margot about traveling alone. She was a woman; she was white. She hadn't listened. Turning her head, she looked off into the rolling green hills.

Once, when we were already relationship-enmeshed, when my life in Cape Town was more than a big vacation, you were in the back yard, minding the ubiquitous braai fire.

Those crazy braais! The BBQ times one hundred! An impossible amount of red meat!

In my case, the braai involved Afrikaners drinking beer and lapsing into Afrikaans.

Your mom and sister were visiting, and I was helping them in the kitchen. "What are you making?" I asked your mom.

"Vetkoek." She was rolling dough before frying it. "Do you know where the word vetkoek *comes from?"*

"Nope," I admitted.

"Vet is 'fat' and koek *is 'fanny' or 'cake,'" she explained. "'Fat fanny' or 'fat cake.'"*

Your sister handed me one: bready, fried, good—something to eat at a state fair.

Imagine, a fat cake that causes a fat fanny! "That's the cutest thing I've ever heard," I laughed. The two women nervously giggled.

I went to find you, knowing you were getting excited about all the red meat you'd soon consume. When I found you prodding the fire, I danced around breathlessly. "I just heard the cutest word, Ben: vetkoek. *Fat fanny." I slapped you on the butt. "Watch your koek!"*

You abruptly stopped playing with fire. "That's not your koek, Margot." *You pointed between my legs. "That's your koek."*

Horror traipsed over my features. "What does 'fanny' mean?"

You searched for the words, settling on some. "Female genitalia."

I blushed. "No! You're kidding! It's a cute word for butt or bum back home." I was stung. "Your mom and sister didn't tell me."

"They probably didn't want to embarrass you."

None of us really understood each other.

When the seriously-pierced British guy picked Margot up on the highway to take her to Coffee Bay, she asked him, "Do you remember another Brit with a buzz cut who came by here a few months ago?" The one with *One Thousand and One Nights?* "He told me to come here."

Rich, the seriously-pierced British guy, looked her over: another American/European/Canadian girl on-the-run, probably from love or student loans. He furrowed his eyebrows. "The diver?"

"No." She shook her head. "He wasn't a diver." Dave was a well-traveled English guy. He read good books and wore turtlenecks.

"Yeah," Rich nodded. "Worked in Hong Kong, had short hair, a goatee."

It was Dave. A *diver?* They had been campfire confidantes for about a week. They had seen giraffe together! Rhino! Dung beetle! What else didn't she know about him?

She stared at Rich, punk rock émigré: sick fascination with the deviant.

About Dave, she said, "Spend a week with someone and think you know him."

About the clay on the Xhosa faces, he said, "It's calamine lotion nowadays."

"So, is it true that everyone smokes pot in the Transkei?" she asked.

"Yeah, it's true." He peered over, holding onto the steering wheel. "You smoke?"

"No."

"Have you tried it?"

"For four years," she lied. "Straight," she added. She had no idea why she said this.

You approached outings with my foreign friends with dread—even if you liked them.

You liked Michelle and Don, two Americans from Jersey. They invited us to their Woodstock rental, and we ate hummus, French bread, and grapes. It comforted me: the lack of meat, the presence of chickpeas, their accents. We told silly stories, like the time Michelle was in high school and she and her friends ditched class, dressed up someone's senile grandmother like a cheerleader, put her in the middle of the front seat of the car, and drove to a drive-through liquor store, where they bought booze without IDs. No one carded them with the senile grandmother dressed up like a cheerleader in the front seat.

"That couldn't have happened," you later said.

"Sure, it could've."

You were suspicious. "You guys always tell these crazy stories."

"But, Ben, postal workers really do *go bonkers and try to knock off entire small towns." I looked at you. "What do South Africans talk about?"*

"We shoot the shit."

"Well, we do, too. That's what we were doing." Shooting the shit.

"In your world," you said with a straight face, "nonsense happens."

To get to the hostel, Margot and Rich needed to cross a running river on foot. Rich took her backpack, and a stoned guy in a sarong held her daypack.

They crossed the river, their legs wet: girl on hostel lawn holding puppy.

They entered the house, their arms full: guy at table rolling joint.

The Coffee Bay hostel looked like a frat house. The puppy had *issues* with that carpet. Another guy sat on the couch, staring at his lap, sucking on a joint.

Following the grand tour, which included a main house and several "cottages" in back, Margot went to the store, a ramshackle, dusty-shelved shop, where she bought bread, peanut butter, water, and fruit cocktail. She hated fruit cocktail.

Back at the hostel, she talked to a few people.

But she was scared; she wanted to be alone. If she left this town, she'd be the only white person within miles. If she stayed, she'd be the only one not stoned. Escaping into her dirty bedroom to write in her journal, she realized some things: she wasn't adventurous like Diver Dave; she wanted Cape Town and the model crowd.

Even worse: it occurred to her that she was a hypocrite, a pretender, a poser. She liked the idea of being a free-spirited, tie-dye-garbed wild woman at home among indigenous peoples—but, in reality, she liked it when beautiful black men adorned her white world. The Transkei, with its bruised history, frightened her. Suddenly, despite her professed ideals, she yearned for the world in which people campaigned against drug abuse with pat-phrases like, "Just Say No."

"I want my MTV," she wrote in her journal with a heavy heart. She was obviously failing at real Africa.

I've been in love with soulful men before, Ben. Men with whom conversation eventually ceases because they don't feel like talking about the things of this world, relationships in which paying bills seems silly when questions like Is There A God? are still being asked. I've had this before, and you, you, with whom I almost fell in love, were not a soulful man.

You were so utterly grounded in this world—ready to jump down the throats of those around you in heated conversations about apartheid, South Africa, Nelson Mandela, and paying taxes. You were so utterly grounded in this world, this world where schoolgirls eat meat pies and schoolboys wear socks pulled up to their knees.

"You're very witty," you said to me the first time I went back to your place. You put your hand on my thigh.

"So are you." I looked at your hand. "Do I also radiate intelligence?"

You considered. "Not really."

"Huh." I twitched my nose. "Usually, I do."

When I think about us apart from our politics and everything else, I still smile.

Waking at six a.m., Margot stumbled into the bathroom, wary of a Kermit-sized toad she had seen in the night. No frog appeared, but the backdoor glass had been broken and the kitchen garbage was strewn across the floor. She climbed a hill to watch the yellow sun lift over cold water, stretching its arms through theatrical white clouds. Soft green grass warmed under sunbeams. Ocean foam hit jagged black rocks below.

She contemplated her next move. She could somehow find a way back to Cape Town. She could go on—maybe getting to Port St. Johns, another Transkei town. That's where the Central European woman had been headed.

The sunlight bathed an emerald coast. Hadn't she proven she wasn't a poser? Wasn't it enough she went without showers, looked like hell, slept in dirty sheets, showered in basins that bred skin disease, ate from dishes that had simply passed under a flow of lukewarm water, carried a backpack across foreign terrain, and even had secrets with strangers who dared to keep vital information from her, like their diving histories? Plus, she had practically gotten stoned on secondhand smoke.

Back at the hostel, Mavis, the maid, pushed garbage across a dry floor, her feet bare. Margot sat outside with the potheads, drinking coffee out of dirty cups and talking about pot (where to get it, if it were policed, how the drug dealers stood around like dealers in movies from the seventies, how one guy raked all day when stoned).

She didn't want to be a person who only wanted beautiful black men punctuating a chic white world. "I'm going on to Port St. Johns today," she announced to Rich when he came out of his cottage at eleven, stretching and yawning.

He didn't even flinch. He didn't ask her to stay or have some pot or anything. "Be ready to go at 12:30." He was taking two kids into Umtata, a city with mini-taxi depots; he'd take her too. "You can pick up a combi to Port St. Johns."

Suddenly, there was a shout from the hostel. "Anyone wanting to go to the Hole in the Wall, come on!"

The Hole in the Wall was a bizarre rock formation that sat in the ocean off the coast about a half-hour away from Coffee Bay. Shaped like a croquet wicket, it was the major tourist attraction in the area.

Margot grabbed her camera and jumped into the back of yet another pick-up truck.

It all happened within a matter of seconds.

They were white. And that was the only thing she knew about them.

The guy driving was about thirty, big and beefy. Next to him in the cab was his girlfriend. She wore blue jeans that tightly hugged a puffy abdomen. That abdomen depressed Margot.

A local guy sat with Margot in the back. He looked washed-up, like he'd done too many drugs and he wasn't even an artist, like he found himself living in the Transkei not out of love for an oppressed people or a damaged country, but because no one bothered him too much when he was in the African backwaters.

The beefy guy kept throwing empty beer cans into the back with them. The grin on Margot's face froze as she realized everyone was drunk. Beefy, intoxicated and red-faced, sped recklessly around blind turns, along dirt roads. A pair of flip-flops joined the beer-can toss; he had stepped in crap and he didn't want the cab to stink.

At one point, he stopped the truck and blasted the radio. He called back to the Washed-Up Guy and Margot, "This is Afrikaner music." It was some kind of techno, hip-hop, rap imitation-club music with a distinctly 1980's sound.

It's shit-for-music, Margot thought.

Then, on a beer run at the local shack/store, Beefy hopped out of the truck and did this arm-and-fist-gesture commonly done by grown men at football games. The white boy jive to very bad Afrikaner techno.

"Nice," Margot said. "It's good," she lied. She was becoming quite the liar.

Beefy stood by the vehicle and turned his back to her when the Washed-Up Guy went to purchase beer. The girlfriend was still in the cab. Beefy unzipped his pants and proceeded to urinate on the side of the road.

Turning towards Margot again, he put his hand on her ankle and moved it slowly along her calf. "Do you shave all the way up?"

She flinched.

Thank God, Washed-Up Guy returned just then.

In the car, Beefy pretended he was going to hit Xhosa kids walking along the road, dodging them at the last minute. The children fled, scattering like spooked animals. He threw a beer can at them and laughed wildly when they chased after it.

You're a pig, Margot thought.

They raced up and down hills, and Margot hung onto the truck, beer cans rolling around next to shitty thongs. She prayed he wouldn't kill any kids.

Meanwhile, Washed-Up Guy said, "The Xhosa are a lousy tribe, unlike the Zulus. The Xhosa don't want to work; they're lazy."

Finally, they made it. Beefy attempted to park perpendicular to a hill; Margot fully expected the truck to tip, tumbling into the sea. They would surely perish on the rocks below.

She jumped out of the truck the first chance she got.

"What's wrong with you?" Beefy asked.

"I want to live," she answered.

After he managed to park, they marched down the path to the obviously overrated Hole in the Wall.

Margot trailed behind with the girlfriend. "We met in Namaqualand eight months ago," the girlfriend explained. Namaqualand was in the Northern Cape Province. Though blanketed in blooming purple, orange, and yellow wildflowers in the spring, at the end of summer it was brown desert. She continued, "At a meat festival."

A meat festival?

"This is the first time we've seen each other since," she said. "I live in Port Elizabeth; he lives in Cape Town."

A meat festival must be equivalent to those odd American events at which big trucks roll over little trucks within coliseums containing men with beer bellies and women wearing tank tops sans bras.

Finally, the Hole in the Wall. A rock formation!

"Damn!" exclaimed the girlfriend. "I forgot my camera in the truck."

She left to retrieve her camera. Washed-Up Guy wandered off. Margot was alone with Beefy.

"So you shave all the way up?" he said.

Margot pretended not to hear.

"You're crazy for going to Port St. Johns alone, unless you're into getting raped," he said.

"I'm not."

"Look, I'm dropping her off in Port Elizabeth. I can take you back to Cape Town."

She pretended to think about it. "Probably not." She changed the subject. "Your girlfriend tells me you met at a meat festival?"

"Yeah. " He became very excited. "This one night, I got so drunk I passed out in the back of my truck. When I woke up the next morning, there was a body next to me. I reached over to see if there were breasts. There weren't. I reached down and this guy was harder than me. I shouted, 'Get the fuck out of my truck!'"

I'm in danger, she thought.

"You should see the crayfish in Mozambique. If you were to lay one on top of your breasts, its tail would curl up between your legs."

Shit.

Margot desperately needed to return to Coffee Bay for her ride out of there. After the girlfriend showed up with her camera and took pictures as if she were a *National Geographic* photographer, Beefy suggested a drink for the road.

By the time they were in the truck, it was noon. This time, she sat in the cab with them. A madman, Beefy whipped through the Transkei, spinning tires and raising dust. Washed-Up Guy stood in the rear and held onto a bar on the roof as if he were surfing, as if he were a dog with the wind blowing back floppy ears.

Beefy, looking over at a frightened Margot, said, "What's the matter? You a virgin?"

What do you say to a guy like this? Margot thought that, perhaps, if she engaged him in conversation, he'd slow down. "So, are you two in love?"

The poor girlfriend stiffened.

"Just dating right now." He was shaken.

Margot turned to her. "Well, this oughta make you think."

With the desired effect, Beefy drove on in silence.

They arrived, alive.

You and Tess didn't like each other. She found you to be a redneck, a little too "Dutch." Similarly, you found her obnoxious and American. She couldn't believe I was dating you, an Afrikaner. You couldn't believe we were even friends.

Remember when we went to a movie together—Tess, some guy she liked, and the two of us? You insisted we take separate cars.

We went for drinks first: lines were invisibly drawn—girls and boys, foreigners and South Africans, Afrikaners and English. You drank beer; the English South African guy drank wine. You wore a pullover sweater; he wore a dress shirt.

As the theater filled, a friend of theirs met us. He was a black man, and this was another difference—they had black friends.

You got to your feet, scooted over, and beckoned me to move.

"What are you doing?" I asked, slightly dense.

This is what you said: "Making room for the brother."

Oh, Ben!

Later, I told Tess what you said. She nearly spit her drink out of her mouth, repeating those words: "The brother!"

The brother.

The truth of the matter was this: despite the archaic language, you were the first one to get up and make sure there were enough seats for the black man to sit with us.

I noticed this. Ben, don't think I didn't notice.

Margot journeyed to Umtata and made it to Port St. Johns, named after another shipwreck. She talked to world travelers and Xhosa holy men, read a Tom Robbins paperback in a hammock, and walked on trails through subtropical jungles.

When she thought about Beefy, she was ashamed for having jumped into his truck only because he was white.

At the week's end, she grabbed a Greyhound bus in Umtata to return to Cape Town, staggering from Africa.

They stopped at 4:45 a.m. in Swellendam, where she had to switch to a new bus. Margot had been to the town before, and it reminded her—in daylight—of Switzerland. The mountain ranges were towering, luxuriant, and shrouded in thick green vegetation; the architecture was quaint and starkly white. The town looked like a grid of Puritan main streets with a continental tinge. Rising above the sweetness of the streets, a South African Alps hovered. The place was so clean it nearly glowed. The townships weren't even visible, concealed within cliffs; they were put away, like secrets; everything was sterile. This was a Dutch Disneyland, an English shire.

She waited for the transfer to Cape Town. Feeling a little chilly, she sat on a bench outside a hotel on a desolate street. She was nervous and alone, except for a young black woman sitting nearby. This woman, too, had gotten off the Greyhound, probably waiting for a ride or a transfer as well. Together, they watched the bus drive away, its lights gradually fading.

The streets were empty. In towns this small, no one was out before dawn. The two women looked shyly at each other. They looked at their hands. They looked at the ground. There were a few stark streetlights that hit them like spotlights, and they both seemed to be pretending they weren't scared.

But it was scary. No one was around. No cars passed. Swellendam was dead. Already, Margot loathed this town for its whiteness, its barrenness before daybreak. She felt for this woman, black the same way Margot had been white in the Transkei.

Margot pulled out a package of lemon cookies she had bought on the road. She looked at the young woman, an outsider in this Swiss South African town. She began to unwrap the cookies, the plastic wrap making disruptive crackling noises in the early morning. Finally, the wafers free, their yellow icing was revealed. Margot looked at the cookies in her hands. She pulled the wrap back and took one in her fingers.

Then she held the package out to the black woman. "Do you want some? Do you want some cookies?" She pushed them into the other woman's palm.

The black woman accepted them. She nodded kindly at Margot.

Without a word, they ate lemon cookies together before dawn.

————

Sometimes, I tell anecdotes which reflect poorly on you, on your country.

I don't know how to talk about the times you drove Patience back to Khayelitsha yourself; I don't know how to tell people what that meant.

I talk about how beautiful Cape Town is. I say there's a price to pay for that beauty: internal dissonance, an uneasiness of the soul.

I never asked you if you felt that dissonance, that chaos. Maybe I was afraid to hear what you'd say.

I feel guilty, too.

For my assumptions, for my labeling, for a lot of things.

*This is my confession: you are a South African man and I judged you—*judge *you. But internal dissonance and uneasiness of the soul are not spots on any map. It's easy to point a finger at a place on the globe; it's easy to condemn a regime. But dissonance can be packed, rolled up tightly, stored in a sleeping bag. You can take it with you wherever you go.*

Ben, I had it in my backpack the whole time. Like my passport, I never let it out of my sight.

The Mickey Rourke Saga

—For Ian Jackman

This is all true, though it happened decades ago, right after Nine Inch Nails came out with *Pretty Hate Machine*. I was thinking, "*Yes*, I *am* a pretty hate machine." Whatever that meant. It sounded fierce, ironic, like a bittersweet lovestruck college girl in the late eighties and early nineties. I was coloring my hair back then: jet black, almost blue. I had an aesthetic, a code; it involved self-destruction and a sad kind of exotic, erotic, and alienated beauty. Though I was unhappy all the time, life seemed *heightened*. It was like I was on drugs, but I wasn't.

This story begins in a Buick.

We're not talking about a cool car. Rather, it's an *inherited* one. The music makes the vehicle throb. It crawls all over you like a violation, like it's raping you. I'm with a guy people call *Jest*. *Jest* rhymes with *blessed*, with *rest*, with *test*. Jest is nineteen, one year older than I. He's prematurely balding, with thin wisps of blond hair over a skull of baby-soft skin. I've never touched his head, nor do I really want to, but that's how I imagine it: *soft*. He has an aesthetic, as well. Despite the fact that we live in the desert, he never wears shorts. This is weird because college students in Tucson, Arizona practically *live* in boxers and tees.

Pants are *hated*. Everywhere Jest goes, he wears dress pants and dress shirts with the sleeves rolled up. His hands are always in his pockets, too—not in some perv way, but rather, like a suave undercover spy or a slick millionaire. He loves Sade because she's so damn sensual and otherworldly; he keeps his dorm room lights off with candles burning. He cooks his own meals in the dorm kitchen; he runs a full bar from under his sink. Plus, he whispers. His whispering makes me think he knows something I don't, like maybe he's in touch with God.

So, I'm with Jest in a Buick and the music is positively earsplitting. This is all part of *Operation Get Mickey*.

Mickey Rourke, that is.

From my dorm room, I got a phone call about an hour ago, around nine on this November night. "Mickey's downtown," Jest whispered. "They're shooting a scene. Get ready. I'm picking you up."

Jest understands desperation. This is his story:

Jest's brother committed suicide when Jest was thirteen. He discovered the body in the bathtub when he came home from school. Wandering from the kitchen towards the back of the house and carrying one of those orange juice popsicles that kids make with toothpicks and ice trays, he called out the names of his brother, his mother, his sister. At the bathroom door, he stopped, noticing it was half-open, noticing the light was on. He stood there, licking his orange juice popsicle. He knocked, calling out, "Phil? You in there? Phil?" Pushing the door open, he discovered the body.

There were several long minutes of mad struggle as Jest tried to pull the lifeless body from the room temperature, blood-red water. The dead body fell through his arms like a slippery fish, slapping the surface of the water and, Jest, a boy, clasped onto limbs, pulled on his brother's torso, and screamed out. The anguish and the wetness and the heaviness and the horribleness overwhelmed him so thoroughly that he sunk to the side of the tub, his clothes wet and pink, his limbs gently skimming the surface of deceptively calm waters. As the struggle to alter the past subsided, Jest's fight gave way to weeping; he knew that this quieter, more thoughtful sobbing would make an indelible mark on his person.

The streets are closed; police patrol. We park near the courthouse. Bright lights, cameras, crew members, and Don Johnson claim an entire intersection. While we're staking out the shoot, Mickey Rourke arrives on a Harley.

I gasp. He looks like—like I don't *know* what. A biker. A bad boy. A problem child. He's dressed in leather; he's got multiple earrings. I see stubble. I can't keep my eyes off his jawbone, his minute waist. *My God*, I think. He looks like scum and I'm deathly attracted to him.

Jest doesn't turn to me while he talks, nor does he seem to move his lips. It's as if he were some kind of ventriloquist. Film people do film things. It's all a great mystery to us. Jest, staring ahead with his hands in his pockets, whispers, "Do it."

I take a deep breath. I'm wearing my special *Operation Get Mickey* outfit: denim short shorts, a tight black top that creates the illusion of cleavage, and the leather jacket I've owned since high school. Staring at Mickey and speaking a good octave lower than my normal voice, I croon, "I'm going to seduce him. I'm going to make him *beg*, and then I'm going to tell him *no*. That, Jest, is *all*." I squint my glam rock eyes in his direction.

"Okay." He spins towards me, slowly. "Go."

Ten-fifteen at night. The intersection is cluttered with equipment. Spotlights crisscross the pavement. I shadow Mickey, walking with him, preparing to approach, wondering if anyone will stop me. He smirks. He smokes. He leans against things. He poses, swaggers, wears his leather pants in a serious way.

I step forward. Mickey lights up a cig and turns in my direction. I let my jacket fall open. I summon all the magic an eighteen-year-old girl possesses on a good day. He takes a long, unhealthy, sexually-charged drag of his cigarette. He casts it to the ground while holding his breath, and shifts his eyes to roll over the sideline crowd. He glances my way. He moves on to other spectators. And then, *then,* he returns to me, the way eyes naturally return to disaster. He sees *ruin*, and I have him. For a moment, it's power, the kind of power I associate with Mickey Rourke: it's crushing. We look at one another through scars, mascara tracks, red puckered lips, and filmic props. Electric lights drown out stars. We absorb each other on this street corner in a desert college town over two decades ago when I was capable of romantic, whimsical feats. This is a possession, an out-of-body experience. It's *mine*.

Mickey Rourke and I have rock-your-world eye contact. He walks forward, and I walk forward, too. No one stops me. No one gets in my way. Film crew, security guards, gaffers and best boys—these people are supposed to hold me back. I arrive and I don't know what to do. I walk this distance between us, this blocked-off road. I bury my hands in leather jacket pockets, finding and clutching a wadded-up napkin from Domino's Pizza in the left. I walk deliberately, strongly, confidently, like I'm in a Milan fashion show. Right in front of me, Mickey Rourke stands like a divinely rejected angel, anticipating my very presence.

His raw sexuality is disarming, and I work to pull myself together. I don't know what to say, how to act. I'm an honors student; I'm dark, sardonic, witty, a staff reporter for the school paper—Arts and Culture, my beat. Okay. I'll interview him—I'll interview Mickey Rourke for the *Arizona Daily Wildcat*! *Operation Get Mickey*? Oh, that's still on, of course, but I have to talk to him first, find out what's going on with that *9½ Weeks* shit. Ask him if he's psychotic or if it's just a facade.

Let's be very honest about all this playacting: I'm a coward and I have no real way of approaching this man.

"Mr. Rourke," I say, all breathy and sexy. "You're in town till December?"

He pretends to try to remember. As if one could forget how long one's supposed to be in Tucson.

To myself, I calculate our age difference. "I'm a reporter," I blurt out.

A sudden flash of disinterest spreads across Mickey Rourke's face. I've blown it. My God, I've *blown* my chance to have Mickey

Rourke undress me so that I can say no to him! Oh, if only I had said something else. I'm a gymnast, a body double, a jazz singer, a voodoo princess. I dance on tables. I'm a good-time girl. I play craps, poker, the xylophone. But no. I'm a *reporter*.

Mickey doesn't let me get any further. "If I have time." He points to a large, effeminate, flamboyant man standing next to him, saying, "This is the person you should talk to. She'll take care of you."

She's a *he*. Well over six feet tall with a clean-shaven face and jowl-like cheeks, he's a Christmas tree in a green sweater and white pants, a red scarf thrown dramatically around his neck. He looks at me with big *I'm your girl* eyes.

I have that hideous, you're-a-loser feeling. "Hi."

"Hi, Hon." He flips over a Kleenex box. "Let me get your phone number."

We complete the transaction, but I'm not done. Mickey stands nearby. He speaks to someone with a clipboard. Gently, like adults I've seen often do, I reach out and touch his shoulder. With my eyes a-glow, I say, "It was a pleasure watching you."

"Thanks." Mickey smiles.

It was a pleasure *watching* you?

I turn around and join Jest who's waiting for me behind the sawhorses used for crowd-control.

Operation Get Mickey has its roots.

There's this guy; let's call him *Keifer*—or how about *Trey*? A brooding megalomaniac type, he thoroughly convinced me upon arrival my freshman year that he was brilliant, sexy, capable of penetrating the heart of many of the world's great mysteries, *and* he understood me like no other man ever had or ever would.

To prepare for essay exams, he'd write essays and memorize them word for word. This impressed the hell out of me. They were on things like Chinese history and the Russian humanities.

On a dare, he walked naked to the showers for a month in our co-ed dorm, using shampoo bottles as post-Edenic fig leaves. Girls would sit and watch. I did too.

He was into the problem of evil, the end of the Cold War, and the selling out of U2. This struck me as especially *profound*.

He'd kiss my lips and it was like he was reading my palm.

Trey was a good reason to stay in school. In short, I *believed* in this guy.

In 1986, before our history began, he saw *9½ Weeks*. This was when Trey had longish hair and occasionally wore eyeliner. "Mickey's a *god*," he declared decisively from then on.

I never even *saw* the movie—I wasn't *allowed* to.

Trey fixed this—we rented it at Blockbuster and watched it on a Friday night in the spaghetti sauce-scented dorm TV room. As we watched, Trey leaned forward the whole time, glued to the screen, whispering the score in my ear. He talked me through it, explaining things, laying the groundwork for our own future devastation. "Listen to what Mickey says," Trey instructed, "and how he says it." Trey got excited as if we were at a football game. "Watch his body language, note where he puts his hands." Mickey, looking trampled upon but lovely, became a sick model for Trey, who was—after all—just a smart boy with a good CD collection.

Trey did weird Mickey Rourke things. He never tied me up; he never made me crawl. He posed dramatically in dark places on campus—I distinctly remember watching him smoke outside the dorm at midnight, leaning over the rusty green rail, looking very lonely despite the fact that I waited inside to take him into my arms and weave him into my being till our organs and sinews were indistinguishable. I remember this.

Once, in my room, it involved food—just like with Mickey and Kim Basinger in the movie. It wasn't very sexy, though, because I only had a six-pack of Diet Coke and a bottle of papaya juice in my knee-high fridge. We dumped soda and juice all over each other and kissed like we were in a Manhattan skyscraper and we were absolutely *desperate* for one another. Unfortunately, he had just eaten a hot dog, and I could taste it on the roof of his mouth. For months afterwards, I had ants.

Besides that, he regularly said enigmatic things that sounded slightly warped and twisted. At night, he'd speak softly. "I love you, but I know if I showed you the extent of my love, you'd run like hell."

This would cause me to respond in kind with similarly enigmatic things that also sounded slightly warped and twisted. Before slipping into my room for the night where a retainer for the teeth awaited, I'd whisper back, "*Show* me. *See* if I run."

It ended badly, after eight months of unbeatable melodrama. Who can maintain clever conversation for that long? Who can be sexy every minute of every day? We had homework to do, classes to take, college philanthropies and fun-runs in which to participate. Much of our disintegration had to do with the inability to reconcile our creepy charade with rituals ranging from taking prerequisites to watching re-runs of "Cheers." When all was said and done, the Mickey Rourke routine proved to be rather, well, *insubstantial*.

Rourke was the other woman.

Had Trey and I bonded without eccentricity and false pretense, had we eaten pizza and frozen yogurt, had we held hands in movie theaters and played miniature golf, we may've been happy. I'll never know. Certain *trappings* got in the way.

But I do know this: a capricious rejection of Mickey Rourke will be a small victory for true love. If I do it quickly and suddenly, like murder, its symbolic value will resonate over the course of my entire life. I'll be conquering flimsy erotic nonsense; then I'll get on with things. I'll get on with love.

When Mickey Rourke and Don Johnson come to town to make their movie, it's a godsend. And I *believe* in God.

———

Things happen at night. For two weeks, Jest and I are nocturnal. I had no clue Tucson is so active after dark. Mickey doesn't call, so Jest and I try to keep track of the film. This nighttime world is like *Blade Runner*, like a John Sayles film, like a Lou Reed song. We go downtown where tiny little cafés stay open till four a.m. We hit empty bars where lone figures drink dry martinis. We go to diners, the bus station, Hotel Congress, Café Quebec. I drink Mexican coffee and wait for Mickey to show up. I walk over railroad tracks to Dunkin' Donuts where Jest buys me powdered sugar Munchkins.

He says, "We'll find him. Tomorrow."

My elbows propped on the Dunkin' Donuts' counter and my lips dusted in white, I say, "What makes you think so?"

Jest whispers one word, "Fate."

I believe him.

Jest finds out they're shooting at the Tucson Convention Center. Arriving around nine at night, we park in back. Two trailers parallel a huge stage door. One is for Don Johnson, the other for Mickey Rourke.

I've changed outfits. This time I wear a dress, also made of denim: acid-washed, backless, a dog-collar neck.

Jest is quiet. Sitting in the front seat with the lights from the Convention Center bouncing off the Buick's windshield, we stare at the trailers.

"I'm going in," I say.

Jest puts his hands on the steering wheel, peering out. "Show some leg."

I open the car door and put a foot on the ground. "Thanks. I will."

It's important to know that, in all this, I never have a plan. I walk to the trailer. The door is open, and chatter emanates from within. Rourke's name is written on the side. I slowly climb the four steps to the entrance.

Sucking sharp air into my nostrils, I reach my fist inside and knock. Scampering, shuffling, and arranging sounds emerge. A voice says, "Come in."

So I go.

I walk into Mickey Rourke's trailer, ready to interview, seduce, and reject. Billy Squier sings in my head. I can do this; I can carry this off. The Christmas Tree with the Kleenex box meets me before I get very far. Over his shoulder, I see Mickey drinking Evian with a white towel hanging around his neck. "Oh no you don't," Christmas Tree says.

"I thought I heard someone say, 'Come in.'"

He looks at me with pity. "You did. Sorry, our mistake."

I gulp and try to make it look coy. "I just wanted to talk to Mr. Rourke."

He checks me out. I feel undone, see-through. "Aren't you the reporter?"

"Yeah?" That haunting statement of truth.

He/she shakes his/her head. "Hon," he pauses. "We'll call you. Okay?"

I back up. I step onto the stairs. "I'm sorry. Really. I'm sorry."

And that's that. I return to Jest in the Buick. The whole thing took five minutes max. Jest puts his hand on mine. We sit like that for ten minutes.

Jest breaks the silence. "I need to do something. When I leave, I want you to slide over and start the ignition, okay?"

I'm a little emotional, having been discarded by Mickey Rourke on top of the travesty that is my life. "Fine," I say. Not only has Trey forsaken me, but so has Mickey Rourke.

Jest gets out; I slide over. When the motor's running, I lower the windows and blast the radio. I flip through stations, vacillating between Dexy's Midnight Runners and Modern English.

I figure Jest is getting me an autograph. I figure we'll have to settle for our range of possibilities. I guess we'll have to get real.

I sing "Come On, Eileen" at the top of my lungs, accepting harsh reality. I hit the steering wheel and shake my fake black hair all over the place.

Then I see him.

Jest, running like he's in *Chariots of Fire*, like he's Indiana Jones and there's a boulder chasing him, like he's trying to outrun a raging Dorothy-in-Kansas cyclone, dashes for the car. I swear to God, the guy, dress pants and all, can *really* run. I watch him, not completely grasping the situation. He opens the car door, hops in, slams it, breathes heavily, and gasps, "Drive!"

A two-second delay ensues. My mind isn't digesting the events. Something is in his arms. Jest shouts, "Drive!"

I shift the car and do just that. Though I have to slowly brake over a few Convention Center speed bumps, I race away. Jest has, in his hands, a leather bomber jacket. I look at Jest; I look at the road; I look at the jacket. "What's going on?"

Jest breathes heavily. "I got you something."

Again, I look at Jest, at the road, at the jacket. "What do you mean?"

"I got you this, so you're not empty-handed."

It takes a minute; I'm extraordinarily dense. "You stole that *jacket*?" I was once a girl scout; I went to private Christian schools.

He holds it up. "It's Mickey's Harley-Davidson jacket. In the movie." I look at it out of the corner of my eyes. First of all, it *smells* like leather, like warm bovine. I can almost taste the open highway in my mouth. Second, it's got *presence*. It's beaten-up, black and orange in color. The words *Harley-Davidson* are written on the front, on the sleeve, and sprawled across the back. A deck of cards revealing a full house fans out over the right breast. Under the full house, a skull with *R.I.P.* and the word *Evolution* are written. A pack of cigarettes and a Zippo lighter are in its pockets. I feel like I'm Dennis Hopper and I'm riding a motorcycle to Venice Beach.

"You stole a prop?" I'm utterly confused.

"It's a one-of-a-kind," he nods.

I look in the rearview mirror. No one's behind us. I gave Mickey my phone number. I am suspect number one. Pulling into a university parking lot, I tremble.

With lowered heads, we walk past the front desk to my dorm room. Jest carries Mickey's jacket. Inside, he sits on my pink bedspread. James Dean, Depeche Mode, and Gunther Gable Williams from the Ringling Bros. and Barnum & Bailey Circus look down on us from their smug places on my wall.

I cross my arms over my chest and pace. I've got stolen merchandise in my room and I left my phone number with the victim. "I'm calling my dad."

My father picks up after three rings. I tell him what happened.

"You're an accomplice," he declares, sternly. "Probably to a felony." His volume rises. "Where's the damn jacket right now?" He's really angry. "Where'd you put it?"

"It's here." I whimper. I'm near tears. "In my room."

"And you gave that *joker* your phone number?" he shouts into the phone.

"Yeah," I admit.

"I don't believe you—I don't believe you did this. And that 'Jest' character—doesn't that idiot have a *real* name? You give him the jacket. You make him take it. You tell him to return it. Tell him to go back and return what he stole. Do you understand? I don't want you keeping stolen property in your room. Do you understand me?"

I sniffle. "Yeah."

When I get off the phone, I push Mickey Rourke's Harley-Davidson jacket into Jest's arms. I tell him I can't keep it. I tell him I can't keep stolen property.

Later, he lets me know how it was, how the film medic took it back unknowingly, how Jest made it look like an oversight, something missed in the scuffle.

———

Two years pass.

Trey lives off-campus. We rarely see each other, but I think of him often.

I don't like to hang out with Jest anymore because he scares me, but occasionally we'll have Mickey Rourke Film Festivals in my room. We'll rent *Wild Orchid* and *Desperate Hours,* I'll make microwave popcorn, and Jest will sneak in beer. We're serious critics of Mickey's performances; we understand method acting and Mickey's many, many moods.

Right before graduation, Jest takes me to Mina's Red Pepper Kitchen for lemongrass chicken and Pad Thai.

"I have something for you back at my apartment," Jest whispers over coconut-scented drops of soup. Jest, too, has left the dorm; we are separated, all of us.

"What?" I ask, picturing his apartment. He has silly black sheets he stole from Sears and a shrine to foreign-born women.

"It's a surprise."

"I hate surprises." My tone is dry and indifferent; by twenty, I'm morose and apathetic.

"You'll like this one."

I have grown to hate Jest. That voice triggers something ruthless in me. If there's a reason for war, it's that voice. It makes me want to point my finger at him and assault him with enemy words. When I hear him speak, I know magic is just a sleight of hand.

Back at his apartment, I sit on his bed, the one with the stolen sheets. "Well?"

"Will you do something for me?" he asks.

"What?" I jiggle my leg up and down.

"I want to blindfold you," he whispers.

He's serious. He's completely serious.

"Why?" I ask.

"It'll add to the surprise."

"Okay." I pause. "Blindfold me." One wonders why I allow it. Besides unrelenting curiosity, it's part of being a girl: at some point in your life, a man's going to want to blindfold you and, rather than risk false accusations, you'll let him do it.

"Stand up," he demands. It's part of a plan he's concocted in the wee hours of the night. I can tell. I see it in his face.

I stand up.

"Turn around." His tone hasn't changed, but I sense *strategy*.

I turn around. I hear him move behind me. A tie swings in front of my face, bringing darkness, and he carefully arranges it over my eyes, smoothing the silk over the bridge of my nose. He presses my eyelids lightly, making sure that my blindfold is comfortable. "Is that too tight?"

""It's okay," I say.

"I want you to be comfortable."

"I know you do, Jest."

I hear sounds like jars opening and flames flickering. Jest passes things under my nose. "Smell this."

"What is it?" I ask, hiding fear.

"Just smell it."

I do. Flowers not in season.

I hear the sizzle of a match and know he's passing it by my face. "Don't move."

"What are you doing, Jest?" I whisper.

He doesn't answer me.

I feel a chill against my skin, metal on my arm. He traces a cold wire along my shoulder. "Raise your arms," he says.

"Like this?" I lift them above my head, the way kids do when they can't stop coughing.

"No. Straight out."

"Like Jesus on the cross?"

"Yes."

The cold wire moves over my wrist, past my elbow, across my shoulders, and down the other arm till it touches my fingertip and disappears.

"Do you know what that was?" he asks.

"No."

"Guess."

"I can't."

"Guess."

"A hanger," I moan, feigning detachment. My mind is *reeling*.

"You're right." He presses leather against my skin. "And this?"

"It's leather," I answer.

Jest drapes his surprise over my shoulders and I feel its weight cover me.

"You're a madman, Jest."

"Let me take off your blinders," he declares.

Jest unties me in front of a mirror. I'm wearing Mickey Rourke's Harley-Davidson jacket. "Why did you do this?" I address his image in the mirror.

"You can forget Mickey," he says, standing behind me while we look at ourselves. "But I want you to remember me."

And this is our final hoax; this is how we say good-bye. We use props and call it quits.

Years have passed, and the statute of limitations has expired. I keep the jacket in a closet, dragging it out sporadically at parties, bridal showers. My dad likes to wear it for pictures. He poses like he's the Fonz.

I went back to my natural hair color, a forgettable brown. Divorced and childless, I'm still at a loss when it comes to the company of men.

Jest and I barely keep in touch, but I know he's in the Peace Corps. When he writes, he tells me about the llama jerky he makes in Bolivia while the people wait for revolution. I'm not sure whether or not he continues to wear dress pants. He's still trying to save his brother's life.

Trey is lost. I don't know what happened to him.

Ten years ago, though, we met in a hotel room near LAX when our business meetings converged. The room smelled like maple syrup and the carpet was a disturbing shade of gray. We met and, this time, Mickey was neither here nor there. We were alone. Undressing one another and approaching each other's naked bodies, we searched for that old passion, that melancholic obsession that used to make us feel so alive. We stopped having sex right in the middle, because it seemed ridiculous, as if we were strangers and not strangers at the same time. Instead of the excitement of unfamiliarity or the comfort of the beloved, we found only disgust and drudgery. When we parted, we kissed like cousins. I haven't seen him since.

I rent Mickey Rourke films rather than seeing them in movie theaters, not wanting to pay for a ticket. I can't figure out that plastic surgery business, either. He's like an old friend, like Jest—someone I care for but really don't want to talk to.

Finally.

This, too, is true: Like Kim Basinger in the movie, I would crawl for love. I would get down on my hands and knees and inch across hardwood floors. I would suffer rug burn. I would crawl and crawl. I would crawl for miles. I would humble myself and let any candle flame, any fire, graze my cheek, if love were truly at stake.

Free Dive

Ginger's lover's leg washed up on the shore in early May. Wet suit stuck to corpse like frayed rubber glove. Foot in useless flipper. A crazy rock lobster attached at the knee. When Etienne and Mark, his diving buddies, skulked onto her Camps Bay veranda with the news, she had been drinking schnapps. She laughed a false wail of a laugh. Her first thought was, *I didn't like being the other woman anyway.*

Rian's leg flashed before her eyes. The sky was washed out; the water was chilly and dirty. She didn't visualize blood. Gore didn't suit Rian. He was a beautiful man, South African sunburnt, muscled, chiseled, given to saltwater swims and callused hands. Too pretty for something as revolting as chewed flesh. And that horrible rock lobster, taking possession of what wasn't his.

So she laughed: head thrown back. Those who saw her thought her deranged or ecstatic.

"That's because they're the vacuum cleaners of the sea," Mark explained, referring to the rock lobster.

"Scavengers," Etienne added. "Bottom-feeders. They eat crap from the bottom."

Ginger sighed. It was high time she left Cape Town anyway. It was the middle of 1998. All the conversations were the same.

Ginger and Rian were not in love, but they were conscientious lovers. When they met at night, he always took a shower to wash the salt from his body and she always made sure their sexual gymnastics were memorable, since memory is the force behind hunger.

He was a free diver and she was an American employed by a Washington-based NGO to observe the workings of the Truth and Reconciliation Commission from April 1996 to July 1998. When they met, it was April 1997; she had yet to meet Desmond Tutu.

On their first date, they went to the Cradle of Civilization, a dimly-lit suburban bar with narrow and steep wooden staircases that made every room feel like an attic. "Let's drink brandy," Ginger suggested. She had already lived in South Africa for a year, so she didn't drag around the awe of a tourist when she entered new places. She did, however, drag around her work. In all endeavors, she was aware of both truth and reconciliation. In all endeavors, the disappointments of the New South Africa followed her. She tried not to embody the disappointment; she tried to distance herself from the guilt of the empowered. Basically, she tried not to think about it.

The Cradle of Civilization, despite its Edenic name, played haven to a disgruntled, moody, postmodern crowd of dispossessed, liberal-minded young adults, who were, of course, white. It was so dark, though, they could barely see each other.

Rian and Ginger exchanged preliminary information, having met the previous week at a party. Then, Rian offered opinion. "I'd rather live it than simply observe it." He combed his short brown hair with the fingers of his left hand. "You're observing and then reporting? How can voyeurism bring justice?"

"That's terribly unfair—" She stopped and then quickly added, "Someone has to keep a record. You do understand the need for justice, right?"

"Now you're being unfair." He winked at her. "I'm a diver. We come in all colors."

Ginger stared into her brandy. She looked up at him, and noticed Rian watching her blond hair catch candlelight. She closed her thumb and index finger over the flame, pinching it out. "What does a free diver do, anyway?"

"Unlike scuba divers, we don't use oxygen. We rely on lung capacity." He looked proud of his declaration.

"No tanks?" Ginger twisted a strand of hair around her finger. "So you snorkel?"

"I free dive." Rian's eyes twinkled. "Let's get out of here. I do other things besides dive."

Six months later, in his bed, Rian said to her, "You enjoy yourself, and that's why I enjoy you." He drew waves and shark fins on the flat of her stomach. "Guess what I drew." He propped himself up onto his elbows.

Ginger folded her arms across her breasts, not really pouting but sulky nonetheless. "I'm not playing anymore."

"Why not?"

"Isn't there a new game we can play? A game no one else plays?"

He looked at her with confusion.

"Let's think of a new game, a game just for us. Or we can learn Morse code and practice on each other's bodies," she continued. "We'll send each other SOSs."

"I don't need any help. Plus, I already know Morse code." He tackled her, pulling her under the covers. She giggled, pretending to fight him off. "Guess what I'm saying." He covered her body with kisses.

Though she was laughing, she never failed to compare the similarities between free diving and free love. They both involved being unfettered. Holding Rian to her chest, she wanted to simultaneously cling to him and push him away. He was seductive, confident, unrepentant, and her work made her long for the irresponsible and the unapologetic. Day in and day out, she witnessed horrors, the kind of horrors that seeped into one's skin and made it hard to live at all. Rian's clear conscience allowed her to get some rest—smile, if need be. But Rian was also hardened, cocky, and pleased by his own accomplishments, despite the desolation around him. He could brag about his diving and show off muscle tone. Her work made her want to punish him severely.

She didn't go diving with him until they had been lovers for months.

He helped pull the wet suit over her hips, the vest over her breasts. He smiled and she felt shy because her body, in the wet suit, was so vulnerable to scrutiny. She let him stand in front of her, his hands pulling the suit over her waist—his eyes on his hands, a look of professionalism on his face. Like he'd seen a million women with slight bellies squeeze into wet suits designed for Aquaman and other superheroes. She watched his eyes for signs of disgust. When she saw none, her eyes roamed. She scrutinized *his* body. She examined the way the wet suit hugged the flat of his stomach and molded to the shape of his chest. She checked out his behind. When he walked away from her, she examined the shape of his legs. He was like a seashell to her, a collectable. A perfect physical specimen.

He picked up a weight belt from the ground and headed towards her. "Buoyancy." He faced her, putting his arms around her to bring the belt around her waist. He tightened the belt and she felt like Scarlett O'Hara having her ribs crushed by a corset suited for the starving. She looked at him in horror and he smiled again. "You'll like it," he said.

They walked to the sea together. The coast was rocky, and he held her hand and pulled her quickly behind him. She moved over rocks in her booties, her arm outstretched in front of her to hold him. She noticed the sun damage to the back of his neck—freckles, a dark-hued sunset. She slipped and, without turning around, he firmly pulled her up. It was only then that he rotated his neck around. "Mind the gaps."

At the sea, they sat down with their legs in the cold water. He gave her the flippers. "These are the most expensive on the market." She regarded them gravely. "Don't lose them."

She held up a finger in the air, as if a light bulb had gone off in her head. "Wait a minute." She twisted her ankles in small circles, rotating the flippers on her feet. "I'm having a flashback." Rian looked with curiosity at her face. Ginger shut her eyes tightly. "Learning to tie my shoes." She nodded with certainty. "But you're not my daddy."

Rian winked. "I could be, if you wanted."

He took his mask in his hands. "Spit and rub." He spit into the mask and rubbed the glass with his fingertips.

Admiration filled her; watching him was the reprieve from the blood guilt, the apartheid atrocities. "You know what you're doing, don't you?" she said.

"Yeah." He kissed her hair. "Just follow me." He lifted his body off the rocks, submerging himself in the water.

She pushed herself into the ocean, trying not to visibly cringe. They swam away from shore. Upon his cue, she floated on her stomach the way he did and placed her face into the water, breathing through the snorkel.

Then, they swam several meters out. "Just look down and breathe, Ginger. You can hold onto a piece of kelp and let your body flow with the tide. I'll be around." He swam away, not far but no longer near.

Ginger held onto the kelp and allowed her body to be pushed and pulled by its movement within the water. She pulled herself from vine to vine. She held her breath to go under, to pull her body down, to climb seaweed. An inverted Jack and the Beanstalk.

At the bottom, she saw the things he loved. The oranges and yellows and purples. The life moving in soft rhythms. Small fish given to the ebb and flow danced nearby. They didn't swim; they didn't exert energy. Like her, they moved with the water's movement. She let go of the kelp and pushed to the surface for air. Her body was like an inflated doll. Her eyes were wide-open in wonder at the underbelly of the sea. Her world, made helter-skelter. She felt like a foreigner. She felt like she didn't speak this language.

Looking up, she searched for him. He was swimming towards her. When he arrived, she held onto his arm and rolled her tongue over her salty lips.

Rian was so happy. She could see it on his face, the big smile, the water in his eyes. There was something enviable and perfect about him. "This is Zen," he said, blowing a spray of seawater from his lips.

She didn't say anything. She had been frightened.

Ginger and Rian sat on the beach as the African summer faded away. She drank Castle beer and played with the edges of the down blanket on which they sat in the sand. Rian watched the sea.

"What about Babette?" She didn't look up when she said it.

Rian had a French girlfriend, who lived in France.

"She lives in France."

"She's still your girlfriend."

"But she'll always live in France."

"You must love her to keep her as you do."

"Do you think I love her if I'm with you?"

Ginger sifted sand with her fingers. "I suppose no man can really resist a French woman named Babette."

Rian watched the tide roll in and out, and he spoke to the sea. "Yes. That's true."

"You're supposed to lie to me."

"I don't love her," he said.

For an entire year in his late twenties, he had gone diving around the world. In England, he read paperback novels on the train and got a job in construction. In Israel, he slept with an Ethiopian Jew. He proudly told people about his one sexual encounter with a black woman. In Egypt, he learned to play backgammon and he met Babette. For the past five years, the French woman visited South Africa every winter and every summer. When she arrived in Cape Town, they would take off for Namibia to see the sand dunes and the pink flamingos, they would camp on the beach in Mozambique, they would go diving at Cape Point, in Durban, everywhere. Babette had tried living in South Africa for six months once. She missed France, though, so she had left after five weeks. She told Rian she felt harassed on the streets. "The men always talk to me," she told him, her French accent sounding pointy on her tongue. At least, this is how Ginger imagined it. "They won't leave me alone," Babette had said. Rian and Babette never really discussed what her departure meant for them. The following year, she visited Cape Town for three weeks, and they had gone diving ten times. Since Rian had begun seeing Ginger, though, Babette hadn't been to town. She was working in the States. Neither Rian nor Babette brought up her living in Africa since that one time.

Ginger watched the orange and purple sky slip into blue. For a moment, she saw them from above: their two bodies in their mid-thirties, bodies that filled space well—unlike the ripe bodies of young people, crying out for discovery, and unlike the wrinkly bodies of old people, like bags of used food in refrigerators. Their two bodies were vigorous, secure, comfortable. They knew how to wear their hair, how to pick out swimsuits, how to sit in flattering positions. "Don't you think it's cruel to keep her as you do?"

Rian tipped his beer back and said—not unkindly, just matter-of-factly—"You do realize, don't you, that if we continue to discuss this, we'll kill the passion between us?"

Ginger blinked. She thought, *Oh.*

Rian stood up next to her. "Tomorrow, the swell will be gone."

169

Rian fell against her body with a heavy groan that made her skin taut and her fingers dance down his spine. They moved carefully, slowly, with a certain amount of unwarranted tenderness and unsubstantiated affection. They listened for cues from each other and, when Ginger lifted her arms up over her head, the motion was graceful. When Rian moved his hand over her ribs, it was with fluidity and confidence. When it was over, they sprawled out side by side on their backs, breathing deeply while sweat dried on their skin. Eventually, the heaviness of their breathing subsided and they slept.

Ginger woke early. She left him in bed. The first few times she stayed over, he would keep her with him, pulling her close, wrapping his arms around her.

Now, he barely stirred. She went into the kitchen to start a pot of coffee. Sitting on a stool at the counter, she flipped through the pages of a spiral notebook she took to meetings to see what she had observed. During testimony from miscellaneous apartheid victims, she had written a complete paragraph in the margins:

We fucked all Easter weekend. I didn't pray once. Fucked through Good Friday. Missed the church Easter egg hunt. Would have fucked through Advent, if Advent had been in April. On Easter Sunday night, we had dinner at a Portuguese restaurant. There was nothing Portuguese about it.

Ginger read it twice. She slapped the notebook down on the counter and the pages fluttered.

She thought about Rian, her job, her life. She was an observer, an accountant of injustices. She bore witness, when she wasn't writing drivel in the margins. Rian was a nonpartisan participant, a doer, a diver, a sportsman. She had been drawn to that, drawn to his no-nonsense pragmatism. He told her once, "I'm in this world but not of it." He was referring to the former regime. He had added, "That's biblical, you know."

She had said, "It's also completely out of context."

Rian, apparently for a lack of a better line, had shot back, "You're out of context."

Now, seeing her wasted witness in the margins and knowing Rian could sleep peacefully despite any crimes against humanity, she wondered if they were equally innocent or equally culpable. How could either of their minds ever be elsewhere?

After that first time, Ginger didn't want to dive again. But last night, after outrageous sex—bodies hither and thither, the toss of her hair, the lost feeling in his legs—he suggested she join him in the morning. This was their champagne brunch.

The water was dirty. When he left her alone, she got panicky. She couldn't see a thing—not even a foot in front of her. The water was murky, smoky, not really blue, not really gray. All she could think about were sharks. Great Whites. She knew that if something were looking up at her from the bottom, she'd look like a seal. Those flippers slicing water. Her body, dark and rubbery. The sharks, Rian had said on more than one occasion, were as big as vans. Toyota trucks. They would see you, take you for a seal, and swim right at you, hitting you from below. When they realized you were human, they'd spit you out.

Ginger lifted her head, took the snorkel from her mouth, looked for Rian, and swallowed salt. It coated the inside of her mouth. Putting the snorkel back into her mouth, she tried to relax. *Nothing's going to happen*, she told herself. The suspension of disbelief, she needed that. She held onto kelp, rocking back and forth with its motion. This nauseated her. She couldn't remember what it was she was supposed to do to enjoy this. She began to swim to the shore.

But when she grabbed hold of a rock, she vomited—and it flushed back in her face. And then it washed away.

She got herself to shore without a hint of Rian's grace, her arms swinging, her legs kicking, the sharks no doubt watching from below.

Being tied to land is a relief, a godsend, she thought. She plodded over earth in those screwy flippers, turning herself awkwardly around, sitting on a rock to wait for him.

It occurred to her, as she searched for the sight of his snorkel or his back porpoising up along the surface of the water, that she didn't truly understand why Rian didn't get rid of Babette. She didn't know what caused him to hang on. She didn't press him since she didn't want to squash that passion. Unfamiliarity bred passion. Except in cases of the sea.

Looking towards the horizon, Ginger couldn't see him. Rian could be gone for hours. That's part of what being unfettered meant.

That night, after sex, Rian pressed his forehead into the sheets and balanced most of his weight on his knees. Ginger was on her back, staring at the ceiling.

Outside, Cape Town winds whipped and spun.

"What are you thinking?" Rian asked.

"Nothing," Ginger lied. She was thinking they didn't have anything to say. So they said this. "What are you thinking?" she returned the question.

"The wind is blowing from the east. I can definitely dive tomorrow."

He was always thinking about diving.

They loaded the car before leaving to pick up Mark, Etienne, and their girlfriends. That morning, Ginger had done something underhanded. She snuck some of Babette's letters to Rian into the bathroom with her. It wasn't difficult. She merely walked into his bedroom, slipped them into the waist of her jeans, and headed to the toilet. And, much to her satisfaction, they weren't very interesting. Even at her worst, she knew she was more engaging than that truffle-eating, Paris-dwelling, *Champs-Elyseés* Babette. She felt mildly guilty about having snuck the letters into the bathroom until Rian started packing the car with his damned spear guns and wet suits for another day of diving. Then, the guilt dissipated.

"So why is it like Zen?" she asked, hauling one end of a cooler to the car.

"I don't know."

"What happens to the body?" she pressed him.

"I think it begins to operate at a minimum level when you reach a certain depth. Body functions slow down. It frees the mind." He arranged gear strategically.

"Does your mind wander?" she asked.

"Yes."

"Do you think about something in particular?"

"No."

"Is it like smoking pot?"

"What does pot have to do with it?"

"The mind wandering. That anti-intellectual feeling."

"It's not like pot, Ginger." The comparison apparently annoyed him. Rian opened the car door for her. "Get in."

"Is it like sex?" she asked, climbing into the passenger seat.

"No."

"Is it better?"

"Different."

"How?"

"Ginger—"

"What do you think about when you have sex? Do you think?"

He looked at her. "How about if you read this map for me?" He opened up the glove compartment, pulled a tattered road map out, and handed it to her. "Tell me where we're going."

They were quiet for a while.

She fiddled with his cassettes. "Are we having crayfish tonight?"

"Yeah, that's why I brought that bucket." He took a cassette from her hands, turned it around, and stuck it in the stereo.

"We can cook them fresh out of the ocean."

He rolled down the window and adjusted his mirror. "If you kill them by boiling them alive, they go into shock and the meat may be tough, slightly acidic. The best way is to put them in cool water. Then, they suffocate gradually from a lack of oxygen. It's much more humane."

"*Sounds* more humane." She exhaled. She paused. "How often does Babette write you?"

He turned from the road and glanced in her direction. "Once or twice a month."

"Do you write her?"

"No."

"And she keeps writing?"

"Yeah."

Ginger moped, hoping Rian would ask, *What's wrong?* He didn't, so she stopped.

She never told Rian she vomited the last time they went diving together, but he never asked her why she didn't dive with him again, either.

"Don't you ever get sick of diving?" The weekend before Rian's death, they drove up the west coast for the weekend so Rian could dive and Ginger could compile her findings.

"Nope." He leaned over the steering wheel, perpetually checking the weather. "Do you ever get sick of your work?"

"Yes. Sometimes, I do."

"The sea is always new. Injustice is always the same."

One hour later, Rian accidentally hit a dog, killing it. They saw its body fly to the side of the road, dead.

"My God." Ginger covered her mouth with her hand. "Aren't you going to stop?" The dog, a mutt, was bloody and lifeless in the dirt. She was thankful for the excuse to cry. She really wanted to cry.

"No."

She wept then. The tears were hot and there was something wild, something inconsolable, about them.

Rian put his hand on her knee and his eyes darted between her face and the road. "Ginger, if I thought the dog would make it, I'd stop. I swear." He squeezed her knee, moved his hand to the back of her neck, caressed her skin. "I'd stop. Stop crying, Ginge. It's all right."

She couldn't stop. The tears stained her cheeks and slipped into her mouth, leaving the same salty taste as the sea.

"It's all right," he repeated. "You don't have to cry."

She covered her mouth with her hands, weeping. "I'm sorry, I'm sorry."

In May, Ginger sat on her veranda, drinking schnapps. She had been reading the report she had compiled, a report on the truth about apartheid. When she finished it, she flipped through pamphlets on the Seychelles, thinking about going there in July because Babette would be flying to Cape Town then. Ginger had to make herself scarce. Maybe she'd go back to Washington altogether. Someone else could do this job.

Mark and Etienne appeared on her veranda. She rarely saw them dry. "Schnapps?" She rose to her feet.

"No, thanks." They both shook their heads, putting their hands up in protest. They sat down and the Seychelles pamphlets accidentally fell to the ground.

Etienne opened his mouth. He looked nervous; Ginger saw it. "Have a drink, Etienne."

Mark grabbed her hand, and held it to his chest. "Ginger, we have some news for you."

When she heard, when she pictured the rock lobster, she decided to leave. Only when she was alone did she weep, and she was mostly crying for herself.

Killing Castro

Mission: Save the World

By the time she got to Havana, she didn't care anymore.

But, in Cuba, Erin held her breath and exhaled slowly. She watched the black-skinned people speaking Spanish; she stepped back to let girls in short-shorts and garish make-up walk in front of her on cobblestone streets; she shied away from striking men with heartbreaking eyes who looked like bullfighters, artists, or paupers; and she marveled at prehistoric taxi cabs squeezing through dense traffic like bumper cars. When her eyes traveled the depth and breadth of the eroding colonial architecture—ready to wash into a salty tropical sea that flushed against the island in slow, steady rhythms—Erin caught her breath the way one would as if a rumble in the earth's underbelly rippled underfoot. She heard music, and words came into her head that maybe didn't fit: *calypso, fusion, flamenco, mariachi.* The music was everywhere, and it was Latin, African, Caribbean. Listening, her eyes wide, her face sedate, Erin felt as if she were on the precipice of apocalypse. Cuba felt like the end.

By the time Erin got to Cuba, though, killing Castro wasn't her mission.

The Political Animal

Erin was born political. Her parents had the opportunity to start a McDonald's franchise in Canada in the late sixties. How crazy is that? Rather, they bought a hardware store in Jersey. What would she have been like had her parents owned a McDonald's in Manitoba? Would she believe in socialized medicine? Would she idolize the Tragically Hip? What would she think of Michael Moore then?

This never happened, though.

This story began prior to the inception of Happy Meals, back when *Sigmund and the Sea Monsters* aired on TV. Other than a recurring dream about metallic sea monsters (Sigmund's were green and spongy), the show seemed to leave no lasting impression on Erin. Except for one thing.

The voice.

This is a test.

This is only a test.

Erin, nursery school material in the early seventies, put down Dapper Dan, Raggedy Anne's male companion. A disembodied shriek followed. And it had not been Dan.

It was the TV.

The voice revealed this: Sigmund was artifice, not real.

What was real? The Emergency Broadcast System, that's what. Apparently, if the United States were being nuked or if the Soviet Union did something manic, the disembodied voice (was it God?) would suggest an escape route, blueprints for the undersea shelter, directions to the canned beans and powdered milk.

It couldn't be denied. *Sigmund* was subject to interruption. The world encroached.

Erin took note.

Domestic Agenda

Political sedition was inevitable.

The Cold War. No Nukes. Jimmy Carter. Ronald Reagan. Oil. The

East Bloc. Red China. Ethiopia. Amnesty International. *Ah, Amnesty International.*

At Rutgers, Erin majored in Political Science. She voted for Dukakis. She wore "Free Mandela" T-shirts and had a bumper sticker on her VW Rabbit that said *Whirled Peas.* She subscribed to *The New York Times.* Genocide bugged her.

Erin had an honors thesis to write about slain civil rights leader, Red Hajj. Red Hajj's wife was alive and pretty well—now the Director of Public Relations for the Marcus Garvey Peace Center in Crown Heights in Brooklyn, the neighborhood in which the Hassidic Jews and the African-American community had recently rioted. Erin called Mary Hajj on the phone, which turned out to be an amazingly easy thing to do, and asked for an interview.

The year was 1992, and Erin had no idea what she would say to the widow of slain civil rights leader Red Hajj. Twenty-two and upper middle class, all about saving the world, a senior in college, Erin got on the train from Jersey to Brooklyn, eager to be a politically-conscious peace activist.

Erin was supposed to meet Hajj in her office at two. She arrived in Brooklyn an hour early, so she ate a slice of pizza in a pizza parlor straight out of Spike Lee. Eating her slice of pepperoni, she thought, *Hey, I'm a city girl. Brooklyn is fabulous. I'm the only white girl here, and that's fine. In fact, it's great!*

Then, she headed over to the Peace Center. Erin was *ready.*

The moment Erin entered Mary Hajj's office, however, something collapsed. Hajj was a powerful figure—roaring voice, grandma body, daunting confidence, cool brashness, amazingly good skin. Erin found herself terrorized—yes, terrorized—by a racial question: *Why do black people age so well?*

Such thoughts must be wrong.

There were at least two hundred cans of Coke stacked in aluminum pyramids under Hajj's desk. Mary wore a skirt suit, the desk was a mess, and the walls were filled with awards and photos.

Erin pulled out a mini-cassette recorder. "May I record our interview?" Hajj nodded, sitting behind the desk. "Do you have any ID on you?"

ID? Erin was a kid from Jersey. "I have my student ID," she meekly said.

Hajj reached a powerhouse arm over to tiny Erin. "Let me see."

Fumbling, Erin handed it over. A sticker on the back indicated gym membership.

Hajj pursed her lips and gave the ID a good look. She glanced back and forth between the ID and Erin. Then, Hajj wrote down Erin's social security number and handed it back.

Erin already had her doubts about saving the world.

The interview began. "How would you describe civil rights in America today? How is this related to your husband's legacy?" Broad, vague, unanswerable.

Erin couldn't understand a word Hajj said. The stalwart woman stopped, started, peppered incoherent speech with *my beloved Red* and *my dear husband.* "Well, you see, the world was not apropos for what my beloved Red was best situated to—"

Huh?

Hopefully, the tape recorder picked up something. "What do you think would be Red's international agenda today?"

Mary shouted. "My dear husband would be inconceivably filled with multifaceted—"

What?

Quaking, afraid Hajj would rise up from behind her desk and reach out to swallow her, like the scene in *Raiders of the Lost Ark* when the Ark was opened, Erin cowered and searched her notes.

And then the phone rang.

The two women froze, looking gingerly at one another in the Peace Center office.

Erin pushed stop on the recorder. Hajj picked up the receiver. "Hello?"

While Mary spoke, Erin stared at photos. She studied Red's old-fashioned glasses and the goatee and the serious face and Mary's straightened hair.

When Hajj hung up, Erin looked over, took a deep breath, ready to hear of noble suffering, and pushed record on the cassette player. Hajj stared at the girl. "You weren't taping my phone conversation, were you?"

Erin was, in one word, *flabbergasted*. Beside herself. Ready to commit hara-kiri. She shook her head wildly. "No—I wouldn't do *that*—"

"Because that was my personal phone conversation—" Hajj looked as if she would fly and swoop down on young Jersey girl, Erin. Like the monkey things in *The Wizard of Oz*.

"Oh, no—I turned it off." Erin scrambled to show Hajj, nearly throwing the recorder in the air. "I—"

"Because," Hajj rushed to say, "that was business with the Hassidics. You know, *peace*."

"Right. *Peace*—I wasn't taping." Erin fiddled with the cassette-recorder like a madwoman. "Do you want me to play it for you? I can rewind it and play it for you—"

Hajj stopped; she studied the girl; she touched her fingertips together. "No. Let's continue."

Erin was nearly hyperventilating. She hesitated over the recorder. "May I?"

"Yes."

What was there to ask? What should she say? Suffering? What have you suffered? Erin took a deep breath. "How have you continued Red's work?"

Twenty minutes later, Erin fled, peace efforts defunct. Brooklyn took on a new hue; the landscape looked *different*, menacing, like a war zone. Blacks and Jews. Blacks and whites. How could all these people *ever* get along? What was she *thinking*? What an idiot.

She was in danger. She had to get out of Brooklyn. It wasn't safe. Now, she felt eyes on her. She heard footsteps behind her. The vitality she thought she had seen before looked like criminality in the afternoon light. Erin picked up her pace and almost ran down the sidewalk. She knew where she was going, and it was away from there, out of Crown Heights, out of these crossroads for black and white, this hotbed, this vortex in which racial violence careened out of control. She sped towards the subway station, passing the pizza parlor where she had naively eaten the slice of pepperoni.

Stepping onto the train, she felt grief.

That night, in college-girl-irony, she went to the top of the Empire State Building with friends who had spent the day shopping on Fifth. Erin, quiet all evening and ready for a return to the distant, chalky halls of Academia, looked down. The City was just a gathering of light— pinpoints and blurs, sparkling glass, indistinct solar systems. From above, she couldn't see the urban wreck. All she could see was the skyline like scattered diamonds, gems on a crown. The injustice, the skin tones, the violence in voice and sparring words: up close, they were so ugly. From far, far away, the people—in all their color, all their cacophony— were simply beautiful, stars in a sky, lights in the distance.

How could it not take your breath away?

Political Idealism

Shaken after Hajj, it took Erin a while to regain political footing.

Back at Rutgers, friends dragged her to a frat party on a night she planned on watching *Saturday Night Live.* She wore an MLK T-shirt. Who really does that?

The boys belonged to Kappa something. Kappa Phi? Zeta Kappa? Kappa Kappa Omega? "I've got a guy I want you to meet," her friend Steph said. "He's really politically-conscious."

Erin was immediately pushed together with Stu, tall, blond. "He volunteers with March of Dimes," said Steph. He reminded Erin of a good husk of corn.

Alone with Stu, Erin spoke. "Hi." She held her paper cup of Diet Coke. A Bangles song played in the background.

"Hi," said Stu, strapping and politically-conscious. He wanted to go into consulting. Erin wasn't sure about what he'd consult. His father worked in D.C. Stu was running for student senate. Erin wondered if he could work the word "stew" into his campaign posters. *Stu will stew you. Don't stew Stu. Make a little Stu.*

A drunk Kappa Tau guy pushed into their corner, driven by the mob and the Bangles. He put his arm around Stu, looked Erin up and down, took in her T-shirt. Kappa Tau, beer in hand, reached out with the other to pull on the hem of Erin's tee. "Who's this guy?" he asked, slurring words, pointing to MLK.

Erin could see alarm in Stu's eyes. "It's Martin Luther King, Jr."

Kappa Omega pretended to punch Stu in the arm. He gave Erin another up-and-down. "That's good, because I thought it was the other guy."

Erin and Stu exchanged apprehensive looks. The conversation could go anywhere now.

"But MLK is a *good* black." Kappa Omega gave a thumbs-up sign. "Not like the other one." He gave a thumbs-down sign.

Stu said, "Hey, Mike, why don't you go check out the kitchen." He turned to Erin and said, "I'm sorry. He's drunk."

"It's okay," she said, waving her hand dismissively.

Kappa Theta, though, was irritated. He got very close to Erin, beer-breath reeking, and said, "So you date black men?"

"I date black men and white men." Or, she would, if dating she did.

Stu was silent; the conversation was moving too quickly.

Gamma Kappa whispered, "So you like that big, black cock?"

Stu stepped in. "Mike—" He pulled Kappa away. Then, as if they were playing Pin-the-Tail-on-the-Donkey, Stu spun Mike around and pushed him away.

Erin, a little shocked, watched Mike disappear: *Good-bye, Kappa Zeta.*

Stu turned to Erin with a red face. "I'm sorry. He's not really like that—"

"It's okay." She pivoted, too. "Good luck with consulting." *You stalk of corn.* And Erin was gone, as well.

She never wore the MLK T-shirt again.

The story was folklore among friends, at once hilarious and vexing.

Political Theory

Degreed, Erin got a job at the Committee on International Policy in Manhattan. It was the nineties, which weren't like the eighties but weren't that different, either. Mildly burdened by adult acne and clinical depression, in possession of a vapid love life and crushing personal debt, desirous of a diplomatic career in some third world country where she could wear scarlet and azure, Erin was pretty in a bony, white-girl way (knobby knees, lovely teeth). She wore business suits and her résumé could have said—but didn't—that her career objective was *world peace.* Whirled Peas. Instead, it read: *to obtain a policy position in humanitarian relief.* Though she wasn't entirely sure what this meant, it could be tweaked to suit any position.

Her boss explained her job like this: "You orchestrate visits to CIP by foreign dignitaries and domestic policymakers. In many ways, it's all about you. You're the stage manager, the press officer, the coach. At the end of the day, you're the one who knows how to run the world." These visits were for CIP members only—a group of mostly curmudgeonly old men who were CEOs and retired government officials. The political bigwigs—no doubt global affairs superstars and international infrastructure celebrities—arrived at the Upper Eastside think-tank with as much pomp and circumstance as the British Royal Family. The bigwigs gave a little sermon on the global landscape. The CIP members asked highfalutin questions, and dinner followed. Membership dues and donations kept the think-tank machinery well-oiled.

During the Clinton Administration, Newt Gingrich saw Erin getting yelled at during dinner. Erin and her ilk—ten other girls with similar bone structure—ran around a mahogany dining room under a crystal chandelier and asked questions like *Would You Like*

More Coffee? and *Did You Need Another Chair?* The girls—they were all girls—had miscounted meals or chairs. Erin's boss, a woman with drive and ambition plus experience in television news and an Ivy League education, had yelled, "Surely, you did your homework! Surely, you counted how many people want braised beef and how many want roasted chicken! Didn't you? *Didn't you?*"

With Newt behind her, Erin held a china plate in her hands. Steamed vegetables and roasted chicken emitted the scent of parsley, sage, rosemary, and thyme. Who needed poultry? Who wanted beef? Was this famine relief? Didn't she graduate in something related to famine relief?

Didn't she? Didn't she?

The guests had continued speaking politely to one another. Say what you will about Newt, he had the decency not to stare. When she resumed the feeding of George Soros, Richard Holbrook, and Thomas Pickering, she was acutely aware of the sound of her Nine West heels clicking on polished parquet floors. It wasn't a bad job, really. She ate free food at a Christmas cocktail party for George Stephanopoulos, stuffing her face on mini-fried things till she puked in a CIP toilet. She got her picture taken with Henry Kissinger and Ted Turner. Madeline Albright asked her for a pen once, and Tom Brokaw requested that she give a note to his assistant. But when she saw Newt Gingrich graciously overlooking the admonishment, she felt the full force of political disillusionment. This wasn't saving the world. This wasn't even trying.

She was in her early twenties, and she asked aloud: *How does one save the world?*

The Discourse

For three years, Erin did CIP. She took the Foreign Service Exam once on Columbia's campus—envisioning herself at a foreign embassy in which she'd wear black velvet and spend the evening talking to a French prince. By the end of the night, filled with shrimp and dizzy from pink champagne, she would have eliminated world hunger and human rights abuses in Africa. They would've talked about forming their own peacekeeping force to send to the Balkans. They would've danced together to Chaka Khan and then ended all civil unrest. For sure, she'd be wearing black velvet.

But she didn't make the cut.

Her thinking changed even as she packed her daily fruit salad. Saving the world wasn't happening. Even a couple food drops to ease global pain weren't on her horizon. With her job at CIP, reducing world suffering had given way to rhetoric, hot puffs of air served with hot cheese puffs. She spent her time arranging chairs and pouring coffee for politicians who were interested in maintaining their own positions. Political platitudes resembled propaganda; idealism morphed into cynicism.

"I'm cynical," she admitted to Steph—now Steph*anie*—as they sat on the veranda of an Upper Eastside bistro. "I need to go to Africa."

"What's in Africa?" Stephanie, now a lawyer, said while adjusting her lapels.

"People who need help." Erin pulled at her French dip. "I want to *do* something."

"By fostering a discourse, you are doing something."

"But I'm not. It's not a real discourse. It's just talk." Erin popped an olive into her mouth. "You learned that word *discourse* in law school, didn't you?"

"How do you know it's just talk?" Stephanie picked at her horseradish steak baguette.

"Sometimes I get scared, Steph. Sometimes, I wonder if I just got into this for the rock concerts. Did I just get into it for the rock concerts? Did you join Amnesty International too?"

And so Erin launched her own letter-writing campaign on CIP stationery, no doubt illegal, asking people for money to fund her volunteer work in Africa.

Realpolitik

In the autumn of 1996, Erin sat at her CIP desk. The phone rang. CIP member George Levitt said, "Ms. Yarborough, I received your letter. How much money do you make?"

Brazen.

She spat out: "Twenty-six thousand."

A pause. A dangerous pause in which Erin assumed a role: poor girl in the Big Apple, bright eyes, big hopes. She became beggar, hustler. A Real Politician.

"May I take you for lunch?" Levitt asked.

Erin found herself at Shun Lee Palace, one of the nicest Chinese restaurants in Midtown Manhattan. While taking off her Land's End winter coat, the hostess announced, "He's waiting for you." She felt like a wench off the street, taken in out of the cold for one last hot meal. She decided to milk it.

George Levitt looked like Marlon Brando in *The Godfather*. He sat in the back of Shun Lee, facing out, drinking something clear, scribbling indecipherably in a little notebook. She approached cautiously in her old dress and grocery store nylons. *L'eggs.*

He seemed cantankerous, probably in his late fifties, most likely a cigar-smoker, and he had terrifically gray hair. Plus, a facial tick: she couldn't tell whether he was smiling or twitching. As lunch progressed, she noticed that the tick seemed to coincide with things she said that *might* be construed as funny—but she was only slightly funny, so it was tough to say.

He ordered Slippery Chicken; Erin had Beijing Crepes. This wasn't a Chinese meal in which they passed around the pork-fried rice and chicken Chow Mein.

"I can't fund you, but I thought I'd buy you lunch." He smiled or twitched.

How Pygmalion, Erin thought. "Well, thank you."

"I'm an American nationalist," George Levitt announced. He gave a short survey of his foreign policy. "I'm a strong proponent of

Realpolitik," he explained. "Morality should not come into play when discussing politics." At the end of the day, nations should decide issues according to security concerns. Survival is the name of the game—not that right or wrong stuff.

He longed, Erin thought, for the return of the Cold War. It was so much fun back then. James Bond. East-West. Khrushchev. *We will bury you.* The Iron Curtain.

Should she tell him about all the Communists she knew?

Should she tell him how Red Scare was no scare at all?

"Wow," Erin kept saying, looking at him over green tea.

"I admire your entrepreneurial spirit. And there's the health concern that AIDS could potentially pose for the U.S." Then he asked, "If a businessman is flying in and out of Bangkok, not engaging in the sex industry, can he get AIDS? From the restaurants?"

"No." Erin tried to keep cool. "It's not airborne."

He pushed away the empty dish of Slippery Chicken. "One has to draw a distinction between foreign policy practices and personal morality. I'll make a few phone calls." He paid the bill. "See if there's anything I can do."

They arranged to meet again. Erin wanted to interview him. She liked the process: the talking, the testimony, the commitment of pen to paper. A slave to discourse, rhetoric.

Two weeks later, she pulled out her trusty tape recorder in the offices of Levitt Incorporated. She had no clue what he did for a living.

"I'd rather not discuss American nationalism on the record," he said, eyeing her recorder. "I'd rather not serve as a representative of it." He paused, twitching, frowning. "I'm not sure I'd like for my ideas to be publicly known."

"Why?" Why would he hide his beliefs if he believed them? Was this the real nature of a political being? "Off the record, then?"

Levitt twitched and surprised her. "Why do you want to hear the thoughts of an old man?"

Then, she surprised herself. "You're a rich old man with political clout."

He leaned forward. "Let me hear your questions."

She read them aloud: What should motivate U.S. foreign policy? When is intervention justified? Why do nations have the right to seek their security interests? Should we define ourselves in another way besides "American"?

He grimaced. "It would take seven hours for me to answer those." He scowled. "I'll give you the money. Go, find yourself. That's what you want, isn't it?"

"I'll take your money," she said.

Game Theory

After Africa, the discourse.

A class called International Civil Society was hers, and—amazingly—it was going to take her to Cuba in the spring of 2004. She also taught, depending on the year and semester, the Political Animal, Domestic Agenda, Political Idealism, Political Theory, the Discourse, Realpolitik, and Game Theory.

Enter Mohamed, a Somalian student in Game Theory. He had been in the States since 1998, and, before that, Kenya since 1991. His English was good, and he had already completed a degree in mathematics. He worked for a relief program that settled political exiles from war-torn countries. He was transferring to Yale in the fall.

She was his advisor. "These courses," he said, "belong at a university, not a community college."

"I don't have a Ph.D." Erin stacked books, lifted a paperweight, didn't do any comparison whatsoever between herself and Mary Hajj, that other woman behind a desk with political interests. At thirty-four, Erin was a low-level academic with an uneasy, too-cynical approach to her work. Students loved her classes. They usually decided to major in something else, often thanking her for her help in making that decision.

"So what should I take?" Mohamed was a little cocky, she thought.

Erin found the sheet of course descriptions and handed it to him, to this boy-man—Muslim, Somalian, Immigrant, Exile, Refugee, Noble Sufferer. He read:

POL 164, The Political Animal: What is the nature of politics? What does it mean to be political? Is it part of human nature? This course, part political science and part philosophy, examines foundational questions and reads from both early and contemporary texts (from Plato's *Republic* to *The New York Times*). No prerequisites required.

POL 165, Domestic Agenda: How do nation-states navigate the domestic landscape within the global environment? This course looks at domestic policy in light of internationalism. One particular issue is how a global phenomenon is rendered or handled on the domestic front. What accounts for the different "political faces" that show up on the world stage? No perquisites required.

POL 166, Political Idealism: Political idealism and liberalism are among the schools of thought that dominate International Relations. Topics for discussion in this survey course include Wilsonianism, American Exceptionalism, Regime Theory, Neo-liberalism, International Organization, Interventionism, and Sovereignty. No prerequisites required.

POL 167, Political Theory: This foundational course includes historical attention to tyranny, monarchy, aristocracy, and democracy—as well as conceptual and contextual analysis of ideas surrounding justice and liberty. No prerequisites required.

POL 168, The Discourse: A course that looks at Political Science as an academic discipline within the Social Sciences, posing the provocative question *For what purpose?* Recommended for majors and those considering a Political Science major. No prerequisites required.

POL 169, Realpolitik: Focusing on the political realist school of thought, this course examines a variety of ideas such as Balance of Power, the Arms Race and the Cold War, spheres of influence, and superpowers. From Machiavelli to Kissinger, the role of morality in politics will be questioned. No prerequisites required.

POL 170, Game Theory: Can mathematics be used to explain political behavior? This course looks at Game Theory and its applicability to politics. No prerequisites required.

POL 200, International Civil Society: There are three parts to this course. First, we look at nation-states. How do nation-states work together? Second, we look at universal values. Are there universal values or norms that govern behavior? Finally, we look at collective international action, which will culminate in a ten-day trip to Cuba. No prerequisites, though permission of the department head is required.

When he finished, he looked at her as if she were slightly mad. He didn't say anything.

Erin found herself squirming. "They're rigorous, scholarly endeavors, I can assure you, Mohamed." Why was she speaking like this to a student? Why was she defending her personal renditions of fascinating courses? These were hers. She was a trusted, responsible, experienced, published academic who attended conferences. Her teaching evaluations were impressive. She rarely ditched office hours.

And why did she always feel like she didn't belong in this arena, like she was a pretender?

Okay, so she was a pretender. She'd never truly been interested in the mechanisms of political science. She'd never really been all that impressed by the cogs turning, the processes analyzed, the chessboard of political machinations.

And Mohamed seemed to pick up on it.

"Why do you do what you do?" she asked, eyeing him intently. "Why are you getting another degree? Why do you work with refugees?" She poured herself more coffee from the stained Mr. Coffee machine. "Do you think another degree will help you help them?"

He wasn't like the other refugees he knew; he hadn't been wandering across a wasteland, starving and poor. "A degree will help."

"With what?"

"I was born in Somalia," he began, "and we were rich. My father was a government official. We had a big house in Mogadishu, with a big gate in front, and fancy cars parked outside. We could wake up, and our parents would tell us we were going to France or England. We had a driver and maids."

"Sounds good," Erin smiled.

But his face changed. "In the middle of the night sometime in 1991, there was a knock."

"What happened?" Erin leaned forward to swing shut her office door.

Now, he was sullen, a refugee after all. "We were all home. I was a kid—thirteen years old. I had three sisters. I didn't know what was going on in Somalia. I didn't even really know what my father did. He was just a government official." He shook his head, smiling. "My mother told my father not to answer."

"But he did—" Erin tried to recall her life in 1991. She was in college, studying the Cold War, which was over. The Berlin Wall had crumbled. The Soviet Union was no more.

"I don't know if he answered, or if they knocked the door down—"

"Who?" she asked. She drank her bitter, cold coffee.

"About six or seven men with guns." He pointed an imaginary gun at her, and then raised its imaginary barrel to the ceiling. "It happened right in front of me." He turned from Erin, maybe with tears forming.

"Will you tell me?" she asked, reaching for his hand, sensing revelation.

Mohamed stared at the hand on top of his. "I will tell you." He shook his head. "I don't know how long it lasted, but they made my mother and me watch. First, they beat my father. They bloodied him, knocked him down, broke bones so he couldn't move, and held a gun on him." Again, he held an imaginary gun; this time he held it in both hands. "Then, they raped my eldest sister—all of them. After that, they killed my father—shooting him in the head."

Erin raised a hand to her mouth.

"They left at daybreak."

"And your eldest sister?"

"She died an hour after they left." He lowered his chin to his chest.

"I'm sorry, Mohamed."

"And then we fled. Right away." His voice changed. The sorrow gave way to vigilance. "And we separated. My mother sent my sixteen-year-old sister away, on her own. My mom was afraid they would rape and kill her, too. She made her go. She said she'd be better off without us. And then my mother, my little sister, and I fled to Kenya. The three of us are here in the States now."

"Your other sister?" Erin raised a hand to her forehead. "What happened to her?"

"She's in South Africa. She made it there. We haven't seen her since."

"I don't know what to do with this."

"No one does," he said. "So now I want to help people."

International Civil Society, Part I: Nation-States

So she went to Cuba in the spring of 2004 with a group of professors and select students on an educational visa. She barely even thought about Castro. Once, Fidel with his angry beard would have been framed in her mind's eye in a portrait gallery of world despots.

On the day of their arrival from Miami via the tiniest plane in the world, there was a huge anti-American demonstration all along Havana's Malecón—the sidewalk that lined the ocean across from the seaside buildings (which were pastel-colored, decrepit, and looked bombed-out, like one might expect to see in war-ravaged cities in Lebanon or the Former Yugoslavia). In their state-owned tour bus with their state-sponsored tour guide, a very attractive Cuban named Oliver, they made their way to their hotel in Havana. Protesting people—*peaceful* and *cheery* protesting people—filled the streets, moving in throngs, their destination unclear. Erin and her group were a little alarmed when they saw posters portraying President Bush with a Hitler mustache, declaring him a Fascist.

"Don't worry. We're safe," Oliver said. "They were told to take the day off to march. They'd be fired if they didn't show. They're against America, not Americans."

Old political pangs stirred, but now they were tempered. Is this how it happened? Is this how national identity formed? Quite suddenly, and a little without precedent, Erin felt decidedly *American*.

Since when did she identify herself as an American?

Was that a sign of increasing conservatism?

Driving through Havana, which would surely be condemned in its entirety if it were a city in the United States, comparing the layers and layers of human life to Mexico City and the destruction to parts of Iraq, Erin felt a mixture of conflicting loyalties and truths.

Surely, *nationalism* was destructive, an excuse for violence and hatred.

Surely, Castro must die. Was it wrong to hope?

Surely, she was happy to be American. It had its advantages. She wouldn't want to live anywhere else. She'd been around the world.

Would she fight for her country?

Would she fight for a nation-state? On behalf of a government? Would she?

How does one fight?

Weapons of mass destruction?

Political revolution?

These were the things she thought about as they drove through an anti-American protest in Communist Cuba, arriving at the Hotel Telégrafo, an upscale—by Cuban standards—hotel in Havana.

International Civil Society, Part II: Universal Values

Cuba worked on her like an epic movie. Communism was monolithic, inescapable, sweeping. Castro's face was everywhere, Stalinesque, militaristic, a father no one wanted.

Oliver gave them a walking tour. Wandering along the chipped streets of Old Havana, lovely in its ruin, Erin peeked into romantic courtyards, seeing blue peacocks wandering by classical guitarists. She walked under wrought-iron balconies with green vines dripping down cracked brick walls. She observed old women dressed in black shawls with lace at their wrists and collars, some in latticed veils. Large piazzas with lyrical Spanish names at the end of cobbled mazes opened before neoclassical cathedrals and cafés serving espresso and dark roast coffee.

Standing in the shadow of a towering image of Castro in a public square, Erin felt more thoughtful about her life in politics than she ever had before. The Cubans, undoubtedly oppressed, were vital and warm. And she was from the land of the free, the home of the brave. She said she wanted to change the world. Did she really? What had politics meant to her? Why did she do what she did? Did she want to help people? Was she like Mohamed?

Erin felt a tug at her sleeve. She jerked her head to find a young man, desperate-looking, with feral eyes in a tank top with yellow sweat stains.

"Miss," he said. "Will you buy milk for my child?" He pulled at her, trying to lead her somewhere.

"I'm sorry," she said, as she had been trained to say in the pre-trip orientation. "I can't help you." She thought about it: *Why couldn't she help him again?*

"No money, miss." He still pulled her. "You come and buy milk with *my* money."

Erin didn't understand. Oliver walked over. "What's going on?" he asked in English.

Oliver and the man rapidly exchanged words in Spanish. Oliver had his hands on his hips. The man waved his hands around. On the corner of the plaza, a uniformed guy watched them. He held what was possibly a gun and looked like a soldier or cop.

Then Oliver pulled her aside and explained. "Cubans are only allowed to spend a certain amount. He wants to give you his own money to buy more milk at the store."

"Should I do it?" Erin asked.

"It's probably a scam." Oliver put his hands in the pockets of his tour guide blue slacks.

"It's milk for his *child*," Erin said, raising her hand to shade her eyes from the sun.

"It's a scam." Oliver's voice was flat, matter-of-fact.

Erin and Oliver stared at each other. He was Cuban, too. He spoke English, French, German, and Spanish. At twenty-six, he worked with foreigners every day. He had a cell phone. His clothes were clean. He was, simply due to his washed slacks, a member of the aristocracy, the elite, the bourgeoisie. Someone had told her he lived in a small house with his young girlfriend near the airport, miles outside of Havana. Everyday, he had to be at the Hotel Telégrafo at eight a.m. to pick up tourists. He stayed with them till late in the evening, serving as their ears and mouths in a country they found backwards and charming, a country that made them dance to Latin music, that made them feel romantic and poetic. By the time Oliver headed home for the night, public transportation had stopped, but he would somehow make it back to his house near the airport—only to return to the Hotel Telégrafo a few hours later, wearing his pressed white shirt and navy blue slacks. He was ready to show peacocks to tourists.

"We'll wait for you," he said to Erin.

"Thank you," she said, turning to the man who wanted milk for his child.

She followed him, as he raced through the streets of Old Havana. Erin had to run to keep up. They arrived. At the store, customers stood at the counter and ordered their groceries. The feral-eyed man rattled off an entire list of items.

"Just milk." Erin looked at the piles of food.

"Just these, okay?" he pleaded.

"Do you have the money?" Erin asked, putting her hands on her hips.

"Just these, for my child." His eyes were wide and moist. "Please."

Erin slapped down the money. Before it was fully out of her hands, the man was gone.

She made her way back to the plaza. The man with the gun was still there. When she told Oliver what happened, he said, "I hope he uses the food, and didn't run to the back door to return it for the money."

After the morning in Old Havana, an Ernest Hemingway afternoon followed. They had daiquiris in his drinking haunt, El Floridita. They lunched on the Hotel Ambos Mundos terrace. Hemingway had lived in the hotel, writing *For Whom the Bell Tolls*. They spent the afternoon at Finca la Vigía, his home outside of the city. Hemingway, like Castro, was larger than life.

In the evening, Erin went for Cuban food at a Chinese restaurant in Havana's Chinatown with a Spanish and Latin American Politics professor from Texas. A beef dish was served inside a pineapple half. The professor, a Mexican-American woman, told Erin how she had been stopped outside of their hotel elevator on the first night. "The hotel manager said, 'No Cubans allowed upstairs.' I had to show them my passport before they let me up."

Turns out, they thought she was a whore.

"I guess that's why Oliver always has to go home every night—he's not allowed upstairs." Erin cut into her pineapple. Bourgeoisie, perhaps. But still Cuban.

At every turn, Cuba begged a political question. How should the nation be governed? By whom? When the academics were given a tour of a hospital that looked like a mad scientist's lab under construction, someone undoubtedly would ask about healthcare under Communism. When the academics bought art on the Prado and planned to take it home rolled up illegally in their suitcases, someone undoubtedly spoke in conspiratorial whispers with the artists about freedom of expression and how to get to Miami. When the academics went to the museum dedicated to the Communist Revolution and Castro looked like a saint, someone undoubtedly pointed out exactly how history had been re-written, eliminating pertinent information having to do with murders and disappearances. When the academics went to the art museum, someone undoubtedly pointed out how the Fine Arts had obviously been stymied by Cuba's fate—much like art under Stalin. Everywhere they went, political issues were raised.

They visited Castro hot spots, seeing the monster-sized images of Che Guevara and Fidel on the Plaza de la Revolucíon; they pointed out Raúl Castro's office building and whispered about his sanity. They walked down a colorful and teeming alleyway devoted to Santeria, the religion of many Afro-Cubans—chicken-neck decor, voodoo dolls, drumbeats, throbbing bodies, rampant erotica. One professor puked. They ate ice cream at Coppelia, waiting in the dollar line which took only minutes while the Cubans waited in the peso line that wound around the block and took hours. They went on side-trips to Trinidad and Cienfuegos and smoked Cuban cigars. Erin took pictures and felt like an American spy.

On the last day, Oliver took them for lunch at a restaurant in the neighborhood where the embassies had been prior to Castro. By now, he was chatty, chummy, dismissing fears that the tour bus was bugged. The Americans were giving him lewd English phrases to memorize and, in exchange, he taught them how to cuss in Spanish.

While they drove through the neighborhood of old, unmaintained mansions—a rotting Beverly Hills—someone asked, "Is this where all the rich people live?"

Oliver was standing up in the bus, looking out the windows. "Not anymore."

"Where do they live now?"

Oliver said, "In Miami."

International Civil Society, Part III: Collective International Action

Sitting in the Hotel Telégrafo lobby on the final night, Erin looked through the postcards and pamphlets she had collected. She had writers' union leaflets, notes about the health care system, a postcard from a Martin Luther King, Jr., Center.

Two professors joined her. One taught a class called World Politics and Religion; the other taught International Organization. They launched a professorial conversation on how they would speak about Cuba in their classes. How would it fit into the discourse? "Do you think Cuba has a future?" she found herself saying. "What do you think will happen after Castro dies?"

Certainly one of them would have an answer. Neither spoke.

"That's the tough part," World Politics and Religion finally answered. "Where do you send the money? What do you do with it? Do you support these fledgling attempts at unions and organizations, even though they're heavily under Castro's hand? Do you support exile groups in Miami? Do you work for the overthrow of the government?"

"Careful," International Organization warned. "You never know who's listening."

"Should we even be here?" Erin asked. "Maybe we should've stayed home."

International Organization looked piqued. "We have to prepare for life after Castro. We need to let the Cubans know they belong to the world. We need to integrate them into global civilization. We should be here, participating in their lives as much as possible."

Erin held up two fingers in a peace sign. Then, without any irony, she said, "Castro must die." Instinctively, all three of them peered about suspiciously. She shook her head. "I'm just talking. I don't know." She stood up, ready to return to her room. There, she could watch a little CNN before sleeping. It was available in the hotel, but not anywhere else. She knew Cubans watched television, though; when she looked out her window, a thousand blue screens lit up, glowing inside the dilapidated buildings—reminding her, in a strange way, of the view from the top of the Empire State Building from so long ago. She turned to the political science professors. "I've always wanted to save the world, truth be told."

When people would ask her later, she'd talk about fresh lobster on the beach, guitar music filling inky El Greco nights, imposing architecture that reached into the sky, fresh mango and papaya and guava for breakfast, beautiful brown people in every direction, a dying tropical paradise exhaling its last breath.

Getting on the plane, having given Oliver one hundred American dollars, she knew Cuba would die. Castro's death knell rang and rang. That was for whom the bell tolled.

As she put on her seat belt, Erin remembered seeing Venice as a summery sophomore. It had been sinking even then, pulsating in baroque rhythms, slipping into canals, a green algae frill around its edges. A different kind of death toll. Parts of the world dying all the time.

Erin remembered, just in her lifetime, how maps had mutated. The Soviet Union, Yugoslavia, East and West Germany, Czechoslovakia: no more. What could be said of the Middle East?

Erin remembered Tiananmen Square, Lech Walesa, Vaclav Havel, Gorbachev, Mandela, even Bob Geldof: her political life unfolding.

Erin remembered passionate outbursts about liberals and conservatives, global and grassroots causes, dissidents and playwrights. Her fires had been quelled: sometimes by disappointment, sometimes by age, sometimes by disillusionment. Her political history was passé.

On the small plane going back to Miami, Erin felt as if she were carrying a weight. She couldn't stow it under her seat.

When the wheels lowered in the States, she thought of boat people—the Cubans who attempted to make it to Florida by raft or boat. Many died. Many drowned. Many got caught and were sent back to their country.

The wheels hit the ground, and it seemed as if the belly of the plane scratched the runway. Realizing she had survived, Erin thought of *Sigmund and the Sea Monsters*, Red and Mary Hajj, Mohamed and Mogadishu, Castro and Cuba.

Who could really rescue the boat people?

Who could really do it?

This is a test. This is *only* a test.

That's what they said, anyway.

Who would really save the world?

Could it be saved at all?

When she found herself at home in the United States, preparing again for another semester of classes, the books and scholarly journals spread upon her desk, that question—decidedly not political—lingered on the tip of her tongue, the roof of her mouth. *Could it be saved at all?*

Nipples Beads
Mealie Pap

nipples beads mealie pap

The television is on and there are reports of war. Zaire will be the Congo by the time I leave Johannesburg. Everyone sits around, drinking coffee, reading books, playing cards, rolling joints, writing memoirs. Everyone in hostels is always writing. The sizzle of static is on the telly and I can hear the drivel of backpackers telling their stories.

My legs—exposed, white—are folded beneath me. I sit on torn-up couch cushions with stuffing creeping out of thick, scar-sized rips along worn cloth surfaces. Underneath my body, I feel lumps—possibly metal springs. I look up from my journal to my thighs, and I see the varicose veins, slight, delicate like fragile cracks in Grecian urns.

I close my journal, having written only one line across the top of a blank page: *This will be the only story for you.*

I pull out a postcard. To whom will I send this?

Perhaps Nick. A postcard for a stranger who gently ripped the past from my bones on starry Mpumalanga nights. Gently, gently. Love beads and thumb rings, fingers in pap. The taste of chocolate on the roof of his mouth. The smell of wine and wet grass.

Oh, but it was not so gently.

If I write, will the words pile up like the stories of backpackers, like body parts rendered lifeless by minefields in African soil?

The TV drowns out my musing: war rages. A war of flesh and blood. I stand, postcard and journal in hand. I leave the room, knowing I am all flesh; I am all blood.

It was not so gently.

sarong Soweto sweet potato
Af-Ree-Kah.

Say it with zeal.

Africa's first draw is its poetry.

Imagine frangipani creeping over red-brown mud. Beasts like giraffes and lions walk through thick jungle. Giraffes eat leaves from vine-heavy trees. Lions barely make the foliage crinkle under big cat paws. Elephants are heavy-footed. The earth is deep, and the thunder of elephant feet is not like the drums of distant tribes, but more like a summer storm. Rumbling, sweet, welcomed. These creatures join others creatures under a sky of jewels.

And that's just the animals. There are people, too. Women. They're enfolded in brilliant, insurgent fabrics. No muted earth tones, no camouflage. If unraveled, they would spin like tops in magenta. They carry things—babies, fruit, wood. They're on the go, rushing past skinny goats, calling out words to happy children.

Africa is *only* poetic. Its people and panoramas are poetic, even its poverty and politics are poetic. It's undeniable. Africa is one great big Shakespearean tragedy. Every book about every agonizing struggle features beautiful revolutionaries with scars etched onto faces. Every protest is led by a man who should be king but has been in prison or stuck in Soweto instead. The stories, the dramas—they are not about criminals. They are about uncrowned princes.

I flee to Africa for the poetry.

South Africa. I don't choose Zimbabwe or Gabon, though those names are more poetic. I choose South Africa, a compromise. It's safe. I can dip my foot in the pool and still run under the cabana. I can shop and barter at markets, but all the grocery stores are well-stocked. I can buy the fabrics women elsewhere wear and hang them on my walls. Their clothes, my art. South Africa is my white world far away from the white world. But never forget this: South Africa is my compromise and I choose it because I am a white woman.

rave shave torch bugs

Sandy sends me on safari. For one month, I wander Cape Town. She hates the sight of me walking down Adderley, coming at her with comments about whites and blacks in South Africa. All day, every day, I sit in cafés, eating salads and dissecting the details of my finale with Zachary. I put together premises, make conclusions. *You said I was your soul mate. Soul mates don't leave. You left. Therefore, I am not your soul mate. You said I was the love of your life. True love is meant to last. You left me. Am I not the love of your life? You have no love of your life? There's no such thing as a "love of your life"? You're a liar? Don't believe a word you say? Don't trust words?*

I've always been a believer in words.

"Here are malaria pills. Start them now." Sandy hands me a phone card with fifty rand on it. "Use this in an emergency." She throws her dirty backpack on the floor. "Pack this."

After five weeks in Cape Town, I fly to Durban to meet a group of backpackers who have signed up to go on a safari with an Afrikaner named Elmer.

bras braais fingers socks

I traced the tribal tattoo on the small of Zachary's back.

But he pulled away. He spoke of the other woman, a friend he'd once told me about. He said, "I'd love her even if she had no arms or legs."

Hmmm, I thought. *You must really love her.* "Is she the one who slept with her brother?" I asked instead.

I got out of our bed, pulling the sheet around me. I turned to him with rigidity. "Well, you better go then."

And the thing I'll never forget is this: *He did.*

moist wet hake curry

I sit around a tree-trunk table in the Coconut Bar of Shakaland in KwaZulu-Natal, where South Africa is green. It isn't really called the Coconut Bar, but it reminds me of *Gilligan's Island* and, if I had my drink of choice, I'd be drinking something milky and sweet from a coconut half. Rather, I sip beer and snack on Spanish peanuts, which have been generously laid out for us by a Zulu woman of indeterminate age.

Stop number one. Shakaland. The old movie set for *Shaka Zulu,* named after Shaka, who united the Zulu tribe. Zulu Disneyland, Zulu Old Tucson.

Ten people met in Durban, loaded their things into a minivan, and headed to KwaZulu-Natal in the eastern part of South Africa. We drove through the rolling green hills where sugarcane grows and the Zulu people work rich fields, walk muddy roads, and carry colorful bundles on their heads. The climate is subtropical; the landscape is thick and green.

Mostly, these people are English with a few German exceptions. There are only three males—Elmer (our Afrikaner leader), Jens (a German), and Nick (a Brit). We are a predominantly female, English-speaking group. We sketch, keep journals, talk about boys, and have secret lives in other countries. But, for now, we are preoccupied with *Shaka Zulu.*

"They used to show *Shaka Zulu* in school." It's the *New* South Africa and Elmer is a *new* Afrikaner. "Like your *Roots.*" He points his chin in my direction. I'm the sole American. I'm never the sole anything.

"Have a beer, Elmer." Nick , the Brit, scrapes a nearby chair on the ground, dragging it over.

Elmer sits.

"*Shaka Zulu*, huh?" Nick's voice is a song. "How was it growing up in a pariah state?"

Elmer runs fingers over a stubbly chin; he's no doubt used to tourist interrogation.

"We don't mean to insult you." An English girl sips her beer.

"When I was a little boy, the black woman who worked for my family slept under my bed." We lean forward over Spanish peanuts. "We were all defying the curfew." The Zulu woman brings him a beer.

"Yikes." Nick licks peanut salt from his lips.

Elmer stands. Our eyes follow him. He's our unifying force, our Shaka Zulu. "Let me make sure the dancing is still going on tonight."

"The dancing?" The German girl sinks into the arms of her German boyfriend. They wear scary, ripped-up concert T-shirts and black combat boots. They seem progressive. "Not dancing." She lets out a moan.

"There's always Zulu dancing." Elmer turns on his heels and leaves. "I'll be back."

We look bashfully at each other. It's only been three hours. We barely know one another. We simultaneously reach for peanuts like synchronized swimmers.

Before the Coconut Bar, we had our *Shaka Experience* which included a clip of the *Shaka Zulu* movie in the Gilligan Cineplex, where the matinee is always the same. "Did you notice that Shaka's mom wore black mascara?" I turn to one of the English girls.

"Pure cheese." Her name is Dylan. She's traipsing from the Cape to Cairo, which has always been a British dream, though she's no imperialist. Dylan's adventures are free-spirited, unruly, uncertain. She answers to no one, the ultimate free-thinker. "Does anyone else feel uncomfortable?"

Just then, the Zulu woman walks by our table and Nick pulls her over, kindly.

There are a lot of people on this safari. They merge and blend and become distinct only later. Now, they only have high-pitched voices or London accents.

"May I ask you a question?" Nick holds onto the arm of the Zulu woman.

We look at Nick, who doesn't blend. He doesn't blend because he's male and we're female and he's pretty and we're traveling, which means all kinds of things you don't tell your mother about.

I stare at him. He's one of those twenty-something backpackers with love beads tied around his ankle and stories to tell about the Mozambicans he met on the beach and the incredible experiences he had with the Xhosa in the Transkei. He uses words like *dodgy* and *lovely* and *cheers*. He wears thumb rings and a goatee and he has a tattoo of the sun on his upper arm. He's not a boy, but he reminds me of an era when boys prevailed. It's the goatee and the thongs with Velcro and the tattoo. He's so PC, so in touch with Mother Earth. He's graying a bit and the two of us are the oldest. He's twenty-nine and I'm twenty-eight. We're old! In the minivan, driving through the sugarcane, we discussed Umberto Eco, Thomas Pynchon, and Sartre. Comparing reading lists is like batting eyelashes. *Touch me here,* I could say, opening a volume and splaying it across my chest.

When he grabs the Zulu woman by the arm, a most delicate touch, she's warmed by his peace-loving smile. She looks like she's swept a thousand floors in her amalgam of Western clothes picked up from charities and wealthy white women cleaning out their attics. Nick looks into her eyes. "How do you feel about people like us?" He holds her arm. One person touching another. It's uncommon for a woman like her to be touched by a man like him.

"Oh, we like you. We like white people."

When she leaves, we are silent. They are frightful, lovely words. Nick smiles in his love-Mother-Earth way. Dylan looks at me, free to hit the road. The others eat peanuts.

The significance of words.

moss malaria butterscotch Ndbele

"Isn't Charo on this boat?" Dylan leans back from her position in the food line to call out to me. I'm five people behind her, scooping spinach into my plate.

Dinner is served in the same fashion as the *Love Boat* buffet. The rest of the world knows us by our prime-time TV. Mealie, cabbage, and curry replace fruit and caviar.

After dinner, a group of young Zulu men, sleek and hard-bodied, scantily clothed and armed with spears, charge joyously into the dining room (shocking the hell out of Captain Stubing) and beckon the delighted tourists to a big round hut for a night of dancing. We skip after the Zulu men like it's the Disneyland Electric Parade.

"This is killing me." Dylan pops an evening malaria pill.

We take our seats on wooden bleachers in the Zulu hut. The dancing begins. It's frenzied, hypnotic, rhythmic. The men dance first and the women dance in response, a debate. Bodies convulse, glowing from sweat.

Some elderly French cower when the Zulu men stomp their feet and rush over wielding spears, and I'm ashamed. The ten of us try not to recoil when the Zulus charge. We try to appear as if we're at ease with the delirium. *This is primitive. This is primal. This is wild. But, hey, I'm okay with relentless, irrational chaos. I'm okay.*

When the dancing is over, I walk to our hut with Nick. He jumps around, hyper like a teenage boy.

"I spent the night with Xhosa witch doctors in the Transkei in April." He walks backwards in front of me. "They did trance-dancing. Spontaneously. This was a bit contrived."

"What do they think when they're dancing?" I stare at the gray at his temples.

"Nothing. It isn't a *thinking* thing." He looks at his feet as he speaks, looking at his Velcro thongs. He's been to the beach, I bet. Camping on the beach. I imagine a scenario in which he sits by a fire on the coast of the Indian Ocean eating crayfish and drinking wine with other kids. He's still the oldest. "It's an act apart from the mind."

"How can that be? How can they think *nothing*?"

"It's intoxicating—the movements, the rhythm. Plus, they're smoking a lot of dope."

I'm really staring at him now. *Male.* Wow.

"It's like Transcendental Meditation." He stops walking, and we stand together under the moonlight. "But better—because you're dancing."

I grin, and we walk together again. We get to our hut. We laugh about Shakaland, about sleeping in grass huts on bunk beds, about smelling shit, about watching out for chickens.

I go to bed with my own relentless chaos. Perhaps Zachary left me for my lack of spontaneity, my fidelity to rationality, my commitment to order. Perhaps Zachary missed the delirium, the dancing. Perhaps he wearied of my allegiance to rules—my wordplay not playful enough. Perhaps Dylan, a free-thinker, free to think anything, submitting to nothing—perhaps her freedom and that dancing speak only of my deficiencies.

What if I let go?

What would happen if I really let go?

Khayelitsha Mapumalanga Xhosa click

I wake to roosters crowing.

Outside, they peck the ground, jerking their bird bodies here and there. I'm under an itchy, mothy blanket. When I reach for my toiletries, my flashlight falls noisily to the floor. No one stirs. Quietly, I sneak over to the Shaka showers. By six a.m., I'm in the Coconut Bar.

Dylan joins me, diary in hand.

"Will you read it later?" I ask. It's a quiet morning in Africa and we whisper. I'm fascinated by her wanderlust coupled with the writing down of her adventures in a permanent record. Freedom and commitment.

"Doubt it." She shrugs.

"Why do you bother if no one's gonna read it?"

Dylan has her legs crossed and she bounces her ankle up and down. She's very blasé. "I don't know. To know where I've been, I guess."

After a while, she leaves. Nick arrives.

shoulder blades sweatpants sunrise sunset

He sits beside me with a disarming gaze. We have no pasts, only presents. Booklists are the only eyes to our souls and we are too well-read for lists to be enlightening.

"I've heard you teach prep school," I say. "For what are you preparing them?"

Nick raises his eyebrows. "You're getting your doctorate in English lit? Why aren't you home teaching classes, reading books?"

"Unpaid leave of absence," I say.

"Me, too." He winks. "Unexplained termination."

I stir my coffee and look at him. Again, I see he's male. He points to the sky, points to the sun rising. It's orange and round; it creeps gently over lush green mountains. It feels like we're in central Africa, Rwanda or Burundi. Birds call out in jarring shrieks. "It's the perfect moment." His index finger seems to touch the edge of the sun. "Hold your breath until it passes." He holds his breath, and I hold mine, too. Then, he says, "What's your area of expertise?"

"In what?" I ask.

"In English." Nick smiles flirtatiously.

"Oh," I say. "South African and American lit. I *was* working on my dissertation. Apocalyptic literature of South Africa and America." I watch for a reaction. "How each literature conceptualizes *the end*."

"Very ... eschatological." He nods, looking serious. "I studied postcolonial theory once." It feels like we're in a bar pointing out astrological signs, but not the Coconut Bar.

"It's a very romantic subject—the whole aftermath of imperialism," I say.

"Yours isn't." He stretches his arms above his head, letting out a groan.

"South Africa was romantic when I started." I put on my sunglasses. "Working out the details after the revolution isn't so exciting."

"But the apocalypse is never romantic." He tightens the laces on his hiking boots. "It's rarely beautiful. Everything is reduced to the mechanical or the technological. Always doomsday. Our visions of the future are inevitably devoid of beauty."

"I wouldn't spend my days reading about it if I didn't expect it to be beautiful." I take on an aura of dramatic perplexity. "*Of course*, I expect beauty."

"Then you are the lone romantic apocalyptic literature fanatic." His eyes are bright, brash, seductive. "Do you want breakfast? A Danish?" He pauses. "You could use some eggs over-easy. I detect a tight-ass."

Hmm. "Sure." I stand up. "I could go for a Danish."

"Orwell was no romantic." Nick begins walking, muttering to himself. "Vonnegut? H.G. Wells? What kind of romantic are you?"

I point to the sun, feeling poetic though I am no poet, feeling giddy though I am no silly girl, feeling young though I am usually old. "Look at that." I point to the yellow ball in the sky.

"Lovely." He touches my arm gently.

wildebeest warthog Zulu shithead

"Send *this* to your grandma." Nick gives me a postcard. On it, a group of Zulus are lined up, bare-breasted and wearing traditional attire. "Happy Zulu People," it says.

"I'm buying it." We're in a gift shop in the center of Hluhluwe-Umfolozi, a game park just north of Shakaland.

"There's time for capturing your thoughts later, professors. Dylan approaches us. "Lunch is being served outside the minivan."

We spend the day driving around Hluhluwe-Umfolozi, stopping by watering holes and watching zebra. We're never allowed to leave the vehicle: lions are out there, after all.

"He's *sooo cute*." I see every creature, and it's always my first response.

The Brits die laughing. "You really sound like an American." Americans, apparently, have a tendency to state the obvious.

"Those guys are adorable!" I watch a group of warthogs.

"When they run, their tails go straight up in the air." Elmer, like every South African, is gifted at maneuvering the vehicle in order to optimize wildlife-viewing.

"They're funky." Dylan leans over me, trying to see better. The warthogs trot alongside the road. Snouts to the ground, babies in tow. "The bohemians of the wild."

"*Aawwhh.*" I let out an American sigh as Nick crawls through the window and on top of the van. The others snap pictures and press against glass for better views.

"That's a great name for a rock band: The Bohemian Warthogs." Dylan elbows me.

"They're so *cute.*" It's a reflexive response. I can't help myself. Everyone laughs.

"You are such an American." When English Catherine speaks, I desire tea and scones.

"Now, what's the sexiest animal?" Dylan has the concerns of someone on the road. Sex. It's all about sex. Africa, animals. You name it: *sex.*

Elmer moves the vehicle forward, trailing after warthogs.

"The buffalo seems like a big stud." I grab one of the many safari guides. Everyone has a safari guide. After reading them, we know whether or not we're having fun. "Big, bullish. Excellent horns." The Brits crack up. In America, I'm never so well-received.

"And, Nick, what animal do you think is the sexiest?" Dylan raises her eyebrows. Nick is our standard bearer for the male species. The German is too quiet and Elmer already serves the same purpose for Afrikaners. Plus, he might be gay. We're not sure.

Nick thinks. "Definitely the impala." He nods his head decisively. The impala looks like Bambi. "That little tail …." He moans like he's either about to eat venison or make love to it. "The way she puts her ass in the air." He speaks seductively. "Her delicate ways. Those soft eyes. *That* is an animal."

"Impala me," I add.

Shrieks from the minivan.

We know Dylan's concerns, but what of mine?

Impale Me.

Wordplay. I'm interested in wordplay.

Do words mean a thing?

shag fuck Bourke's Luck

We spend the night on the border of South Africa and Swaziland. It's beautiful. Deserted. Green. Lush. This time, the sun sets in orange.

Lena, hair flowing, body speaking, says something in German to her boyfriend and walks to the edge of our lodge pool, seemingly self-contained. "Lena's a Botticelli." Catherine, who always has her sketch pad, puts down her pencil to watch. Lena stands perfectly still. After a minute, she jumps gracefully into the water. Catherine is almost breathless. "Bravo!"

Lena is so self-possessed, so confident. I've never been like that.

All the women watch in silence as Nick peels off his shirt and dives into the deep end. Then, we look at each other.

Dylan's eyes settle on a bicep. "Why do you have the tattoo of a sun on your arm?"

"Sign of the Aquarius."

"Are you a follower of astrology?"

"Just another possible reality. Sometimes, I'm into it."

I feel like I'm in college. I feel retro, like I'm with Zachary and he's about to soliloquize on relativity and the lack of a fixed truth. I feel a surge of blood pump through my veins because I'm both wholly attracted and wholly repulsed by those who soliloquize on such subjects.

"Ahh …." Ingrid closes her eyes. "An existentialist?" She is rosy-cheeked, wistful.

I'm back in the late eighties, the early nineties. Zachary's carrying around copies of *The Catcher in the Rye, The Stranger.* I'm a traumatized coed, wondering, wondering where he is.

"I don't know if I would go that far." Nick floats on his back. "There are alternative truths—everyone arrives at his or her own."

I wince internally. We are so *On The Road*, so serenely beatnik. I'm forever bewitched by the *I'm OK, You're OK* crowd.

"I would never assert there is one truth." Nick treads water.

Flower power, acid trips, friendship beads, thumb rings.

He pulls his upper body out of the water and balances on the edge of the pool. The water drips from his torso. The sun is about to disappear behind the mountains. I see the tattoo of the sun on his arm. Dusk approaches. "Jillian, look over there." He directs his gaze to the sunset. "You're about to see another perfect moment."

hair beard tremble shiver

At night, we play a card game called "Shithead." The object is not to be Shithead. We drink wine outside on wooden picnic benches with mosquito repellent covering our exposed body parts. We laugh aloud and argue about the aphrodisiac effects of chocolate.

I share a cabin with Meredith of South London. She's saucy and she smokes. She used the word *cunt* two times in the first three hours we were in the minivan, which threw me. In between our two beds, there's a lampstand made from an impala leg. It's a leg, a lampshade, and a bulb. Meredith and I giggle as we turn off the lights to sleep.

I'm happy. I haven't been happy in ages.

In the morning, we begin again our adventures, fantastical, escapist.

I sit between Nick and Ingrid in a Range Rover. Dylan sits with the Swazi game park ranger in front, the Germans are in back, and we're in the middle. Jens, a quiet man, is wearing a Sex Pistols T-shirt and Lena, the self-possessed Botticelli, is wearing one with the Sprockets from *Saturday Night Live* on it. We're in Swaziland, in the Mkhaya Game Reserve. We're waiting for the Range Rover to move. We want to see animals. All desires in life boil down to this.

Nick and Ingrid are debating whether or not truth is Absolute. I didn't start it.

"Look." Nick's annoyed. "There *are* no absolutes. Meaning is *relative*." Ingrid is chomping at the bit, which scares me. I'm afraid of combat. I look off to the side of the road. A goat nurses her kid.

Nick isn't done. "My experience determines what's real. My world rests on my interpretation and I can only know the world by what I have experienced." He doesn't seem too upset about it. He's a happy existentialist. I've never met one who's happy before. It disturbs me. Jolts me. Where's his misery? Why doesn't he threaten suicide? Metaphysical ambiguity usually bothers people.

"You're egocentric." Ingrid is matter-of-fact. "Surely you can't live as if you're the center of the universe?"

"That's all I have."

Philosophy, philosophy. We're all gonna die.

Our Swazi guide starts the car. The other half of our group is in another vehicle. The Germans say nothing, indifferent observers to our melodrama. They cuddle while we argue. Dylan twists her head back. "You stop now. Fuck the questions." Dylan just doesn't care.

Nick and Ingrid are almost panting. The Range Rover begins rolling. I whisper—I don't know why I whisper—to Nick, "I respect existentialists." Our legs touch. The proximity is tantalizing. "In fact, I slept with one for eight years."

He whispers, too. "I could argue about it all night long."

"Maybe, later, we will."

We never do. We drop it. We drop it because it only seems like fun. We take this—that I have slept with an existentialist and that he is one—as the thing that makes our proximity electric. Not the difference of opinion. Argument isn't really sexy.

The Range Rover drives through Swazi jungle. I've never seen anything like it. Hluhluwe-Umfolozi didn't do it. We fall in love. We fall in love with Africa, with each other, with animals, with the planet. We cannot help but love. We see elephant, giraffe, zebra, rhino, ostrich, hippo, buffalo, impala, and bohemian warthog. "The ostrich is the Toulouse-Lautrec of the bird kingdom," I say. "Those feather skirts, those skinny legs." We get out of the vehicle because our guide tells us we can. Slowly, quietly, we step over branches and weeds and grass to follow elephants. We make no noise except for crunching sounds with our feet. The elephants touch each other with their trunks. "Elephant foreplay." Nick looks through his binoculars. Our mouths open wide in unadulterated smiles. Their hulking elephant bodies are beautiful. The giraffes, in graceful swoops, whip long necks against each other. The rhinos frighten us, make us tremble, and it's an awesome fear, a fear without ugliness. We are fragile. We are delicate. We're no longer so certain we're the center of the universe.

Ingrid snaps photos. "This is what the fear of God must be like."

flick lick Sabie River

We share a tent.

We arrive at Mlilwane Animal Sanctuary in the middle of Swaziland. "Pick your tentmates wisely." Elmer hands out tent poles. "You'll be sleeping with him or her for the next ten days." We pick each other. I don't feel strange about it until I notice the other women looking at me. *I'm not a slut*, I want to say.

Elmer makes pasta and we eat inside the campground recreation room. We play Shithead again, but this time we call it "Impala." Whoever loses has to imitate an impala. The first one to lose is Jens. He refuses to imitate Bambi. Ingrid, pink from too much wine, gets down on her hands and knees, puts her behind up in the air and says in a proper English accent, "You do it like this, Jens."

We drink wine and play. The conversation gets increasingly lurid. Dylan, over her cards, when others are engaged in an ongoing chocolate, sex, and women debate, looks over at me. "Nick?"

"What?"

"Impala?"

"What?"

"Potentially?"

"Pardon me?"

The other girls catch the tail-end of the exchange. Catherine stares at us. "What? What are you guys talking about?"

"They're being catty girls." Nick puts down his cards. I bet he heard the whole thing.

"Are we?" Dylan acts insulted.

I stay up till two for fear of bedtime. Finally, I can't take it. "I have to go to sleep." I rise, shy like a bride, and Nick catches my eye.

"See you later." We exchange goofy smiles.

He gives me a head start. He leaves me alone in the tent for a good fifteen minutes. I rush to take off my jeans and put on sweatpants. I rush to get into my sleeping bag and zip it up. By the time I've casually arranged myself, I'm in a sweat.

He crawls in quietly and takes his shoes off by the light of the moon. When he zips up the mosquito net and tent door, it's pitch-black inside. I hear him get into his sleeping bag. We can't see each other. There's no source of light.

"Tell me the most extraordinary moments of your life." That's what he says.

"You go first." I push my socks off with my feet.

I listen to the sound of Nick's voice, think about Nick's presence. Here he is. Man. Male. Then there's me. What if we can do whatever we want within these tent walls, and there is no consequence, no lasting effect—only the phenomenon of skin on skin, the hiss and lick of rapture: sexual, sanguine, quickly over? What if it's *only* that?

"The preliminaries first, okay?" Nick's voice is like a PBS special.

"Okay," I say.

"My parents are Oxford-educated. My siblings and I were expected to do well in school and we lived up to expectation. Of course, I turned around and used my *hard*-earned degree to launch the *non*-lucrative career of world traveler. In between backpacking, though, there is *some* room for teaching."

"Where have you been?" I ask.

"On every continent, except Antarctica."

"Tell me about one place."

"In Thailand, I took this three-day trek on the back of an elephant." I feel like he's close to my body, my face. "Then, we left the elephants and took up canoes. I remember floating through caverns that were so low we had to lie down in the canoe and the top of the cave almost touched our faces." He pauses, thoughtful. "It was like floating on the edge of the world."

"Was that one of the most extraordinary moments of your life?" I put my cheek on the pillow so I'm facing him.

"No."

"Where were you before Thailand?"

"Baton Rouge, where I learned to do cocktail tricks."

"And where will you go from here?"

"I should settle down." Melancholy slips into his voice. "I would write, but every time I have a great idea, I read it within days in someone else's book." Futility. Next to uncertainty, it's killer.

"What would you write about?"

"I don't know. The Romantics, tribal differences among African groups, Asian philosophy, Rodin, how to make a lemon martini. Have you ever had a lemon martini?"

"No."

"I'll make you a lemon martini." He's next to me, propped up on an elbow. "I've been in love twice."

"You're lucky for that." I stretch out on my back.

"Have you been in love?"

"Yes."

"How many times?"

"Only once."

"I think I've already experienced the best love—I'm afraid I'll spend the rest of my life approximating the kind of love I had and lost, all before the age of twenty-nine." He stops. "Losing it bothers me."

"You had it twice."

"It's never enough."

"No, I guess not." I know he's close, but we're invisible. "Tell me more."

"My family isn't very affectionate. I can make my mother blush if I hug her too tightly."

"And why are you so affectionate?"

"I don't know. Are you very affectionate?"

"No, I'm a cold fish."

"I enjoy sex very much."

"Do you?"

"Yes. Shoulder blades and collarbones are a weakness."

"And what about your childhood?" I change the subject.

"I was a good boy. Reading by flashlight in the middle of the night, watching *Scooby-Doo* in the morning—hoping that Fred and Daphne would finally get it over with and shag."

"When did you stop being a good boy?"

"Only later. Only later did I show signs of irresponsibility, leaving jobs and girls." Wearing silly things like thumb rings, friendship bracelets. "I'm occasionally depressed." He sighs. "But it's not pervasive—or detrimental. Tell me who you are," he says. "Who are you?"

mosquito net chocolate Hluhluwe

I'm the girl who gets the boy. We fall asleep, his body against mine in a way that suggests accident.

We arrive at Kruger National Park, the premier game park in South Africa. The "Big Five" are there: lion, leopard, buffalo, elephant, and rhino. Roughly the size of Israel, there are a few campgrounds in the middle surrounded by barbed wire.

"Did you hear about the guy in Namibia?" Nick erects the tent and I hold sleeping bags.

"No." We don't even pretend to push the bags on opposite sides of the tent. I throw them together in the middle.

"Apparently, some guy at a park wanted to see the lions at night, so he sat up on one of the benches inside the campground, just behind the barbed-wire fence."

"Yeah?" I say.

"He must have decided to take a little nap. The lions jumped the fence and ate him.

I recoil. "That's disgusting."

"Don't think a little barbed wire is gonna stop those guys. If they want you, they're gonna to get you." He zips up the mosquito net on our tent.

In the afternoon, we take a one-hour drive while the sun is setting and it's spectacular. It's Africa. A brilliant red sun and a purple sky over the bush. We see hippos, lions, elephants, impalas, a lilac-breasted roller, giraffes, baboons, a vervet monkey. We take pictures as the sun goes down in streaks of rich color, as the rain clouds roll in, as the sky turns a dark shade of blue.

It rains in the evening.

When it stops, Elmer feeds us grilled hake and cabbage. The fish and the rain and the stars and the warm coffee are everything I want. We head over to the recreation area and it's already dark and glittery. I imagine wild lions jumping barbed-wire fences. When Ingrid gets up to leave, I stand.

"Where are you going?" Nick looks concerned.

He thinks I'm leaving. "Nowhere. I'm taking Ingrid's place."

"Good." His facial features relax.

We play cards, trading smiles, sharing glances.

On our way back to the camp, I veer off and head towards the bathroom. "See you at home," he says.

The malleable heart.

It's a starry Mpumalanga night and there's the razor-sharp sound of leopards, the jackal cry. We zip up the tent to be alone.

"Don't use your flashlight." I stand in the pitch black, pulling down my shorts to slip on sweatpants.

"I'll just use my imagination."

Cape Town Kruger Shaka Mlilwane

The days have been filled with bird varieties, with starling and Marabou stork. They've been filled with animal sightings and changes in landscape, sunsets in burgundy, golden, and sapphire. Our nights have been filled with the sound of crickets and birds and jackals and hyenas. Our concerns are over who washes the dishes and who sits where in the minivan. All of our needs are provided for—from meals (Elmer prepares beef curry) to toilets (Elmer knows where every bathroom is from Cape Town to Mpumalanga). We haven't spoken about white complacency or Johannesburg suburbs or black townships. We don't want that kind of encroachment. Instead, we wake early to see animals. We go to sleep late under stars.

We look at a vervet monkey.

"He's kind of fun." I take the monkey's picture.

Catherine turns her whole body around in the minivan, just to look at me. "What, exactly, does *fun* mean in America?"

"The same thing it does in England." There's a bite to our words.

She continues sketching the vervet monkey.

While Elmer makes cheese sandwiches at a picnic spot, Dylan and Ingrid and I sit off to the side, discussing politics. It's the first time in days—since Nick touched the arm of the Zulu woman—I've thought about South Africa in terms of its political situation.

"I'm not anxious to return to my other life." I picture that other life: an empty apartment, unread books.

"There aren't any politics in this world." Dylan squints her eyes at the sun.

"This sort of existence isn't sustainable." Ingrid sips her water. "It's so—" She searches for the word. "*Tentative.*"

"We can repeat it till it's not, make this our life. An overland safari to Namibia." I check out my sunburnt shoulders. "Ward off the ephemeral." Make it certain. I look at Dylan and Ingrid. "Don't you guys want to go to Namibia?"

Dylan puts her hair into a ponytail. "I'm going to Victoria Falls after this, Jillian. I can't make it, love."

"And I'm really a dentist." Ingrid counts her South African money. I look at Ingrid. "I didn't know."

"Of course you didn't." Ingrid pockets the money. "I didn't tell you." Her eyes are hard on mine.

In the distance, the others run around. Elmer slices tomatoes. Nick plays Frisbee with Catherine. He prances on top of the grass with his T-shirt lifted up over his torso, like a kid. I dream of Namibia: red sand dunes striking hard against cloudless blue skies.

"When we get to Jo'burg, I may immediately go to a travel agent." I lift my arms over my head. "Sustain it for as long as possible." I think of making permanent what is fleeting. It's like struggling to make Zachary love me, like re-tracing tribal tattoos. Dylan checks her datebook. Airline itineraries stick out. "You've been a lot of places, Dylan."

"I have. Namibia isn't one of them." She looks up at me. "And what will you do after Namibia?"

"Botswana?" I stand up to get a cheese sandwich.

Repeat it till it's true.

pen paper words books

On the seventh night, I undress in the silhouette of the moon. We listen to the constant roar of crickets and grasshoppers from inside our tent. "Imagine. They live to shag and die." Even when Nick says *shag*, he sounds sophisticated.

"It's not a bad life," I say.

I answer the last of his questions.

"What will you do without him?"

"I'm fine, Nick." I panic when he asks. "I'll love someone else." That he even thought to ask alarms me.

I can't see him. I feel him hover. I feel him move a hand over my forehead and through my hair. He moves away just as quickly.

He is consoling me for my losses because my words sound like lies.

words words words books

We arrive in Graskop, a quaint town in the Eastern Transvaal. Little shops and a pancake place are the main attractions. We look at art galleries during the day and go to a bar at night. Inside the bar, everyone's Afrikaans. There's something about the bar that reminds me of Texas.

"What are you thinking, roomie?" Nick comes up behind me with two pool sticks.

I take a stick. "I'm thinking we haven't been in the company of others in days." I grab chalk to rub on the end. "It's strange to be among other people. It's strange to see everyone else among other people."

"If you forgot what to do, watch me." Nick moves to the other side of the table.

That's exactly what I do. I watch women look at him. I watch him look at women. I watch him play pool. When I see others reacting to his presence, I want him. Tonight.

Nick comes over, carrying his pool stick. "You're up. Your turn." He winks and stands close to me. He wants me, too.

We play pool and it's silly. We play act and it's thrilling. I shoot pool not to win, but to bend over—to reveal cleavage like a waitress at Hooters. We pass each other and mouth the words to songs that play loudly over the radio and we watch each other through the eyes of others. It's like seeing one another anew. I move hair out of my face when he's looking. He pays attention to where I stand in the room. When it's his turn, I give him my full attention.

An hour later, we're both called over to the corner. Ingrid, Catherine, and Dylan are drunk. Dylan says, "Jillian, what do you find physically attractive in a man?"

Nick hangs his pool stick on a rack. "Personally, I like shoulder blades," he interjects.

I feel confident tonight, like what I think is mine will surely be mine. I'm one big shoulder blade.

"Arms." I pick up the chalk. "You think I can take this home?"

Elmer drives us to our campsite and Dylan, Nick, Ingrid, and I sit on the edge of a ravine, passing around a bottle of Cape Velvet, the South African version of Baileys Irish Cream.

We talk about sex. Casual sex.

"I'm through with it." I'm lying. I've never had it.

"The best sex I ever had was casual." I think Dylan lies, too. She's not very convincing—only drunk.

Nick takes a sip of the Cape Velvet and passes it around. "I'd prefer if it weren't casual, but beggars can't be choosers." We laugh nervously, shyly.

"I guess I'd just like something a little more certain." The chocolate liquor coats the inside of my mouth. My tongue is sweet. "I hate uncertainty."

Nick looks over at me, yawns, stretches. "I'm going to bed."

"I am, too." I fake a yawn.

He grabs the bottle of Cape Velvet and takes it with him.

"I feel a little drunk," I say when we get inside our tent. But I don't. I know what I'm doing.

"Cape Velvet is lovely." I hear Nick move around. I can't see him, but I hear him rustling through things. He gets into his sleeping bag. I'm standing over him, towering over him.

"I'm undressing." I float above his body in the dark. "My clothes are coming off." I kick the legs of my jeans away. "There go my jeans."

"Wait, wait—you're going too fast." He laughs aloud.

They're already off, though. I'm standing in the dark in bra and underwear and I can tell he's on his back, listening. "Here. I'll do it again. This time, slower." I don't re-dress. Instead, I take the zipper of my fly and run it up and down. "Do you hear that?"

"Did you put your pants back on?" he asks.

"Yeah."

Nick laughs. "You're a bit of a nut."

I dangle the legs of my pants over his face, creating a breeze over the bridge of his nose. "They're off again." I move around the tent and nearly step on his leg. I almost fall, but don't. "Whoops."

He grabs my ankle. His hand takes hold of my body. "You *are* a different one."

"What do you mean?" I'm flirtatious. It feels like I've never done this before.

"You're—I don't know." He releases my ankle, mumbles something. "Perhaps it's better if some things remain unsaid."

I fall to my knees and crawl into my sleeping bag, without zipping it up. "No secrets between us. No pretense, either. Let's say what we mean."

"You're—" He pauses, thinks about it for a second. "*Spicy.*"

I giggle like an innocent. "Where's the Cape Velvet?"

"Over here." In the dark, he hands it to me. We feel our way. I grasp the bottle, feel his hands, climb over them with my fingers, hold the bottle, take it, and drink. He takes a sip, too.

"You're full of contradictions, Jillian."

"Am I?"

"You hate to trivialize sex and yet you'll sleep with me tonight—"

"You shouldn't say it."

"No pretense."

"Thank you." My eyes are open and I feel his face next to mine.

"I can't see where your face is to kiss you." He draws close to me.

I show him. It's without awkwardness. We taste of chocolate. We kiss and it's a very good kiss.

strung together pulled apart

There's something silly about it. The things I say to the stranger, the things he says to me. His voice, jarring. I want silence—I don't want to hear him speak because then I remember I don't know him. When he says my name when I touch him, shortened on his lips, I'm unnerved. "Jill." He doesn't know that no one calls me Jill.

I say, "That was metaphoric." I think. "Or is it metaphorical?"

He doesn't ask, "For what?" Rather he says, "Lighten up, love."

We smell of mosquito repellent, chocolate, liquor. Our clothes are in piles and our sleeping bags are turned inside out. Everything about the way he feels is different. I tremble from the difference. In the midst of it, he says, "No one would ever call this casual."

No one would ever call this casual. It's a sense of matched intensity, a coordination of movements, the elimination of freak accidents and false starts. It is, though, *only* casual.

"That was intense." He rolls away from me.

I think, *Was it?*

"I like it that way." He speaks to the tent walls.

"I do too," I say.

At three in the morning, I make my way through the darkness to the bathroom. I stare at myself in the mirror, feeling sort of tainted, feeling something sad, feeling the sadness go away.

"No weirdness in the morning, okay?" I crawl back in on hands and knees.

Nick is already in his own sleeping bag. "We'll see what happens." An honest answer.

I think, *I could put my arms around him—I could do that.* As the moonlight creeps through our tent door, now open, now peeled back and thrown up over the walls, I know I can't—I can't put my arms around him.

shout metaphor simile

There is no weirdness in the morning or on any of the mornings after that.

We never tell anyone. It's a secret. Every day is charged from then on and when our tent is sealed at night, it's ours. It's mine.

On the last night, everyone stays at the Rockey Street Backpackers in Johannesburg. In beds, in rooms for girls and rooms for boys. We eat African food at a tiny restaurant down the street.

The group splits sun-dried mopani worms and crocodile spare ribs. "I wish they had lion paw or lion tail on the menu." Ingrid focuses on the menu's appetizers.

I eat ostrich. "I devour art, I eat beauty," I say, thinking of Toulouse-Lautrec.

Nick eats impala. "I eat women."

"There are boy impalas, too." Dylan unfolds her napkin.

"Not the one I'm eating. All girl." Nick's eyes sparkle.

We exchange addresses and promises and glances and I know it's magical but temporary and part of its magic is this exchange, these promises, these glances.

"I'll send you doubles." Dylan re-loads her camera, speaking to me.

I doubt I'll ever see any of these people or their photographs again, and it's not because I don't like them.

Nick follows me into the hostel bathroom when I get ready for bed. He wraps his arms around me as I bend over the sink. I push back against him, welcoming his embrace. I turn around and we close the door to the bathroom with us inside. I press my body against his, and our kisses are like exchanging addresses with people we'll never write. It's the removal of meaning from gesture, the dismissal of significance from action, the denial of truth. Arms thrown around strangers. Take me today only.

"You can sneak into the girls' room with me."

"No." He kisses my forehead. "I won't get any sleep."

This sort of existence isn't sustainable, Ingrid had said.

I look into his eyes and smile. "You need rest before your long flight tomorrow."

I ask once, twice, even times three

In the morning, everyone leaves, except for Nick and me. Everyone flies to Durban, Cape Town, London and Berlin. Nick's flight to Heathrow is at four and I'm scheduled to return to the Western Cape at the end of the week.

We wander down Rockey Street in the Yeoville section of Johannesburg, holding hands. We've never held hands before.

"Maybe I'll get a tattoo." I pull Nick forward as we wander in and out of used bookstores and record shops.

"No, don't."

We stop at a café, have coffee, not talking about anything. We go to rave shops and tattoo parlors and places to buy trinkets.

"You and Ingrid and Dylan were my favorites." I make him pose for a picture.

"I don't play favorites." He looks at me out of the corner of his eye and I try to hide my injury. A smile creeps up from the corners of his mouth and he puts his arm around my neck, pretending to wrestle me, laughing.

At two-thirty, we exchange notes—nice notes, devoid of pretense, full of affection, offering simple promises and no guarantees.

I stand with him in the front of Rockey Street Backpackers as he prepares to take a cab.

"I liked you, Nick." I hold his hand, facing him on the sidewalk.

He kisses me and I kiss him and it's still a nice kiss.

do these words, though, mean a thing?

I'm still wearing my dirty camping clothes stained with moss and earth, insect repellent, saliva and other bodily fluids. I already miss that gossamer world, my tentative, short-lived sensations, those dreams of Namibia.

I sit on the couch at the hostel with the "Happy Zulu People" postcard and journal in my lap. I hold the pen poised over the journal I was writing for Zachary. It's empty. I haven't written anything, except for this one line: *This will be the only story for you.* I close it.

I flip over the postcard. Should I send it to the stranger? I can send him this card and invest my words with meaning—till we carefully measure the things we say. *Then,* we will have to consider the weight of words. *Then,* there will be resonance to our words. *Then,* we may mean something to each other.

What if I say nothing instead? What if I resist linking one word to another? Renounce committing meaning to language, compose in haphazard fashion? Just write down a bunch of *nothing*. Then, anyone—anyone at all—can cut my words to pieces. They can take a razor blade to my paper and make delicate rips. They can separate the things I say, the words I have, and spread them out across the table. They can toss them around, say something new—make my poetry relative. Kill the certainty.

With that, nothing is exclusively mine.

With that, there is no truth.

I stare at the pen in my hand. I touch its tip to the card, thinking how this minute act bespeaks commitment, cries out the certainty of language, of meaning, of all things recorded. I do not have words for Zachary, for the stranger.

Still I write:

nipples beads mealie pap
sarong Soweto sweet potato
rave shave torch bugs
bras braais fingers socks
moist wet hake curry
moss malaria butterscotch Ndbele
Khayelitsha Mapumalanga Xhosa click
shoulder blades sweatpants sunrise sunset
wildebeest warthog Zulu shithead
shag fuck Bourke's Luck
hair beard tremble shiver
flick lick Sabie River
mosquito net chocolate Hluhluwe
Cape Town Kruger Shaka Mlilwane
pen paper words books
words words words books
strung together pulled apart
shout metaphor simile
I ask once, twice, even times three
do these words, though, mean a thing?

Missing
Northern

I went without for over thirty years, but now I was back. I got my daily dose in the morning, sometimes even before coffee, and Elmo came up in conversation at least once every twenty-four hours. He was new to me, but I accepted him as my own.

Oh, Elmo. Elmo, Elmo, Elmo. My incantation.

You know you're in trouble when you start carrying a diaper bag as a purse, and the baby isn't even with you. That was what I wrote on the yellow sticky, the one Eli found on the kitchen counter and asked me about. "Are you all right?" he said, looking at me funny before he returned his attention to the American Express bill.

"At least he read it," my friend said later, when I told her.

At least.

"It's just a line I thought up," I told him, shrugging falsely while sterilizing pacifiers in the microwave. "Something I can use later." When I got around to using the quips I collected on yellow Post-its for purposes as yet undiscovered, like issuing my own special line of mixed messages in fortune cookies for trendy pan-Asian restaurants that served tofu and the like. I said, "I wonder if we're giving our baby a dose of radiation by microwaving these."

I was *not* all right.

Would someone turn on the TV?

My father was a salesman. During his lifetime, he sold many things: baby clothes, blue jeans, hand-knit diapers, and, of course, cars. When I was a kid, we parked the silver station wagon with the peeling paint in the stadium lot near the horse track and the ghetto homes with chain-link fences and snarling dogs, then we opened up the hatchback and peddled knit socks. I loved those days, waking early and getting a thermos of hot chocolate, walking around Park 'n' Swap to shuffle through used books and records, eating Indian fry bread out of the backs of trucks. Pulp fiction and Peter Frampton, Ian Fleming and Eartha Kitt. Old toys, old coins. Refried beans, cotton candy. One could find anything. One could collect anything. I was too young to wonder if he felt shame, embarrassment.

Every morning, he'd do a thousand push-ups and leg-lifts. Nothing stopped him, neither respiratory infection nor charley horse. He'd sprawl out on the office floor in the room next to my room, and I—still in bed—would hear him huffing and puffing, a rhythm that maddened me. The man was *driven*; I was sure he did them the day he died.

The only sales job I've ever held was selling coffee for Gloria Jean's Coffee Bean. I did a few push-ups once.

Irony: *we are the same, that dead man and me.*

Ask anyone. Ask my mother.

The thing about sales is that it's performance; things aren't what they seem.

My parents married in their early twenties. Eli and I married in our late thirties. We didn't exactly *grow up together*. We married after Eli lived with five women in various locations like the Ozarks and Nantucket; and after I had been to fifteen different countries, studied up on classic rock, acquired multiple advanced degrees, and seen a million movies with my single female friends. In our marriage, co-dependency wasn't a problem; self-sufficiency was. Both of us tripped and sputtered helplessly over words like, "I *need* you." We said it when we were dating, of course; but, hey, that life was *over*. We didn't *need* anyone! *Needing* was for sissies! Marriage fit us because our premarital lives had left us desperate for lasting commitment and everything, but we were jolted, out-of-sync with reality. All those demands on our time! All that sharing! All that communication—you had to say stuff when you woke up, when you walked in the door, when you sat down for dinner!

And, of course, we had to instantly reproduce.

Eli and I went to see *The Forty-Year-Old Virgin* when I was eight months pregnant, and there I was, all Pillsbury Doughboy in maternity overalls, next to the man who did the deed, knowing no one would mistake me for a virgin. Suddenly, in the dark theater, in between references to the eighties which did me right, I felt nostalgic—not for the eighties, but for my virginity: those days when love, life, everything seemed far off, sweet, magical. Ah, my virginity: a time when the world was black and white, a *before* and *after*, an interlude between Casey Kasem and important bands. Ironically, that was the eighties.

By the time I put on my maternity overalls, had the sweetness vanished? Did I still feel the pang for things distant, just-out-of-reach? If I thought about it, squinting my eyes and squeezing my temples, I could almost remember the intensity of wanting something I didn't believe I would ever get.

Oh, the *wanting*!

The magic: the future spread before me.

What did I want again?

Songs made me think of my dead father. Chicago's "Saturday in the Park." Silly songs like "Mellow Yellow." The soundtrack to *Songcatcher*.

Other music, too. Jethro Tull. Richie Havens. Traffic's "Low Spark Of High Heeled Boys."

I forgave him his New Age stage, since he saw Bob Dylan with me. I thought of him when I saw albums spin, when the Commodores played, when I saw old pictures of Elton John, Earth, Wind & Fire, even Led Zeppelin.

Play that funky music, white boy.

A nineteen-year-old girl came on to Eli at the Toronto airport when their flight got canceled. He was there on business. Biotech stuff.

As the passengers rushed around, trying to book new flights, cell phones abuzz, she suggested they share a hotel room. She did so bashfully, looking—I imagined—like Skipper, Barbie's young cousin, who I thought resided in some beachside co-op. The come-on girl's long, natural blond hair flipped like wind sails over bronze shoulders. Rose-tinted blush on her cheeks. Sparkling teeth like a model in a gum commercial. Apparently she hadn't noticed the gold ring on his finger. "We can share a room, if you'd like."

Eli told me he said to pretty Skipper, "Uh, that won't work." I could picture him responding this way, looking overhead at departure flights.

I too had a brush with infidelity. Once, when Aubrey was sick and Jordan wasn't even around yet, Eli stayed home and I went to a wedding alone.

Among the glamorous, I felt like a *hausfrau.* My roots were showing. We weren't talking *dark* roots; we were talking *gray* roots. Though thin, my body resembled a flat tire. For the first time ever, I understood why women wanted boob jobs. Frankly, I didn't have breasts anymore. My stomach had a ripple of a C-section scar slicing it like a marsupial's. I tried to figure out when I started looking like someone's mother.

Was it only when I became someone's mother?

I spent the night explaining to wedding guests in sequins, silk, and gowns, "I'm a stay-at-home mom." I'd say it, watch for the reaction, and follow up. "I used to teach and write for a magazine." I thought about adding, "I'm starting my own business: fortune cookie messages."

A religious crowd, we were about to pray before dinner. Angeline the hausfrau, for whatever reason, dropped her dishwater hand into the lap of the man sitting next to her! Right into his lap! He politely picked it up, held it the way everyone was holding hands during the prayer, and she was quick to pull away. Hausfrau didn't look at him for the rest of the night.

She wondered if Eli would care. Would he think about it? Did he picture her as a woman capable of coming on to a man? Did he picture her as lovely, or as a hausfrau? Did he see her in maternity overalls? Did he remember she had no breasts?

What did he think of me, anyway?

There was a common theme in the pop culture of the seventies: *Imposters*.

The Stepford wives? *Imposters*.

Episodes of *The Bionic Woman*? Someone's face would rip off to reveal robotic insides. *Imposters*.

Creatures were constantly feigning humanity to obscure hidden perversions, alien intentions. Though the original *Invasion of the Body Snatchers* came out in 1956, the remake in 1978 made a huge impact on me. I would forever picture Donald Sutherland letting out a Body Snatcher howl at the end. Oh, who could you trust? Wasn't that the question, after all? If Donald Sutherland turned out to be a body snatcher, who was safe?

One of my childhood friends, Stacy Something-or-Other, was spooked by the trend. "Have you told your parents?" I asked. We were in second grade.

"I don't like bringing it up." Stacy did a penny drop off the monkey bars.

"Why?"

"They might get the wrong idea." She landed in the sand like Nadia Comăneci, legs properly spread, arms outstretched. "I don't want them thinking I'm an imposter."

"Oh." I was electrified, riveted.

"I'm also pretty sure I was adopted. But I'm not bringing it up."

I smiled, giving her a wink of confidentiality.

Oh, who could you trust?

Was Lassie even a real dog?

Aubrey, three, blessed people when they sneezed. Already the baby waited for God's benediction when she let loose.

What do you say? I prodded my kid, sometimes.

We'd be sitting in the kitchen, our haunt. Jordan, ten-months-old, in the high chair with the zebra on the cushion and the fruit puffs stuck in every crevice, Aubrey in the booster chair with grape halves tucked underneath, me in the kitchen chair stained with unidentifiable food items—all of us huddled around an array of breakfast/snack/lunch/snack/dinner/snack items: macaroni and lactose-free cheese, smooshed banana bits, a pulpy apricot piece, the ubiquitous Cheerios—some smashed to bits on the kitchen floor. Sippy cups askew, sticky juice puddles gathering. A PediaSure bottle resting on its side in a circle of strawberry. Jordan—my truly beautiful bouncing baby—sneezed, Aubrey—gorgeous eyes aglitter—froze, our world akimbo, somehow reminding me of a Van Gogh still life. And then, then, it happened: Jordan radiated bliss in anticipation.

What do you say? I whispered: a breath, a hint, a clue.

Aubrey, knowing it was her moment, proudly offered, "Bless you."

The world was set aright again.

The funny thing was that when I sneezed, Aubrey did nothing, *nada*. Continued playing with her Dora the Explorer figurine or rubbing her stuffed dog's nose. Jordan's expectant look faded. All three of us grazed into the next moment of our lives together.

Yes, we *grazed*.

I'd asked myself this: Was it like the sound of a falling tree when no one was there to hear? Did the tree make a sound? Did my sneeze make a sound?

Did I even sneeze?

And sometimes I asked: *Did this mean Angeline Wells was without God's blessing?*

In the beginning, Eli brought me chocolate chip muffins and steaming pots of coffee. Every morning, there were e-mail epics in thrilling, well-written prose. We played games with the car radio, pressing station buttons, guessing the artists of rock and roll songs. We told each other about our fetid pasts, relishing disclosure. Our first kiss made walls shake. He was smart, bookish, and not a misogynist. Despite his love for the Doors, he also loved the blues. He taught me the difference between Chicago and Southern blues. He showed me that not all Republicans were racists.

Eli and I once made love in the car in the parking lot of the church at which we got married. Afterwards, I ran around outside without panties on. Naked in a church parking lot, asphalt on my bare feet, while my husband put on his blue jeans in the shotgun.

I used to wear go-go boots. Actually, that's not true. I *thought* about wearing go-go boots.

He recently said, "You're *cosmopolitan*."

"Thank you," I said, though I didn't think he meant it as a compliment.

"All these dichotomies you set up ...." He poured an inordinate, non-cosmo amount of hot sauce on his pizza slice.

Hmm, I thought. I was a *cosmopolitan*. We were a *group*. We didn't do hot sauce on pizza. Maybe a little crushed red pepper.

He continued, "Between love and romance, motherhood and womanhood, sexy and straightlaced, the ordinary and the extraordinary—they're false dichotomies, Angeline."

"You think so?" I asked, curious to hear what he'd say.

"To marvel that one has chosen motherhood or being a stay-at-home mom rather than pursuing professional endeavors, at least to me, is to rehearse a singular quandary of a singularly modern, cosmopolitan era, for that singular brood who has been taken with it since feminism and the sixties." Eli could be very articulate, particularly for a non-cosmopolitan.

"What did you just say?"

"It's like metaphysical schizophrenia," he concluded.

Yesterday, Aubrey teased, "Is Big Bird a duck?"

Back to imposters.

"He might be," I answered, playing along. Aubrey, at three, had no doubts over Big Bird's duckness.

When Aubrey began watching *Sesame Street*, friends delivered tirades against TV, bad values, talking birds. But after my lengthy hiatus, I couldn't wait to see how the characters had fared. Gordon, Maria, Luis, Susan, Bob. For a while, I couldn't get over the fact that these actors had spent their whole careers with Muppets. At one time, did they dream of movie stardom, rather than public television for kids?

"Well, they sign yearly contracts," a friend reminded me. "They could've left."

But they didn't. So *Sesame Street,* thirty years later.

Snuffleupagus was no longer a figment of Big Bird's imagination. I knew about Mr. Hooper. But David—how did I miss the news?

Now, *Sesame*-obsessed, I searched the Web. Northern Calloway, despite his winning moniker, was bipolar and maybe psychotic. Did he do sit-ups incessantly? Did he frequent the Humane Society like a ghost in chains from a Dickens' novel? Did he have a penchant for Dairy Queen?

These, my dad's demons.

Psychiatric wards, heart failure, violence, asylums, cancer—rumors surrounded him.

But Northern Calloway *died.*

Though Mr. Hooper's death was written into the show, David's wasn't. Like a tree falling in the forest, like my sneeze in the kitchen. Nothing, *nada.*

Metaphysical schizophrenia was falling in love in your mid-thirties, abandoning everything you'd supposedly worked for, and signing up for infant CPR. Good-bye, mini-skirts; hello, maternity overalls.

Who was the imposter now?

I walked into Eli's office while he fixed the printer. I wore low-rise jeans and a black lace bra; he didn't even look up. While staring at an ink cartridge, he answered my staged question: "Have you seen my sunglasses?"

"Nope," he said. "Where'd you last put them?"

I thought: *Who were we once?* I thought: *I'm virtually naked.*

Last night, he came into the bedroom, wearing a full-length bathrobe. He sat down on the bed. I was already under the covers, reading.

Touching his back, I said, "Your robe is a turn-on."

When we first got married, I had this elaborate theory on how sleeping in the nude fostered marital intimacy: It's good for a man and a woman to sleep naked on a small bed and constantly bump into each other all night long. Eli, into nudity, was never quite into the bumping-into-each-other part.

The other night, when I rolled over and bumped into him, I discovered boxers and a tee.

"If I sleep with clothes on, my allergies aren't as bad," he explained in the morning.

"Oh," I said.

But there he was the other night, and he had spent the previous Saturday putting baby-proof outlet covers on all the plugs. "I feel like the Cleavers." He turned to look at me in bed, naked but not particularly beckoning, my sex drive analogous to my breasts: *plummeting.* "How was your day, June?" He smoothed down his robe. "I'm worried about the Beav."

During the summer my dad died, I taught a seven a.m. introduction to magazine-writing class at a community college. Drought parched the land and wildfires disfigured the earth; similarly, my own days spoke of thirst. Thirty-two, living at home, about to move into a gross apartment, no love life, ovaries rotting, good looks fading, an increasing need for sleep. I saved every cent of every paycheck, and packed an occasional box to make the future seem real. As far as I was concerned, I would forever wake at the undignified hour of five a.m., I would forever teach prerequisites to bored students, and I would forever argue with my father about the way I took care of my car. For a while, I even forgot I was an adult. Angeline Knox in her thirties—already not the same Angeline Knox of her twenties. The depressed thirties followed the roaring twenties: after college and pseudo-romances and faux-careers in other parts of the country, I crawled back to the desert to teach close to home.

"Your new apartment isn't safe, it has termites, the appliances are older than I, and the neighbors look like they might kill you," my dad said. "And when was the last time you washed your car? Or changed the oil? How do you expect to pay for the alarm system you're obviously going to need?"

"You know, dad," I'd tell him, "I can hear you on the phone from outside the house. That's how loud you are. You're screaming into the receiver."

Sometimes, we'd take a break and go for pizza and a movie. Both of us liked pizza. Both of us liked movies. That summer, we ate much pizza; we saw many movies.

One day, while driving home from work, I saw a car on fire. One of those seemingly random, weird things one encountered in urban landscapes. Very *Mad Max*. The driver pulled into a gas station and police cars gathered. I wondered if I'd make it through the intersection before the explosion, the inevitable fireball that would mushroom into the sky. I wondered if al-Qaeda were behind it. My mom was out of town; I wanted to tell my dad about the possible terrorist attack. Wired on coffee, I went home to grade papers and tell him. "We're at war," I'd say. This was my summer of anxiety, my season of an unknown future.

But nothing is as it seems.

The future took shape without pyrotechnics. In the beginning of August, when my bags were packed, my father died in a car accident. No mushroom cloud, but I envisioned a tumbling, rolling truck. *Tumbling, rolling, tumbling, rolling, tumbling ....*

It happened while I was teaching. When I came home, he was gone. On *Sesame Street*, David was already dead.

Angeline Knox would be someone else in a couple years.

Back in the classroom, maybe only a week later (because, amazingly, *you still needed to go to work*), a student wrote an essay about heartbreak: boy-met-girl, boy-dumped-girl, girl-all-alone.

The student described her loneliness as "the sweet scent of solitude."

I repeated it aloud to myself: *the sweet scent of solitude. The sweet scent of solitude. O the Sweet Scent of Solitude.*

I bet she was proud of that one.

Despite the alliteration, I had a few questions: What does *solitude* smell like? And how was it *sweet*?

Could it be worn as perfume?

After my father's death, my mom had to clean out his medicine cabinet. She found his half-used deodorant stick. She pulled off its top. She inhaled a whiff. Walking over to where I sat on the couch, she asked, "Do you want to smell your father's deodorant?"

This was the sweet scent of solitude.

Show, don't tell. Even when you were talking about death.

Imposters everywhere. Perhaps, Big Bird—our collective big old Big Bird—was just a mutant duck. Posing as a fun-loving city bird.

When my dad died, he was driving home from the gym. One of those hulking and impossible four-door trucks skipped over the median and rammed into the driver's side of his car. "Killing him instantly," the police said. It was a phrase we'd hear over and over, apparently meant to comfort us. A Natalie Merchant album was stuck in his CD player.

Later, I drove to the site of his accident and spoke to the women at the automotive parts store nearby. I went alone. It was only a couple days after his death. I parked my car. I got out and walked into the store. Quiet, deliberate, falsely strong. A brave imposter.

The women inside were stereotypes: girls with chipped or missing teeth (did they get punched in the face?), thick makeup with blue licks of acrylic eye shadow, cheap yellow gold jewelry, rings on every finger, halter tops revealing wrinkly cleavage, short-shorts with butt cheeks spilling out, bleached hair.

Middle-aged stuff.

They cried when I told them who I was.

They cried.

Who was he? they asked. Did he have a wife, kids?

What kind of man was he?

My mom never drove down that road. She'd go around the block to avoid it. Whenever she spoke of his death, she said, "When he was *killed* …." She never said, "When he *died in a car accident.*" I thought she was trying to make a point. Someone *killed* him.

He also had the soundtrack to *O Brother, Where Art Thou?* in the car, but he was listening to Natalie Merchant. Now, forever, I was left with Merchant spinning without sound in the destroyed and bloodied car.

I still thought about those automotive parts women, the way they cried, the mascara trailing down their old cheeks, not stereotypes at all, how they wanted to know who my father really was. Was that just an imposter in the car?

O Brother, where art thou?

I didn't feel particularly ennobled by my role as stay-at-home mom. I could wear go-go boots if I wanted. I just didn't.

Sometimes, I cried to Eli, "I can't do it. I can't do it. I can't do this motherhood thing. It's too much." I wasn't cut out for babies, for hanging out with other moms, for Walmart, for nozzles in sippy cups, for teaching them how to do things we all knew how to do—using a toilet, holding a fork, not rubbing yogurt all over our legs. I wasn't cut out for two-year-old conversation. Something went wrong, horribly wrong. I was a lousy mom. I was supposed to do something else, something solitary. I was once lovely, remember? Stark? Alienated? Untouchable? Aloof? Unhappy, yes—but lovely. Don't forget, *lovely.* L-O-V-E-L-Y. And now, now, look at me.

Imposter mom.

Eli, a faithful man, bit his lip, endured. Suggested sex.

Sometimes I found his response admirable, righteous.

Sometimes I wanted to yell: *You Passive-Aggressive Fuck. Do something. Help me. Can't you minimally say I'm still lovely?*

I am my father's daughter.

He always wanted to be a history teacher. "If I could do it all over again," he'd say. He spent his whole life saying, *If I could do it all over again* ....

I am my father's daughter.

A few months prior to his death, my father told my mother, "I hate my life." It wasn't the first time he said it. My mother and I didn't tell people. Our dirty little secret.

In *Scooby-Doo*, the villains always ripped off their masks to reveal their true identities. It was like *The Stepford Wives.* Underneath the masks, horrible things lurked.

I am my father's daughter.

I kept thinking about how Gordon and Maria and Luis renewed their *Sesame Street* contracts, forsaking the movies. A steady income. A good life. Did Bob incessantly say to himself, *I could've been Harrison Ford? I could've been Keanu?*

I am my father's daughter.

I used to envision myself as something else. Someone with more verve, more play. Now I sneezed, waited for Aubrey to notice.

At what point did you admit to yourself, *This is my life?*

That was then, this is now.

Judy Blume? S.E. Hinton? Thank you, S.E. May I call you *S?*

So, post-death, post-apocalypse, I would be unrecognizable to my own father.

Who was the real Angeline Knox? Would she please step up? Remember that show, something with Wink Martindale? *To Tell the Truth.*

That was then, this is now.

I shopped at Walmart, even though I was a snob and it jarred my sensibilities. I lived for pictures of my kids, trailing after them with a camera in one hand and rechargeable batteries in the other. I went to sleep at ten, unable to comprehend a word my husband said after dark despite the fact he didn't say much during daylight. I bought Chips Ahoy! cookies and I'd try Nutter Butters next. When I was in the airport or some place where people unabashedly stared at each other, the thing I was struck by was this: I looked like a mom now, like someone's wife—not one of those sexy wives husbands liked to take out on the town or passionately embrace; rather, like the wife who made a shitload of peanut-butter-and-jelly sandwiches, and lost her sex appeal somewhere in the laundry.

I could see the disappointment in my husband's face. A romantic, he was always hoping for a domestic beatific vision: Aubrey would be throwing her helmet-clad head back in laughter while safely racing down the sidewalk on her tricycle; Jordan would be precociously scrutinizing a book called *Arts and Crafts for Rainy Days*, about to begin a collection of popsicle sticks and non-toxic glue; and Angeline, his beautiful Angeline, would joyfully be singing "Zip-A-Dee-Doo-Dah" till the sun went down. Then Angeline, his scrumptious Angeline, would transform into a high-sexed masseuse.

My lack of enthusiasm troubled him. A faithful man, he bit his lip and endured. Suggested sex.

Recently, he said he'd like for me to plan a romantic Friday night for us when the kids went down. I nearly keeled over. "Well, you asked what I wanted to do," Eli said, innocently.

I had asked; that was true. *What do you want to do?* But I was thinking, *Do you want to watch the Will Smith movie or share the chocolate bar in the fridge, or—ideally—both?*

Romantic evening after the kids go down? At nine o'clock, when I finished the dishes? After I wiped up the soggy fish crackers stuck in the tile grout? After I showered off the possible pee on my skin, the definite YoBaby yogurt in my hair, and the soggy fish crackers from under my fingernails?

No, my father wouldn't recognize me. He knew the young Angeline, the child Angeline—not the mom who wanted to watch Will Smith movies and eat chocolate on the couch.

Imposter songs: "Once In A Lifetime" by Talking Heads. "Jessie's Girl" by Rick Springfield. Anything by Wham!

Sometimes, Eli cracked me up. He'd shake a chair to scare Scrappy or Scooby and say, "Whoa, Nelly." He tried to move one of them from a pillow and say, "Dude, move." We'd be talking about art, about Peter Paul Rubens, and he'd ask, "Is he the guy where you've got a boob over here, and some grapes over there?"

"Pretty much," I'd say.

Aubrey, too, filled me with adoration. She'd run into our bedroom, naked after a bath, declaring herself a ballerina while doing a pirouette. She'd say, "I'm like this because I'm doing this." She'd reach for my hand while taking a walk, Jordan in the stroller, and she'd say, "I like walking with you. We're two mommies." She'd hand me a masticated hard-boiled egg and say she didn't like it.

I'd ask, "Which part?"

She'd answer, "The egg part."

And Jordan's killer routine of crying at five in the morning till I put her into our bed, where she sucked her fingers and looked at me as if I were a true child of God: If I could do it all over again, would I?

Would I be stark and alienated but lovely?

Or would I renew my contract like a *Sesame Street* cast member?

I am my father's daughter. Don't think he would've done it differently.

The other night, at ten-fifteen, I approached Eli in the kitchen. We stood by the refrigerator, and I fixed my red terry cloth bathrobe around my body. I had just finished cleaning the living room, and so I held two pink piggy banks that oinked when a coin fell through the slots in their backs. I said, "Are you coming in?" Which was my super-duper, post-apocalyptic lovemaking battle cry.

The poor man looked at me, not exactly stupefied. Maybe reconciled.

I let my robe drop open, revealing my nightshirt that said "Crazy Cat Lady" on it. We didn't even have cats. I saw him looking at it. "This is what we've got." I sighed.

"What? Two pigs and a bathrobe?"

We laughed so hard, falling against kitchen cabinets, shaking walls.

—————

No one toasted me at my wedding.

It was this awkward moment, punctuated with dead-fatherness.

Two years after the accident, I got hitched. Soon, I'd have two kids he'd never know.

I'd say this outright. Though I seemed remarkably over his death, I was left with a couple great sorrows; one of them was that my children would never meet my father.

Not to mention, my mother—who had to reinvent herself. *At least*, she thought when I married, *Angeline was taken care of.*

So my wedding: *no toast.* Of course there were logistical reasons—I told one friend I didn't want anyone toasting me, she believed me even though I was full of it, she told my other friends, everyone believed it, and no one did it. End of story. Period. Dead Father.

My wedding was perfectly lovely. Traditional, pretty, no tripping, no gasping, no secrets revealed. Even some special college friends showed. Just the presence of the dead father, the presence of an absence.

That, and the cake sucked. But we ate it anyway.

I was finally taken care of.

We were home from the hospital for one day. Aubrey was still at grandma's doing the wild toddler thing, and Jordan was asleep in the bouncer, doing the newborn loll.

"Mrs. Wells?" the voice on the line asked. No longer Knox. Post-apocalyptic Wells. Angeline Wells, fatherless, a wife, a mother. I had just had number two.

"This is her," I said, staring at the room, my domain, my baby. Jordan had a full head of dark hair, my little sleeping princess.

"This is Carol from Sunny Farm."

My vet's office. "Hi, Carol." Carol loved cats, dogs.

"We were going through our ashes, and we came across Token's."

She wasn't trying to be particularly delicate. But Token wasn't mine. "I think you have the wrong Mrs. Wells," I said. "This is Angeline Wells." Scooby and Scrappy were mine.

"Oh, okay," Carol said, as bright and cheery as can be. "Bye."

No apologies.

The phone went dead, and I stood there, contemplative.

Was it *token*, *Tolkien*, or *tokin*? Were the dead pet's owners gamblers? Members of the literati? Deadheads?

Just who were these people who had a dead pet named Token? Didn't anyone want to know?

When my husband was a little boy in New England (where trees grew, snow fell, brooks bubbled, dust never settled, kids played happily, et cetera), he used to go to the dump with his dad.

"Didn't I tell you this?" he said one night, after the girls were theoretically asleep, when Eli and Angeline Wells were theoretically adult married people.

"I don't think so." I dropped my swollen ankles onto the coffee table, all set for romance.

We were talking about garbage.

"We used to go to the dump every few months; it's not like it is here, where you don't do that stuff." My husband left his adorable New England homestead and landed, cheekily, in a hot urban landscape sans *Mad Max*. Phoenix, Arizona.

He hated Phoenix, Arizona.

He never let me forget it. "I'll never be able to leave," I've said. "My mother is alone."

Trash. We were talking *trash*.

"We'd go to the dump and the attendant or whatever those guys are—"

So, since I grew up in the urban landscape, I quickly pictured *Sanford and Son*. Weren't they garbage men? Delightful, charming, inner-city garbage men? Junk dealers?

Eli continued, "He was a sharpshooter. We'd throw a penny up, so high we wouldn't even see it. But, then, we'd hear a 'clink,' and he'd shoot it—he'd hit it mid-air."

"Wow," I said dryly, not as enthralled by the sharpshooter as I was by the idea of going to the dump. "You guys went to the dump? What did you do there?"

"Dropped off things," he said, ever perplexed by my naiveté.

What, no bulk trash days? "Where's our dump?" I suddenly felt hot and clammy.

He began painting a picture. "You wouldn't believe how *vast* it is." *Vast*. "It just goes on and on and on," he explained. "There are bulldozers and heavy machinery just pushing the trash around—you're not sure where—but trash is always being pushed around. It's endless."

As he spoke, something happened to me. All that trash. Being pushed around.

"I used to love it." A dreamy look on his face. "I'll take the girls when they get older."

I felt nauseous. Nervous. *Where was the trash being pushed?* It was *vast*.

Not my girls.

What happened to all that trash? What the hell happened?

So, thinking of displacement and abandonment and trash, I recited Matthew Arnold's "The Buried Life" for Eli.

He looked at me with the same look I gave him when he talked about the sharpshooter. "How *Cosmo*. Put on the cat shirt and let's watch Will."

It occurred to me now, since imposter movies had given over to random sexual liaison comedies, that the imposter complex was really a duplicity complex, which was really a concern for authenticity, the desire to be known. Who was the "real me," and who knew her?

Perhaps I lost the *Bionic Woman* fans.

What I knew about my dad, the *real* Seamus Knox. Struggled with duplicity, felt as if—all his life—he wasn't quite himself, like he should have done something differently.

There was another secret my mom and I possessed. On the last night of his life, he did something strange. My mom sat on one couch, her legs outstretched before her. There was a cat on her lap, or maybe the newspaper. The TV was on, prime time hours, a habit my mom did away with when he died. My dad was on another couch, a couple feet away. His legs were on top of the coffee table; he was eating a very big bowl of ice cream out of a black glass that looked like a goblet, purchased at a Crate and Barrel in the seventies, during the imposter era.

But this was the secret. He reached over to my mom, touched her arm, maybe her hand. Deidra Knox, about as authentic as you could get. He said to her, "I've loved you since the day I first saw you."

I'd heard the story many times, the story of my parents' meeting. It was the sixties in Chicago; my old mom was a looker—tall, skinny, mini-skirts, real go-go boots, platinum blonde hair down her back, a Twiggy/Marianne Faithfull thick-black-eyelash thing going, probably a necklace of daisies around her neck. She was the boss's daughter in a downtown Chicago men's clothing store that thrived, famous for selling the Jackson Five bell-bottom pants and shirts with paisleys and snaps. There was something radical about that store, Steamy Syd's. A cross between chic and nouveau pimp, lives intersected—or clashed—and spun off into stories, epics, novels. And there, the boss's daughter walked in one day and needed a ride home. So the boss turned to Seamus Knox, a skinny-ass kid from the metaphorical wrong side of the tracks. Both Seamus and Deidra had immigrants for grandparents, but Seamus's were grocers and Deidra's went into sales.

Seamus took her home that day. My poor father always wanted to be a history professor. Instead, he got married, had a kid, went into sales, too.

One could call me a romantic with my memories and poems. Most wouldn't.

I found more yellow Post-its when my girls slept. Forget fortune cookies. I'd launch Marsupial Moms, products for post-apocalyptic moms. Pen in hand, I wrote, *Traded in go-go boots for nipple guards? These boots were made for walking? These boobs were made for chapping! Marsupial Moms Nipple Guards. Keep 'em pretty.* On another, I wrote, *Posh? Preggers? Go Cosmo: Marsupial Moms Maternity Overalls. Wear for nine months and then fold into stylish diaper bag and latte holder. You gave up coffee? Also holds juice box!* On still another, I scribbled, *Angeline died. They buried her in her maternity overalls. She wanted to be cremated but no one wanted to burn the duds. Marsupial Moms made them.*

I went to a pool party, consisting of mothers and kids and a few miscellaneous young women—all of them good-looking. The men conspicuously absent, working, not invited. Aubrey held onto me, having just finished her own private swim lesson. She wore her hair in a ponytail, and her bathing suit was red, white, and blue, triggering a comment from another mom, "You look very patriotic today." Jordan was being held by one of the miscellaneous young women who happened to be good-looking.

I couldn't help but study the young woman, scrutinizing her, wanting to be near her. She was so lively, so pretty. She bounced up and down, doing underwater ballet or tap. "I gotta dance," she said. "The water is great for it, and I'm taking dance classes."

"Oh?" I asked. "Which ones?"

She did some sort of cha-cha, Jordan happily springing and bounding with each move. "Salsa and swing."

"How fun!" I said, a happy imposter—really staring at her boobs. They were great! Perky! I was very aware of my tattered bathing suit, my maternal thighs.

We got on the subject of marriage. She declared, while salsa-ing underwater and holding my baby, "I've done a lot of things people want to do before marriage. I've lived in Europe—"

I lived in Europe, too! A couple months in the nineties! "Where?" I asked, entranced by her salsa and breasts. Aubrey wanted me to swish her around the pool like I was a much younger motorboat, and Jordan was perfectly content with the energy radiating from the good-looking girl. Another miscellaneous young woman floated by. She had short chic hair and big hoop earrings. On her back, the words "Forever Young" were tattooed, and I was pretty sure she was referencing Bob not Rod. "How long were you in Europe?" I asked.

She lived in Paris for a year with a rich boyfriend who owned a club. Barely out of high school, the relationship left her feeling vacant and insipid but fluent in French. She wished it had been different. She could have danced!

Well, there's nothing quite like a beautiful young American girl living in Europe for a year. As Oscar Goldman might have said at some point to the Bionic Woman, Jaime Sommers: *Watch Out!*

But now, she was older, ready for marriage. "As long as he lets me dance," she said.

Without dance, she'd just be an imposter.

We got out of the pool, the salsa dancer, the Forever Young floater, the ThighMaster flunky, and the two gorgeous kids. After getting the two gorgeous kids out of their swim diapers and positioning them in chairs with juice boxes, I sat down, still stung by the impression of the miscellaneous young women.

My envy, of course, eradicated their miscellany.

Aubrey woke me from my, um, *reverie.* "Mommy, mommy, mommy."

"Yes, babe," I turned to my star-spangled daughter.

She pointed to another little girl. "Where does No-Mommy live?"

"Do you mean *Naomi*?" When you were a kid, it was all about mommy, who had one, who didn't, and where yours was. "She lives with her parents, her mommy and daddy."

Aubrey looked thoughtful, as if trying to configure how the name and the existential reality coexisted.

"Just like you live with yours," I added. "I'm your mommy."

I wondered if Northern Calloway sat around thinking, "I'm nothing like David." Did he die thinking about the duplicity of simultaneously being Northern in real life and living on Sesame Street in fiction?

I wished my father had lived long enough to accept his fate. Though he would never teach history, I pictured him in histrionic proportions.

When I was three, my parents moved to the other side of the country. They packed up the pets, the Volvo, the Peugeot. I rode with my dad, and my cousin Scott and the pets rode with my mom. We drove from Chicago to Phoenix, and I was told I talked non-stop. I remembered a few plastic games for the car. I have a vague memory of looking out the window while my dad drove, talking, talking, talking.

I remembered something else, too. Another car-on-fire event, but this time it wasn't an urban landscape. And Mad Max was definitely not around. The details were lost in post-Peter Paul Rubens Impressionism. We were on a dusty, empty highway—between towns and landmarks. Something horrible had happened involving a massive truck hauling big, rolling tanks of gasoline; a VW bug flat like an empty tin can; and a truck and trailer with a horse in it. In my impressionistic vision, about as reliable as my impression of the dump, the gas truck and horse trailer ended up on their sides, and the VW bug was crushed with four people inside. I remembered many dead, including the horse.

Here was the heroic, blockbuster part: in my mind's eye, my father helped the gasoline truck driver. Despite fire and impending explosion, he pulled a girl from the VW bug. She lived, while three died. And then there were the infernos and detonations. The orange and blue and black filling the air. A dead horse, the silver cylindrical tanks, the VW bug not even visible. Yes, as incredible as it sounded and probably was, my father was a hero, emerging from fire, holding a girl.

Even though I periodically asked my mom what really happened, this was what I remembered.

This was my dad.

When I was not even a teenybopper, just a pre-teen, pre-bopper girl frightening in my lanky-limb-womanly-suggestiveness, my parents relented and took me and my friend Kristy to see Rick Springfield's movie debut, *Hard to Hold*. Again, I remembered very little about it, except that Rick played a rock star named Jamie. And there was this scene on a balcony.

Rick and his love interest looked into each other's eyes, having found true love that circumvented all existential angst and potential explosions of fire, and the woman said something like, "Jamie, isn't life nuts?"

For the next decade, my father would occasionally turn to me at key moments with a very solemn look on his face. He'd grow serious. Then, after the dramatic pregnant pause, he'd say, "Jamie, isn't life nuts?" And he would burst out laughing.

And what was a post-apocalyptic mom? An imposter mom? A duplicitous mom? A cosmopolitan-turned-*hausfrau* mom? A mom who survived the explosion, the mushroom cloud, the fire in the sky? A mom who associated existential angst with the dump?

Was the apocalypse catastrophic? The end of the world?

When one finally met God and said, "*This* is my life?"

Aubrey asked me about my dead dad. We told her about the resurrection of the living and the dead. "Will your dad play with me?"

She pored over old pictures that rendered him forever young. "He's playing with Jesus now?"

I told Eli about my occasional dreams. "He's alive, and it's just like normal." Eli, despite his attempts to understand, only knew me as a woman without a father. I looked at him, and whispered, "*I see dead people.*" He laughed; he knew the movie.

At the apocalypse, the metaphysical schizophrenia was healed and the false dichotomies dissipated. At the apocalypse, there were no imposters. The post-apocalyptic mom was the mom who waited for the resurrection—all the while missing the dead. I missed the dead.

I am missing the dead.